MATCH MADE IN HEAVEN

MATCH MADE IN HEAVEN

Bob Mitchell

KENSINGTON BOOKS
http://www.kensingtonbooks.com

KENSINGTON BOOKS are published by

Kensington Publishing Corp.
850 Third Avenue
New York, NY 10022

All Kensington titles, imprints and distributed lines are available at special quantity discounts for bulk purchases for sales promotion, premiums, fund-raising, educational or institutional use.

Special book excerpts or customized printings can also be created to fit specific needs. For details, write or phone the office of the Kensington Special Sales Manager: Kensington Publishing Corp., 850 Third Avenue, New York, NY 10022. Attn. Special Sales Department. Phone: 1-800-221-2647.

Kensington and the K logo Reg. U.S. Pat. & TM Off.

Library of Congress Card Catalogue Number: 2005924289

ISBN 0-7582-1269-0

First Printing: May 2006
10 9 8 7 6 5 4 3 2 1

Printed in the United States of America

To Susan:

Ours is a match made in heaven.

Lessons through suffering.
        —Aeschylus

The heart has its reasons
that Reason doesn't have a clue about.
        —Blaise Pascal

A Wounded *Deer*—*leaps highest.*
        —Emily Dickinson

As you walk down the fairway of life,
you must smell the roses,
for you only get to play one round.
        —Ben Hogan

PROLOGUE

THE GURNEY CARRYING Elliott Goodman careened down the corridor of Boston's Mass General Hospital with the purposeful velocity of a Juan-Manuel Fangio Maserati.

I can't even believe it. Not now! Ohhh maaan . . .

"He needs another blast of morphine," Nick Lindsey, the cardiologist, barked. "Five milligrams, *stat!* What's his BP?"

"One-forty over eighty. Heart rate's sixty," the nurse answered.

Elliott was experiencing a panoply of classic symptoms, including nausea, sweating, and a crushing chest pain radiating to his jaw and left arm, all accompanied by disorientation, acute fear, and utter panic.

It didn't take a brain surgeon—or even a heart surgeon—to determine his condition. Elliott had already pronounced the instant and correct lay diagnosis.

Heart attack. The Big One.

Elliott Goodman—husband, father of two, jock, and professor of comparative literature at Harvard—had just turned fifty. As his gurney turned the corner, barely avoiding a wheelie, he closed his eyes and felt an unspeakable sadness at his apparently imminent demise.

Special moments from his life beckoned to him.

Playing make-believe ball games with his beloved Spaldeen in the driveway. Watching early heroes like Willie Mays and Elgin Baylor and Gale Sayers and Pancho Gonzalez and Ben Hogan. Executing a perfect drop volley on a rich red-clay court. Opening his letter of acceptance to college. Travis-picking his Martin double-oh-eighteen. Discovering Leonardo and Rembrandt and Blake and Goya and van Gogh and Picasso. Making love for the first time. Getting stoned for the first time. Devouring Shakespeare and Poe and Dostoyevsky and Mallarmé and Rilke and Neruda. Earning his Ph.D. Listening to Beethoven and Gershwin and Georges Brassens and Francesco De Gregori and The Beatles and Cocker and Fleetwood Mac and James Taylor and Leo Kottke. Savoring Hires Root Beer and Guinness Stout and Barolo and Balvenie. Falling in love with Paris and London and Barcelona and Florence and Amsterdam and Marrakech and Rio. Falling in love with Joy, and then the joy of seeing the twins, Jake and Molly, grow up and flourish . . .

"BP now?" Lindsey asked the nurse.

"Sixty palpable, heart rate's now thirty. Looks like complete heart block."

Nick Lindsey knew the urgency of getting the patient into the OR for an emergency bypass. Otherwise it might be just a matter of seconds before . . .

Still consumed by terror and pain, Elliott again closed his eyes.

It is late spring, the robins are chirping, hope is in the air, and seventeen-year-old Elliott Goodman is taking a Latin final, his last exam as a high-school student. He is mulling over a devilishly difficult passage from Virgil's Aeneid, *gleefully meandering through forests of dactyls and spondees, and he is in heaven. How he loves Latin! Its cockamamy syntax, its mysterious grammar, its illogical logic! It was in this same Latin class that he first realized the linguistic coincidence of his initials—e.g.! Elliott Goodman . . . exempli gratia . . . "for example." Was he supposed to be, as a human being, an example for others to follow? Would he be, someday, somehow, in some way, chosen by someone as . . . some sort of example of . . . something greater than himself?*

When the gurney finally reached the OR, Jim Dash, the cardiac surgeon, arrived at the scene. "Let's go, people. This guy needs to be prepped and draped. *Stat!*"

Elliott was in bad shape, and he knew it. His mind grasped for any tiny flotsam in its ocean of fear.

Perched on the roof of his college frat house, a copy of Dante's Paradiso *in one hand and a tankard of suds from the house keg in the other, twenty-one-year-old Elliott Goodman senses that life couldn't be more idyllic if it tried. The air is filled with the bounties of floral perfume: lilac, jasmine, wisteria, honeysuckle. From somewhere below wafts the glorious cacophony of students bantering on their way to a seminar, a Dusty Springfield LP, campus canines copulating. It's about as good as it's gonna get. And as he sips and reads and ponders and soaks in the sensuousness of the scene, he ruminates on what he will become.*

At college, he has been preparing for life in his own way. Refining his technique on acoustic guitar. Perfecting the fine art of dating. Participating in sports of every kind. Taking courses from every cranny of the curriculum. He has become a jack-of-all-trades, and while most of his classmates have mapped out their careers—medicine, law, business—he has no clue of what he will do in life. This ongoing quest for focus will take him on a merry chase, via the Peace Corps (Nicaragua), six months apiece studying in Florence (Renaissance art) and Oxford (philosophy), plus a glorious year in Paris.

Ah, Paris! There he will sit for hours on end, at the Café Apollinaire on the Boulevard St-Germain, slowly sipping Martinis rouges (rocks, twist) and slowly puffing on Campanella mini-cigars. He is thinking about teaching literature. He loves the concept of sharing ideas, of spreading the contagion of his passion for words and thoughts. . . .

Jim Dash reached for a sublingual tablet of nitroglycerin and tucked it under Elliott's tongue. In three seconds, the pain was gone.

Amazing!

"How're we doing?" Jim asked, as he prepared for the by-pass. A quick glance at Elliott's contorted face told him that the agony had returned.

"Goddammit, he's arresting!" Jim snapped, as he initiated CPR.

Deep in the bowels of Harvard's august Widener Memorial Library, just-turned-fifty Elliott Goodman walks through the maze of stacks to a book titled The Heart Has Its Reasons: The Individual vs. Society in Western Literature. *He had written it just a year ago, and his ego is curious to see how many students have checked it out since. Turning to the back of the book, he is dismayed to discover that only one due date is stamped on the withdrawal slip.*

As he stares at the solitary date at the back of his book, his eternal questions resurface. What does it mean to achieve something? Why has he been put on this earth? What's the value of all his education? Was Pascal right, after all? Who are we insignificant creatures, in the grandness of God's universe?

Walking through the stacks, he feels adrift in the halls of academe, a misfit. In his heart, wouldn't he rather be far away from libraries and classrooms, picking his guitar or playing golf or having fun with his family? Then: Has he been a good enough husband to Joy? Has he spent enough time with Jake and Molly—having catches in the driveway and helping them with their homework?

His left hand still clutching his book, he crumples to the floor in the library stacks. He is seized by fear, but not the fear of having a heart attack nor the fear that no one will find him there deep in the bowels of Widener. Rather, it is the fear of ignorance, of not knowing why this is happening to him. After all, he's fit and trim, he doesn't smoke. So why him? *He isn't a religious man, but somehow, his thoughts are directed toward a higher being, someone who might listen to him in his pain and his solitude and his ignorance.*

The pleading voice of Elliott Goodman echoes down the library corridor. "Why me, God? Why me?"

Elliott felt his heart stop for a brief moment, then beat again as Jim Dash breathed life back into him. The CPR had worked, but he felt strange, disoriented.

Did he make it? Was he dead?

He detested the idea of giving up.

Oh, God, I'm not ready to go. *Not yet.* I want to live! *Let me have my life back!*

The force of his internal pleading opened his eyes wide.

"And just why *should* I?" a voice responded somewhere from above.

"Wha . . . Who's that?" Elliott asked. "Is that *you*, Doc?" While Elliott tried to locate his interrogator, he felt as though he were trapped inside a weird variation of Rembrandt's 1632 painting *The Anatomy Lesson of Dr. Tulp.* There was the dark operating room; the surgeon and his assistants huddling around him, their bodies bathed in a ghostly shadow; and, emerging from the chiaroscuro, an imposing form floating eerily above them all, as if suspended from the ceiling.

"Well, why *should* I?" the floating figure repeated.

"Why should you *what*?"

"Why should I let you have your life back?"

Wait a minute, who am I talking to? What's going on here? Is that Mephistopheles up there? Am I bartering my soul for another shot at life? *Hey!* How'd he know what I was thinking? That I wanted my life back? Could it *be*? Am I talking to . . . ?

"Are you . . . ? You *can't* be . . ."

"Yep, I sure am. It's me, all right. The Almighty."

"*God?* Is that *you?*" Elliott inquired, incredulous.

"The one and only," God answered. "So why should I save you, Elliott Goodman?"

Elliott couldn't believe the conversation he was having. He was on the brink of death, maybe taking his last gasp, his chest was about to be sawed open, and here he was shmoozing with his Maker!

With his life on the line, he had to come up with an answer, and a damn good one at that, one that would justify his entire existence on the planet.

"Well, let's put it this way," he temporized. "I'm not a bad person. I'm a pretty good husband and father and friend. I—"

"That won't cut it, Elliott," God interrupted. "You could be any one of several billion people down here. So why is your *particular* life worthy of salvation?"

Elliott peered up at the ceiling to get a better look at the Almighty. Perhaps because of the morphine and his emotional and mental states, the details were fuzzy. He did notice a white beard, a bit shorter than he thought it would be, and instead of a robe or some such Old Testament garment, it appeared that He was wearing a burgundy golf shirt and tan Dockers. God's voice was deep and resonant, with a faintly Charlton Heston accent.

"Well . . . ," Elliott fumbled, "as a teacher of great literary texts, I've helped many students to appreciate the important thinkers of Western civilization. . . ." Elliott couldn't believe the vapid claptrap he was spewing. No, he'd have to come up with something more human, more empathetic.

"And . . . and . . . I love life and I love animals and I never kill anything, except maybe, occasionally, a mosquito or a fly," Elliott blurted.

He racked his brain furiously in an effort to come up with something else that would make sense, that might satisfy God, that could . . . save his hide.

Maybe something more appropriate to the occasion?

"And . . . I go to synagogue for the High Holidays and still light the Chanukah candles with the kids and . . ." Elliott realized he was in a deep hole from which he'd have to try something desperate in order to extricate himself.

Perhaps . . . the truth?

"Actually, I don't know why. I'm still thinking things through. I'm still a little confused about exactly who I am and what I've done with my life and what it all really means. Honestly? I . . . I don't know why I'm worth saving. . . ."

After what seemed an eternity, God spake.

"Well, Elliott Goodman, this is a tough one. I know you still haven't figured things out, and that's par for the course. But because I'm a just and merciful God, and because I find your case intriguing, I'm going to give you a chance to save yourself. And also a chance to work out some of the issues you've been struggling with all these years.

"Here's the deal: We're going to play a golf match. It will be match play, eighteen holes. If it ends up all square, we'll go to . . . [*a sly smile creases His lips*] sudden death. The stakes? It's for all the marbles, Elliott. If you win, I'll give you back your life. If you lose, you won't make it through the surgery.

"I'll even let you choose the course yourself. So close your eyes, get yourself ready, and we'll see you on the first tee. Ciao!"

Elliott lay on the operating table, stunned.

Had he heard right? A golf match against God, to save his life? After fifty years of living and loving and teaching and trying and succeeding and failing, had it all come down to *this*?

He gazed up to take one last look at God, but by then the Almighty had vanished into thin air.

Was this a dream? Was he hallucinating?

Fading fast, all he could see was the empty OR ceiling, and then the vague outline of the surgeon. He could barely hear Jim Dash's voice.

"Scalpel . . . Now I'm making the incision. . . ."

Elliott Goodman closed his eyes, slowly . . . slowly . . .

FRONT NINE

1

NICE CLUBS

WHEN HE OPENED HIS EYES, Elliott was astonished to find himself not in the OR or even the ICU, but in the men's locker room at Inwood Country Club, on Long Island. Wearing nothing but Jockey shorts, he was seated on a smooth wooden bench in front of a locker that sported a strip of adhesive with his name carefully scrolled in red marker pen: GOODMAN, E.

So it *did* happen! So it *was* God!

Elliott's mind was cluttered with desultory thoughts and questions. He was breathing normally and, best of all, felt no pain. In fact, he'd never felt better in his entire life. Somehow, God must have healed him, at least for the time being, presumably in a grand gesture of fair play.

He must also have read Elliott's mind (again!) and known that he'd chosen Inwood, the site of the '23 U.S. Open where Bobby Jones came from three strokes behind on the seventy-second hole to force a playoff, then beat Bobby Cruikshank 76 to 78 the next day, as his course of preference. After all, that's where he'd learned to play the game as a kid, and he knew the golf course like the back of his hand.

Then the torrent of questions.

How am I supposed to beat God? Are we going to play even, or is He planning to give me some kind of handicap—you know, the one a person gets when he has to pit his skills against those of . . . *the Supreme Being*? If so, how many strokes per hole will I be granted, to compensate for miracles? Let's see, last time I played, I was a 10-handicap. Does that mean I'll get five strokes a side, or is God less than a scratch golfer? Is He a plus-10, for instance?

Is God going to hit from the blue tees and I from the red? If He is perfect, does that mean He'll have a hole-in-one on every hole and shoot 18? On the other hand, what would it be like to watch God flub a shot? Has He ever played Inwood before? Are we going to use a cart, or will we walk, accompanied by caddies? Does God *need* a caddie? Why did the Almighty choose golf as the game upon which my salvation depends, rather than, for instance, tennis or squash or racquetball or badminton or billiards or bowling or ping-pong or pennyball?

Shrugging off these questions, Elliott concentrated on getting dressed and preparing mentally for the match. He opened the locker and found, hanging neatly on hooks, a pair of olive Dockers, a golf visor with the inscription MASS GENERAL HOSPITAL, BOSTON, and a light green hospital patient's collarless V-neck scrub shirt with his name embroidered on the left breast. On the floor in front of the locker were some forest green socks rolled up in a tight ball and resting comfortably on a pair of brown-and-white-saddle FootJoy golf shoes.

How very spiffy!

Elliott put on his togs with great care. As he slowly tied his shoes, he grew aware of a complex of feelings coursing through his veins. Relief, from being out of the hospital and out of the pain and anguish of the infarction. Nervousness, from the ramifications of the imminent match. Confusion, from his ignorance of the rules. Most of all, exhilaration.

He put his head in his hands and tried to gather his thoughts, to catch his breath, to give himself a little pep talk. Okay. This is it. You can *do* it. . . .

Holy kamoley! I'm playing golf *against God!* With my *life* hanging in the balance!

Despite the jitters, Elliott pursed his lips and screwed up his face. He was a fighter, and nothing was going to keep him from giving this his best effort.

As Elliott walked toward the exit door, he noticed that he was wearing the conventional metal spikes he used to wear and not the soft ones presently required by most golf clubs. This made him smile, because he'd always loved the sound of the spikes against a hard surface. The tiles of a locker-room floor. A concrete cart path . . .

It occurred to him that, like the adhesive on the front of the locker and his feeling of complete health, the spikes might just have been another nice touch by God, and a sporting one at that.

When Elliott stepped outside, he was greeted rudely by a stiff breeze. Situated smack on Jamaica Bay, Inwood could be a bitch of a course when the wind picked up. It could add ten strokes to your score, easy. Elliott figured God just wanted to enhance the challenge and that it would be the same for him as for his Esteemed Opponent, so he didn't give it a second thought.

Instead, he headed toward the pro shop to get some tees and a scorecard. Awaiting him there was none other than Al Peppe, the old caddiemaster at Inwood who had, in fact, passed away in '77. Elliott was astounded to see Peppe, but then, in light of everything else that had just happened, he assumed it was simply one of those things God could do.

Boy, it was good to see ol' Peppe again! He was the same jovial guy, with the body of a sixty-year-old and the spirit of a teenager. His face was, as always, filled with character and the wrinkles of joy. Dotted with birthmarks and imperfections, it had a magnificent dark olive hue, reflecting both its Mediterranean roots and its constant exposure to the sun. As a kid, Elliott could always count on Peppe for an encouraging word and a quick tip before he teed it up on number one.

"They's waitin' for ya, kid," Peppe said, in his Italo-Brooklynese accent. "I knows ya can do it. They ain't got a chance!"

Elliott smiled and gave the caddiemaster a wink as he left the pro shop and walked confidently toward the tee-box at number one. It bothered him, though, that Peppe had referred to his opponent in the third person plural.

They?

Approaching the first tee, he looked up and saw a cart with two bags strapped to the back. The course was empty, except for a lone figure on the tee, his back to Elliott, taking practice swings. Noticing from behind a longish white beard, Elliott naturally assumed that the figure was God.

On closer inspection, the beard appeared to be longer than the one he'd seen in the OR. Longer, and less kempt.

When the figure turned around, Elliott could swear he'd seen that face before. The long, scraggly white beard. The tousled white hair, nearly bald at the top, just like Alastair Sim's in *A Christmas Carol*. The bushy eyebrows. The rings under the eyes. The ruddy complexion. And, protruding from the weather-beaten face, the noble nose that erupted, like Etna from the Sicilian countryside.

Of course! It wasn't God at all. It was . . .

Elliott could scarcely believe it. That face, just as it appeared in the famous self-portrait he had studied for hours in his carrel in Widener while preparing his "Imagination and Literature" seminar! His opponent wasn't God at all, but . . . *homo universalis,* the prototypical Renaissance man, the genius from the village of Vinci.

Leonardo!

Elliott felt a huge sense of relief. He didn't have to play against God after all! Not for the first hole, anyway. But another question had just been added to the heap piled up in his brain.

Why Leonardo?

Having spent a good deal of research time in Italy over the years and having taught texts by writers like Dante, Petrarch, Boccaccio, Machiavelli, Leopardi, and Pirandello, Elliott knew enough Italian to get by. Walking up to the great thinker, he doffed his visor and smiled nervously.

"*Buon giorno, signore, e come stai? Mi chiamo Elliott.*"

"*Bene, bene, io so . . . ma . . . parliamo inglese,*" Leonardo answered, with his scratchy yet noble voice.

Elliott felt like a total doofus.

Of course Leonardo da Vinci speaks English! *Du-uh!* Along with twenty or thirty other languages, probably!

He couldn't believe he was getting ready to tee off against possibly the greatest thinker the human race had yet produced.

"Excuse me," he began. "I hope I'm not offending you, but may I ask why *you're* here? I was expecting to be playing against God, actually."

Leonardo smiled his wise smile. "*Ascolta.* God has decided that to make even the field of play, he would not make you to play against Him. Instead, in His wisdom, he is sending down eighteen of us—how to say?—*substitutes* to play against you, one for each hole."

Elliott almost burst out laughing, not because of the information Leonardo had just imparted to him, but because the severe Tuscan accent had summoned to his mind's eye the image of *SNL*'s Father Guido Sarducci.

Once recovered from his near hysteria, he wondered why God had chosen Leonardo in particular for this opening hole, and who would be his (equally extraordinary?) opponents thereafter.

"The honor, she is yours, I think."

Elliott accepted, although he couldn't figure out why he would be given the honor over Leonardo. Had God given it to him because, after all, it was *his* life that was at stake? Would it be the last time in the match he would have it?

Determined not to be bothered by these negative thoughts, as well as by all the jetsam bobbing around in his head, Elliott approached the cart, grabbed a Big Bertha Titanium 454 driver from his bag, and walked to the tee-box. As he Velcroed on his off-white FootJoy StaSof glove and propped up his Titleist NXT ball on a yellow tee, his eyes slowly surveyed the terrain ahead of him.

The first hole at Inwood is pretty straightforward, a short, 345-yard par-4. (They'd be playing the blue tees today.) Most of the trouble is on the right, in the form of an expansive driving range that Elliott had gotten to know intimately in his slice-filled youth. For some reason, it had been designed immediately adjacent to the first hole.

Farther down lurks a massive area of marshland and reeds, beyond which is the dreaded Bay. Definitely OB. A sliced drive is obviously big trouble. Your ball would either land in the driving range, surrounded by thousands of old range balls with those thick red circles painted around their circumferences, or, if you really tagged it, be lost for all eternity in the mucky fen.

The left-to-right wind picked up considerably, making a slice even more disastrous, as Elliott took his stance. He was trying hard not to be overwhelmed by the aura of his opponent, or by what was at stake in the match. On the take-back, he thought only about pronating his wrists and drawing the ball, or at least not slicing it.

Keep it straight or left-fairway. Turn your wrists. Back to the target . . . back to the target . . . back to the *target!*

Just as Elliott uttered the penultimate syllable, his wrists exploded at impact, pronating as he had wanted them to, a fraction behind his lower body. This enabled him to avoid opening his clubface and slicing the ball. He couldn't control every drive this way, but to his relief, he did this time.

The ball jumped off the tee like a rocket and described a magnificent arc that he had effected in the past only occasionally. Starting out to the right, it corrected itself at about a hundred yards, veering gently to the left against the wind. *A perfect draw!*

To Elliott's delight, his Titleist landed 240 yards down the fairway, center cut.

It was Leonardo's turn now, which allowed Elliott to make a more detailed study of his opponent. He noted that Leo—he liked the idea of calling the great man Leo, if only to himself—was clad in surprisingly modern garb, all Italian, of course. A stylish navy-and-white-striped polo, by Fila. White Armani slacks. A pair of handsome cream-colored leather golf shoes, obviously handcrafted in the land of Buonarroti, Garibaldi, and Valpolicella.

My God! It is him! I'm playing against the creator of the Mona Lisa, The Last Supper, *and* The Virgin of the Rocks! *The author of* The Notebooks! *The student of anatomy, botany, optics, mechanics, geology, aerology, hydrology, and meteorol-*

ogy! The creator of the underwater diving suit and the flying machine! Painter, sculptor, architect, engineer, scientist, musician, innovator, inventor!

Elliott had to calm down from the realization that he was actually playing against this icon. Watching Leonardo tee up his ball, Elliott reflected that, in a bizarre twist of irony, a mere six months ago he had been driving through France—Normandy, Brittany, and the Loire Valley—on a research grant and had stopped for an hour to gaze upon the rectangular stone tomb, at the château at Amboise, of . . . *Leonardo himself!*

He ruminated on a few other things as he watched the man from Vinci take his practice swings.

He's a lefty. *Of course* he is, which is why he was so good at that mirror writing. His tempo isn't as smooth as Bob Charles's or as athletic as Russ Cochran's or as compressed as Mike Weir's or as pure as Phil Mickelson's. In fact, it's sort of gawky! Short, compact backswing, a bit herky-jerky through impact, off-balanced at the follow-through . . .

What concentration! I've never seen anyone so completely into the moment, so totally focused.

And those clubs! Made of ancient wood, maybe an Italian analogue to hickory? They're gorgeous, but primitive-looking, and the grooves on the driver have almost disappeared, probably from many centuries of use.

I wonder if . . . Could Leo have designed them himself? *Could it be?* Did golf thus originate in the late fifteenth century in the rolling hills of Tuscany, and not around the same time in Scotland, as common knowledge supposes? Am I actually observing the man who, along with all the other impressive items on his résumé, is also the inventor of . . . *the golf club?*

Leonardo was set. While Elliott observed, unprepared for

what came next. Leonardo's swing may have looked a bit odd, but there was something calculated about it, as if it were the result of a great deal of observation and thinking. After an unprepossessing waggle, the arms took the club back crooked—sorta like Miller Barber's or Jim Furyk's backswing, Elliott thought—but returned to the ball on precisely the same arc, not one degree higher or lower.

Then—*tock!*—the club propelled the ball into the fairway, as if it were thrown by some great, primitive catapultlike contraption. Elliott looked at the moving sphere in awe. It was not a great shot, nor even a pretty one, but he had never seen a golf ball sent forward into a blustery wind as straight or as true. It was as if, rather than hit the ball, Leonardo had projected it the way an assembly-line machine would expel the product of its fabrication.

The ball landed softly in the fairway, a modest 180 yards from the tee, but in what seemed to be its precise mathematical center.

While Elliott watched the drive, a quote surfaced in his brain (as one often did), from Leonardo's *Notebooks,* the section discussing mechanics and its various components—weight, force, percussion, movement, impetus. Elliott had never realized it, but when Leonardo wrote about force 500 years ago, he might just as well have been talking about golf: "Force is nothing but a spiritual energy, an invisible power, which is created and imparted, through violence from without, by animated bodies to inanimate bodies. . . . Retardation strengthens, and speed weakens it. It lives by violence and dies from liberty."

Elliott realized that he was actually witnessing the powerful idea in practice!

"*Molto bene.* Nice shot." Elliott didn't wish to appear patronizing or starstruck, but, after all, it *was* a nice shot. The two replaced their drivers in their respective bags, and Elliott got behind the wheel.

"Mind if I drive?"

"*Per piacere*, I beg of you."

Despite the distance advantage his drive had given him, Elliott felt queasy.

Was the pressure of *having* to win already starting to take its psychological toll? Perhaps it was the strangeness of playing against you-know-who? Or not knowing what to say to this awesome personage?

To break the ice, Elliott proffered the following profundity: "So . . . nice clubs!"

As soon as the words tripped off his tongue, he realized how banal and idiotic they sounded.

What kind of a moron are you? What could you be *thinking*? Here you are, sitting beside arguably the world's most creative mind ever, a genius about whom you've often lectured, and you ask him not about how nature works or the artistic organization of the cosmos or even how he had developed the painterly technique of atmospheric perspective.

But . . . *nice clubs?*

Leonardo, however, seemed pleased by the compliment.

"*È vero.* They are nice, no? I designed them myself, around 1485, I think, in the private forge of my friend Ludovico Sforza. They are pretty old, but they still work pretty good."

Elliott was stunned to have his hunch about the clubs confirmed, but he was distracted by the wind, which by now had become a gale. He did all he could to hold the cart on its course as it teetered down the fairway.

For the first time, he noticed the dashboard, which was filled with accoutrements God must have made available to both him and Leonardo. On his side were a can of Dr. Brown's

Cream Soda, a small spray bottle of nitroglycerin lingual aerosol, and some extra tees. On the passenger's side were a bottle of arthritis pills, a canister of throat lozenges, two tubes of ointment (Desenex, Preparation H), and an empty artist's notebook.

This was a great deal more than Elliott would have wanted to know about Leonardo, but he liked the fact that the Almighty had graciously provided amenities for a number of potential golfing emergencies.

Eager to follow his earlier verbal gaffe with a query of greater substance, Elliott asked, "What is it about golf that appeals to you?"

Leonardo responded without giving the question a millisecond's thought. "I love this game. Been playing it for over five centuries now. She has taught me much, but the best thing is that I get to use both sides of my brain when I play!"

"Yes," Elliott acknowledged, "I've always admired you for your ability to use your left and right brains with equal facility. It's a rare gift."

"I don't know about that, but when I play golf, I am able to think and also to feel. It's a big challenge!"

"But don't you find that difficult to do?" Elliott asked, partly anticipating the reply.

"No, not really. You see, the universe, she's a great big work of art, with all the pieces fitting in just right, like so." The old man clasped his hands together with his fingers intertwined, to make the point. "And all the things in nature are part of a big painting I have up here," he continued, pointing to his forehead. "Yes, everything fits together, art and science, logic and instinct, whether you are inventing an airplane or playing golf!"

Elliott thought it over, then commented, "Makes sense. After all, science isn't really the opposite of art, but, from the Latin *scientia,* just another form of knowledge."

"Bingo!"

Arriving at his ball, Leonardo jumped out of the cart and perused his bag. His old Pinnacle lay quite a distance from the green, about 165 yards away, but it seemed a lot farther in view of the left-to-right wind whipping across his face.

Leonardo surveyed the situation slowly, methodically. Then he grabbed his weather-beaten three-iron and, to Elliott's amazement, faced toward the third fairway, nearly ninety degrees away from his target.

Licking his chops, Elliott waited to see how the old man was going to pull off this bizarre shot. There was his own ball, sixty yards past Leonardo's, and here was the old guy aiming toward the wrong fairway!

Leonardo took a practice swing, a low, three-quarter kind of lunge. At address, he took a slow, deep breath, then pulled the club back carefully and made violent but controlled contact with the ball. The projectile took off like a shot, into the teeth of the wind and, at the start, forty yards off course. It was a strange, low, bump-and-run shot, perfectly appropriate for these Scottishlike conditions.

The wind took the ball in its grasp and turned it over, left to right, in such a way that when it finally landed, never rising above the ground more than six or seven feet, it did so twenty feet in front of the apron and in the center of the fairway—whence it took three teeny bounces and hopped onto the green.

Unluckily for Leonardo, the green had been so hardened by the wind that the ball bounced through and landed over the collar and into the right bunker.

Elliott was dumbstruck. Even though Leonardo had left himself a difficult third shot, it was amazing to him that the great thinker had even *attempted* this shot, much less almost pulled it off.

"How did you do *that*?" Elliott asked, as Leonardo climbed back into the cart.

"*Ecco*, as I once said in my *Notebooks,* force, she is only a desire of flight. Always she desires to weaken and to spend herself. Herself constrained she constrains everybody. Without her nothing moves."

The oblique yet incontrovertible wisdom of this observation rendered Elliott speechless, but he still had his own second shot to contend with.

With the old man in the bunker, all he had to do to clinch victory at this opening but crucially important hole was to get the ball safely on the green, or at least in its vicinity.

Driving up to his ball, Elliott addressed Leonardo again in an attempt to break the tension. "So what's the *real* story behind Mona Lisa's smile?"

"Ah, *La Gioconda,*" the master answered, his eyes lighting up. "What a *bella donna*! She don't smile because she's . . . wearing braces. No, no, just kidding!

"Actually, if you think that golf is mysterious, try figuring out women! That smile, she is the smile of all women. She is no big, no small, no happy, no sad, no open, no closed. I paint it, out of *amore,* to be—how to say?—between the smile and the *no*-smile!"

Elliott suddenly pricked up his ears and tilted his head, like a Doberman listening to a potential intruder. Flaring his nostrils, he became aware of a curious odor emanating from Leonardo's clothes.

On closer inspection, he identified the admixture: the faint, pungent aroma of cigarettes . . . a hint of oregano . . . a trace of Amaretto . . . a soupçon of *formaggio*. It was the smell of . . . Italy!

Like a bolt out of the Proustian blue, Elliott's mind—shocked into action by this olfactory jolt—leaped to his favorite table at his favorite café at his favorite square in the world, Rome's fabled Piazza Navona.

It was a research trip in the late eighties. He was working on a book about the little-known Italian poet, Giacomo Leopardi, and, for the first time, he discovered the restorative wonders of the Piazza. How he loved to sit there for hours, slowly nursing his fiasco di Chianti, *gazing at the stately church of S. Agnese in Agone and the splendid-looking Romans as they walked by his table, listening to the mesmerizing splash of the water as it cascaded down Bernini's Fountain of the Four Rivers. . . .*

Elliott's dream balloon burst when the cart reached his ball.

Let's see . . . about 105 . . . wind's still pretty stiff, left to right and against . . . I'd say an eight-iron . . . maybe a seven. . . .

In truth, Elliott had no inkling of what club to hit. The wind was vicious, and he wasn't sure whether to hit a hard eight or an easy seven or how far left to aim the ball or how low to keep it.

Frozen with indecision, he decided it might be prudent to hit a shot like the one Leonardo had just pulled off. He knew he had to avoid all that junk lurking to the right of the green. He also knew that his distance advantage had vanished.

He took his club back and swung with no commitment. No hard, no easy, no high, no low, as Leonardo might have put it. The ball skidded off the toe of his eight-iron, barely three feet off the ground, and disappeared into the ugliest patch of deep, gnarly grass you'd ever want to see outside of Scotland, landing in front, and to the left, of the green.

Elliott clambered dejectedly back into the cart, put his foot down on the accelerator, and, out of pure frustration, *floored it*. The cart took off, jolting Elliott Goodman and Leonardo da Vinci backward.

Remembering with whom he was driving, Elliott resumed a normal speed.

"You play often?"

"Well, actually, yes. About four or five times a week."

"What do you do on the other days?"

"Oh, I putter around up there, do my drawings, invent a few things. I always keep busy."

"And with whom do you play golf, if I may ask?"

"Different people. You know, Buddha, Henny Youngman, Harry Truman, Michelangelo, Gertrude Stein . . . But I do have a regular foursome."

"And who's in that?"

"Let's see, there's me and Mozart and Alexander the Great and Henry Miller."

"Some group!"

"*Ma certo!* We enjoy playing together. I like beating Mozart, that little squirt! Alexander, if you want to know the truth, he's not so great! And Henry, he's always fun. Except when we play with Cleopatra or Virginia Wolff—then we must keep the eye on him!"

Elliott was still hopeful of winning the hole, but when he reached his ball, his hope was smashed into smithereens. There sat his Titleist, buried in a hyper-nasty clump of weedy, gnarly, overgrown, jungly, gorsy, furzy *garbaggio*—which the course superintendents, Pete and Kevin, had been kind enough to let grow out.

Another quote popped into Elliott's head, appropriately, Dante's inscription over the Gates of Hell: ". . . *lasciate ogne speranza, voi ch'intrate.*"

"Abandon all hope, ye who enter," indeed.

Elliott chose sand wedge from his bag and addressed his ball. At impact, the thick grass took hold of the wedge's hozzle and directed the ball left, to the back edge of the green, some thirty-five feet from the cup. Still, Elliott was pleased with the shot and hoped he could two-putt for a bogey and the old man would have trouble exploding from the bunker.

As Elliott walked up to mark his ball, Leonardo trekked to the bunker and stared back at the green and, beyond it, at the rest of the hole. It was as though he wanted to study the entire surroundings of the hole itself, to get some perspective on his shot.

After jotting down some notes and dashing down some quick squiggles in the notebook he had brought from the cart, the old master spent a few seconds in thought. Elliott couldn't understand why Leonardo didn't just grab his sand wedge and hack away.

His opponent walked back to the cart and grabbed . . . *his putter!*

It took all of Elliott's muscular dexterity, including a cute little maneuver he deftly crafted with his sphincter, to suppress a smile that was begging to erupt.

A putter, from the bunker? Leo must be out of his *gourd*!

What Elliott didn't know, and what the old man had slyly figured out, was that there was hardly any lip on the left side of the bunker, and the terrain going past the bunker and up through the apron and onto the putting surface was relatively flat and bumpless.

Furthermore, the line of this particular shot, if struck properly, was directly into a hump on the green, which, if the speed and angle were judged correctly, would ricochet the ball—in the manner of a miniature-golf obstacle—due east and on a direct line to the cup.

To Elliott, all this would have seemed Rube Goldbergian, but to Leonardo, it was as natural as sucking up a plate of rigatoni. Conversely, an explosion shot, even if hit properly, probably wouldn't hold the green, which sloped away from the bunker and toward the fairway. So the only way of exploding close to the hole would be, in fact, to put the ball *in* it.

Leonardo had learned all this crucial information from a careful observation of natural laws, which allowed him to approach his bag confidently and withdraw from it the only possible club demanded by this particular shot—his 521-year-old, battered but trusty flat stick.

The universal man dug his expensive shoes deep into the sand, took a few practice putts inches above his ball, and inhaled slowly. "*È difficile*," he whispered to himself inaudibly, "*ma non è . . . impos*SI*bile!*" Exactly on the *si*, he struck his ball cleanly and squarely. [*Jump . . . roll . . . roll . . . roll . . . bump! . . . turn . . . roll . . . roll . . . roll . . .*]

Astonishingly, it landed an inch from the cup.

Overcome with amazement, Elliott realized that Leonardo was good for an unbelievable par 4, and that he needed to drain his thirty-six-footer to halve the hole. Stepping up to his ball, he felt his heart flutter. Was it the excitement of the moment? The amazement at Leonardo's play? The pressure of having to make the putt? A myocardial relapse?

Elliott lined up the putt, read it from his crouch, took his stance, and muttered to his imaginary caddie: "Left to right . . . about three inches outside the cup, I'd say . . . green is pretty hard, so it'll be fast . . . just get it to the hole. *Never up, never in.*"

The putt started three inches to the left of the hole, as advertised, and held its line perfectly until it got to within five feet, when it began curling . . . curling . . . At the cup, Elliott's ball refused to turn farther and moseyed past by a mere centimeter.

It was *that* close.

Elliott's knees buckled, and he felt a twinge of nausea rising from his toes. Gathering himself, he walked over to Leonardo and, conceding the putt, extended his hand.

"*Molto bene . . . mi rallegro con voi.* Congratulations!"

"*Non c'è di che!*" Leonardo responded, smiling modestly. "*Ma che peccato!* You played very well, my friend," he added. "Just that one mistake, or it would have been—how to say?—*even-Stefano!*"

Elliott bent down to pick up his ball, and when he looked up to bid farewell to Leonardo, without warning, and to his great bewilderment, the old man had simply vanished into thin air, leaving behind him only a vague trace of garlic.

Elliott was left standing alone on the first green, in a state of mild shock, his brain teeming.

How he had loved meeting and talking to Leonardo! How he wished he had spent more time chatting with him! He reminded himself of Tallulah Bankhead's great quote— "There have been only two geniuses in the world. Willie Mays and Willie Shakespeare"—and made a mental note that she should definitely have included Leonardo in that select list.

Elliott reviewed the hole, shot by shot. Why had he lost it? He had hit three wonderful shots and could easily have won or halved the hole with his bogey. It was just that one bad shot into the teeth of the wind. What had happened?

Wasn't it his indecision before selecting the club that had done him in? Hadn't he lacked a plan for which shot to hit or how hard to hit it or how far to the left to aim? Leonardo, on the other hand, had been decisive where he'd been hesitant. The Great Inventor had *planned* his two amazing shots before making his club selections, so that once he'd chosen a club, all there was left to do was to execute.

Hadn't Elliott failed on this first hole—this first test of his character?—on the very issue that had confronted him his whole life, the conflict between thinking and doing? Usually, he had a Hamletlike tendency to think too much and not do enough, but on his second shot, hadn't he failed to think at all, acting without any concept of what he was doing?

Strange how golf uncovers our weaknesses.

Was *that* why the great Renaissance man was selected by the Almighty as His lead-off substitute? Elliott couldn't stop thinking about how perfectly complementary Leonardo's left and right brains were. The rational and the intuitive. And he reflected on the importance of having both, in golf and in life. Have a plan, think it out clearly. Clear your mind, and just *do* it.

Another thought crossed Elliott's mind. Had he in fact underestimated his opponent? Had he gained some degree of false confidence by perceiving Leonardo as gawky or weak or a lefty or an old man using old clubs?

This is going to be a lot trickier than I thought. After those two miraculous shots by Leonardo, am I playing against God, after all?

Elliott trudged, head down, humbled, toward the second tee with the depressing realization that he had gotten off on the wrong foot. He was one down in the match.

He tried to focus his thoughts on what he had just learned from the play of this amazing man (and inventor of the golf club!), this great Thinker and Doer, when yet another thought crossed his mind. Which "substitute" would follow Leonardo in God's All-Star Lineup?

Who the devil could possibly be awaiting him at the second tee?

2

SEAGULL

"BEELZEBUB!" BELLOWED A VOICE that was, of all the voices in the history of the world, unquestionably the most unmistakable.

Elliott didn't have to look up to ascertain who his next opponent would be. It was *he*! The self-proclaimed Great Man! The one, the only . . . [*drum roll*] . . .

William Claude Dukenfield!

Replacing his ball on the tee from which it had been unceremoniously unseated by a mighty gust of wind, W. C. Fields resumed his diatribe against the uncooperative force of nature. "God-frey Daniel! Blow winds and crack your cheeks, will you? You almost cracked mine, you vile jabbernowl!"

Returning to his pre-shot practice routine, he spied Elliott out of the corner of his eye. With a double-take hitch of his shoulders and a look of mock surprise in his eyes, the Great Man acknowledged the presence of his opponent.

"'Zounds! It is you, young whippersnapper! Yes, it is none other than the eloquent, the eleemosynary . . . Elliott Goodman. What a euphonious appellation! What a beauteous cognomen! It is a distinct pleasure to meet you at last, my dear rapscallion!"

Elliott was flabbergasted. First Leonardo, and now W. C. Fields. How bizarre! How extraordinary! "Hello, but I assure you the pleasure's all mine."

Fields was dressed in his customary golf attire: top hat, gloves (old golf gloves on both hands, with holes at the tips, from which his stubby fingers protruded), a robin's-egg blue polo shirt with a martini-glass logo on his left breast, navy plus-fours, turquoise-and-red argyle socks, and black-and-white wing-tip golf shoes.

"Yes, I'm sure . . . I'm sure. . . ," Fields's voice trailed off.

The juggler from Philadelphia continued his practice swings without missing a verbal beat. "It appears from what has transpired on the previous hole that I have usurped the privilege of initiating the projection of the pulchritudinous pellet. In short . . . I have the honor!"

Elliott could hardly contain his glee at seeing his favorite comic actor of all time. *The great Fields!* He'd laughed himself silly through all of Fields's films, every single one of them. He'd even written a scholarly article, appearing in the *Publication of the Modern Language Association,* titled "Euphony and Euphemism: Canorous Circumlocution in the Language of Shakespeare, Mallarmé, and W. C. Fields."

Elliott knew that his opponent was no duffer.

Hadn't he made four films—"The Golf Specialist," "The Dentist," "The Big Broadcast of 1938," and "You're Telling Me"—in which he performed his hilarious golf shtick, demonstrating extraordinary dexterity and coordination? Hadn't he been a longtime member at Riviera in L.A., one of the world's finest courses? Hadn't he been successful at everything he'd ever undertaken, from juggling to stage acting to film acting to finances?

This was, however, no time for adoration. Elliott was one down, and he had to win this hole to square the match and stop the bleeding.

Relax. It's just another hole. No big deal. Just take it one shot at a time. He may be W. C. Fields, but he ain't Leonardo!

The wind off the Bay was really whipping now, and once again, Fields's ball tottered and fell from its wooden perch. "Mother of pearl!" he yowled, teeing it up for the third time.

The second hole at Inwood is a 362-yard par-4, not particularly difficult unless you slice the ball or otherwise don't keep it on the fairway. When the wind is up, it's about a par-6.

Directly in front of the tee-box and sixty yards down the fairway is a sizable man-made pond, the year-round home of various winged creatures and amphibia. It doesn't come into play except for the fact that it is *there*.

The hole is a dogleg right, with trouble, *big* trouble, on the right from tee to green, in the form of cattails, marshland, and Jamaica Bay, which swallows up thirty-five golf balls on a slow day. To the left of the fairway is no picnic, either, although by far the lesser of two evils (no OB). Over there is hardpan, maple sugars and sycamores, plenty of blind shots, and a slew of bunkers. If you airmail the green on your second shot, well, put a fork in you, you're done. More quagmire, reeds, mucky bog, and the ubiquitous Bay.

As William Claude completed his practice swings, Elliott couldn't help but marvel at his physical prowess. Not that he had a fluid swing or a magnificent physique. Far from it. Fields was on the short and dumpy side and had modest physical endowments. But there was a delicacy about him, an aura of magician and juggler, a sense that at any time, through sleight of hand, he could produce some sort of legerdemain with his golfing wand.

The Great Man addressed the ball, with a waggle of his

hips that spoke volumes about golfing experience and confidence. He gripped the driver gently, with his fingertips first wiggling on, then caressing the leather like a retriever pressing a pheasant in his teeth, with a firm gentleness so as to secure a hold without causing undue damage.

Just as he took the club back, he stopped dead in his tracks, put his left hand in his mouth, and, winking at Elliott, pulled out a brand new Callaway HX Tour golf ball. "Just in case I am guilty of some unanticipated peccadillo!" he explained.

Resuming his pre-shot routine, he talked to himself out loud. "Yes-indeedy. What a gorgeous day. What effulgent sunshine. It was a day of this sort the McGillicuddy brothers murdered their mother with an ax!" Although Elliott had heard the line before somewhere, he felt the beginning of a giggle well up inside, but, observing golfing etiquette, he managed to contain his mirth.

The instant Fields had finished speaking, he took his club back again and struck the ball with a delicate and fluid "hand swing," his talented and dexterous hands in total control and his rotund body just tagging along behind for the ride.

It was not one of his more impressive drives. The upper half of the ball made contact with the lower half of the club-head, producing a shot that had overspin and no trajectory. The good news was that it traveled straight down the fairway. The bad news was that it was moving four feet above ground level, diving fast, and heading directly toward the pond in front of the tee-box.

As Fields held his follow-through pose, his mouth dropped wide open in disbelief. The ball hit the surface of the water, then skimmed out like that flat stone you used to skip on the lake when you were a kid. It landed smack in the middle of the fairway, although only 100 yards from the tee.

"Suffering sciatica!" Fields harrumphed, annoyed at his near-miss but dumbfounded by the stroke of luck of which he was the recipient. Tipping his hat as he strode past Elliott, he warbled, "A bit of fortuitous prestidigitation, I'm afraid. *A toi,* little nipper!"

Elliott's mind was abuzz.

He had barely recovered from the experience of playing with Leonardo, and now this! How could he focus on business while playing against this Master of Amusement? How clever of God to pit him against people he had read about, studied, admired from afar! Was this going to be some kind of perverse test? Had he been chosen as some modern incarnation of Job?

Why had the Almighty chosen golf? Was there something about the game that was especially relevant to this life-and-death final exam? Did God know something about Elliott in particular that led Him to choose the golf course as His testing ground? Is every human being on the brink of death challenged by God to a golf match to prove their worthiness for salvation? Or just Elliott? Are some placed on a golf course, some on a tennis court, others in front of a chessboard, and still others before a written exam like the SAT? Like Leonardo, why had Fields been chosen as one of his opponents? Had God put all these unanswerable questions in his head just to thwart his concentration, to take his mind off the present moment, to make this whole ordeal more difficult?

Elliott also had to wonder about the result of his opponent's first shot. It could easily have landed in the water, with Fields teeing it up again, hitting three. It could have even bounced out into a horrible lie in the thick rough in front of the fairway. Was God continuing His "little game" with him, the one He'd begun with Leonardo's pyrotechnics on the first hole?

En route to the tee-box, Elliott glanced down at his scrub shirt. Through the past twenty minutes or so, he had forgotten about his heart attack, his collapse in the stacks of Widener, his being brought to the hospital and wheeled down the corridor, and the bizarre scene with God in the OR.

When he noticed his hospital shirt on his own body for the first time, the recent past became reality. He paused to check whether his heart was still beating and his pulse was normal. They were.

Could this all be a dream, or was he actually playing a golf match against Leonardo and W. C. Fields and God knows whoever else was in store for him, just to save his life?

He placed his Titleist NXT on a tee and addressed it. His mind in disarray and unprepared to tackle the deadly serious business at hand, he stepped away from the ball and stood there, trying to compose himself. All he could think of, in the presence of his opponent, this madcap genius, were the hysterically funny words of another comic genius, Art Carney of *The Honeymooners*. Attempting to figure out what the golf manual meant by "addressing" the ball—on behalf of Kramden, who needed to learn the game quickly in order to play with his boss—Norton calmly walks up to an imaginary ball and ad-libs, "*Hel*-lo, ball!"

Elliott wiped the grin off his face and tried to clear his mind.

Forget about the heart attack. Forget about the OR scene. Forget about the match and its consequences. Forget about Fields. Just concentrate on that little white, round sonuvabitch down there!

With the wind still howling left to right, making a slice even more deadly, he positioned his stance so that he was aiming twenty yards to the left of center, drew back his TaylorMade r5 Dual Driver, paused at the top, and let 'er rip.

Elliott watched in disbelief as the ball sailed down the fairway, straight as an arrow.

Doesn't this always happen to me? When I want to hit the ball straight, I end up fading it or slicing it, and when I want to hit a fade and aim way to the left, I end up hitting the ball dead straight!

He had hit the ball a ton, probably 260, but it never made that right-hand turn and, instead, flew through the fairway, over some bunkers, ending up practically on the third tee.

"Nearly perfection, my young scalawag!" a voice boomed from behind.

The two opponents made their way to the cart, on which were attached the Great Man's anachronistic set of old hickory clubs and a spanking-new set of TaylorMades for Elliott. On the dash were the same golf paraphernalia designated for Elliott as on the first hole, but on the passenger's side sat a flask full of clear liquid and a martini glass containing several mammoth olives.

"Yes, take the wheel, my boy, I never drink and drive!" Filling his glass with liquid from the flask, Fields purred, "Ah, my sweet apple jack! My tonsil varnish! My nose paint!"

After a sip, he became even more chatty.

"Speaking of the shot I just hit, did I ever tell you about another near-escape I had on a golf course? Well, it was on one of my peregrinations, I believe I was playing at a club on Lake Titicaca, yes. Hit a screamer of a drive, but it commenced to hook, and darned if it didn't hit a geezer on the sconce!

"Well, this old moon calf comes running after me, screaming imprecations, and when he finally catches up with me, whaddya know, but he bops me on the proboscis. Yessirree, right on the ol' beezer. Probably why it's a bit on the voluminous side to this day!"

Arriving at his ball, Fields took another sip, placed his glass on the dash of the cart, and hopped out. "Ah! Terra firma at last!" he crowed, seeing his ball nestled safely on the fairway. "Should've brought a telescope to see the green, though," he muttered, referring to the fact that he still had over 250 yards of fairway to negotiate.

Grabbing three-wood from his bag, he stepped up to his ball, still muttering. "Hope I didn't hit any fishies on the noggin. . . . Yes, a narrow escape . . . a narrow escape indeed . . ."

Fields did his waggle, drew the club back smoothly, and made solid contact. The ball started out straight and true but then began slicing badly and was heading toward the dreaded out-of-bounds marshes to the right. Elliott was already figuring that Fields, having to drop a second ball in the rough, would soon be hitting four, well short of the hole—while he, even if his lie were bad, was lying only one, way down there and not that far from the green—when something dazzlingly improbable happened.

In mid-flight, the ball hit a wayward and unsuspecting seagull, who was apparently not paying much attention to the proceedings below, ricocheted off it, bounded forward, and landed smack in the middle of the fairway, only eighty-five yards short of the green.

"Ye gods! Must've hit the poor beast on the fetlock!" Fields intoned. "Eight-ball in the corner pocket!"

Jesus! First he damn near hits a fish, and now a bird. What's next, a rhino on his third shot?

Fields returned his club to his bag and eased himself back into the cart. "After this fortuitous stroke of unintended serendipity, I think I shall give my tongue a well-deserved ablution," he cracked, as he took another sip of his virtually vermouthless martini. Then, "Did I ever tell you of the time I was playing on this course in Lompoc, and . . ."

Elliott half-closed his eyes in an attempt to regain his focus, to reduce the tension of absolutely having to win the hole.

If you're testing me, God, you're doing a good job. Looks like you're pulling some pretty nasty stuff from up your sleeve, but you know what? It's not gonna work. Okay, he lies two, but he still has some work to do to reach the green. I'm only one, way down there, and I am not, repeat *not,* going to lose this hole!

". . . and I just barely escape with my life!" Fields concluded, nearly shouting, then took another hefty sip.

Jolted from his reverie, Elliott put his foot down on the accelerator and burned rubber. Brilliant juggler that he was, Fields managed to catch his toppled hat with his left hand and hold on to his glass, without losing a drop, with his right.

Suddenly realizing that he was driving around the golf course and not the Brickyard, Elliott decelerated the vehicle and reestablished contact with his opponent. "Bill . . . may I call you Bill? I've always wanted to know one thing about you. Did you and Mae West ever . . ."

"Ah, yes. Good ol' Mae. A tough paloma if ever there was one!"

"Well, did you ever . . ."

"Did we ever do the beast-with-two-backs? Commit the dirty deed? Consummate our filmic dalliances?"

"I was just wondering, with all that on-screen teasing and bantering, did you ever come up and see her sometime?"

William Claude took another generous sip and refilled his glass to the brim, even as the cart negotiated rough and moguls and tree trunks.

"My dear Good Man, a gentleman never divulges the secrets that exist between himself and a lady," Fields confessed to his opponent, concluding with a wink, "but Miss West, truth be told, weren't no lady!"

Although Elliott was longing to hear more, he had reached his ball and was more preoccupied with the lie he had drawn. As he approached it with more than a little apprehension, his worst fears were confirmed.

There lay his Titleist, in an area of hardpan and surrounded by a sizable collection of maple leaves. He was only ninety yards from the green, but, besides the questionable lie, his direct line to the pin was blocked by several overhanging maple branches, barely four feet off the ground. He stepped a few feet behind the ball to survey the situation.

Elliott tried to focus only on the shot, but his hyperactive mind started spewing Latin sayings, aphorisms he'd committed to memory long ago that related to his present dire circumstances.

Alea iacta est: The die is cast. What is, is. I overcompensated to avoid the slice, and now I have to face the music.

Per aspera ad astra: To the stars through adversity. I could've driven my ball in the fairway, but *no!* So here I am on this pile of leaves, with a blind shot to the green, and I've got to meet the challenge. . .

Virtus victrix fortunae: Character conquers chance. So what if Fields caught a lucky bounce out of the pond? So what if he hit the seagull? So what if I have a horrendous lie in no-man's-land?

Elliott came to. He knew how important the shot was, since he could easily go two down if he blew it. He got down on his haunches and peered below the branches to get a line to the pin, which he could barely see. He had two choices. Pitch out safely and duel Fields pitch for pitch, putt for putt, not knowing what other magical tours de force W. C. had up his sleeve, or go for the pin, which required a delicate touch and the heart of a lion.

If he made the latter choice, he would have to punch a

low three-iron from out of the leaves and the hardpan, off his back foot and choking up on the club to the end of the grip, nipping the ball cleanly and landing it just in front of the apron and past the traps on the left so that it would roll up and feed to the hole. It would be a bitch, but, even at this early stage of the match, he *had* to go for it.

Elliott walked up to his ball and addressed it gingerly so as not to disturb any of the leaves. He bent down to get a final look at the pin and raised himself back up.

Looking down at his ball, Elliott experienced an epiphany. Although he believed all these words and thoughts rumbling through his mind, *that's all they were!* Here he was in a real jam; and this time, with his life on the line, words and thoughts weren't worth a wooden nickel.

Elliott closed his eyes and cleared his mind and, probably for the first time in his entire adult life, willed his thinking process to cease.

His brain now completely empty, he took the three-iron slowly but only halfway back, then punched the ball, making perfect contact. Maple leaves flew, the heel of his club nearly buried itself in the hardpan, and his wrists were ringing from the impact.

Elliott's ball exploded out, flew barely under the menacing branches, continued its low trajectory three-and-a-half feet off the ground, landed just short of the apron, and began rolling onto the green. And rolling . . .

His Titleist NXT ended up three inches from the cup.

It was the finest shot he had ever hit. At the moment of impact, he had hit it with a clear mind, uncluttered by any thoughts or hesitations or cerebral distractions. Just pure, unadulterated *focus.* Unlike on the previous hole, he had planned this shot out, unburdened his brain, and executed.

He had also done it with the hounds of lucky shots and bad lies and what-ifs nipping furiously at his heels.

"Drat!" Fields exclaimed, nearly choking on his olive.

Elliott bounded back into the cart, still floating from his heroic shot. When they reached Fields's ball, it was W. C.'s turn to continue *his* magical journey to the hole. He took another sip of his nectar, rolled out of the cart, and selected nine-iron from his bag as Elliott reflected placidly.

Hmmm. Can't see my ball from here, but it looks pretty stiff. Say I'm in for a bird. He lies two and needs a chip-in to halve the hole. If he misses, the match is all square.

Elliott surveyed the skies for wayward gulls and the fairway and green for any unexpected forms of wildlife wandering around. The coast was clear.

The man from the City of Brotherly Love swaggered up to his ball, eyeballed the pin, and did his trademark graceful waggle.

"Once holed a shot like this at the municipal course in Kokomo. Yes. My caddie was tending the flag—he was a mere lad of twelve—whilst my shot was airborne. Ball comes down, hits the whippersnapper right in the family jewels, and bounces twice, right into the cup. I do believe that many years later, the young nipper became the oldest choirboy ever to sing for the Church of St. Agnes of the Meadows."

Fields straightened his top hat, which had been jostled by the wind, addressed his ball, wiggled his fingers on his grip, and took a delicate swipe. Elliott watched as the ball headed toward the hole as if it were moving in Slo-Mo. He knew that Fields had hit a good one, not only because it was dead on line, but also because the Great Man was holding his follow-through as if frozen by the triple forces of awe, bravado, and self-admiration.

Elliott's look changed from one of confidence to one of pure shock.

Was God performing yet another one of His little tricks, through the medium of this joker, this . . . prestidigitator? This time, there was no intervention of wildlife, just a damn good shot. But was there some other force directing the ball toward the hole?

The ball bounced softly onto the slick, smooth green and began to roll toward the flagstick. The line was dead straight, with no undulations or ridges or mounds around the cup. The only question now was speed. Had the Great Man given it enough juice? With his jaw dropped and his eyes wide open, Elliott continued to watch as the ball rolled onward inexorably. . . .

"Shades of Bacchus!" Fields yelped as his ball screeched to a halt, five inches short of the hole. Elliott thought he was having another heart attack, so great was the pounding of that coronary muscle.

He had weathered the storm.

This time, he had picked up the outrageous gauntlet thrown at him by unknown forces and had performed brilliantly. To think that he was a single revolution of a ball away from having this glory denied him!

Without exchanging a word, the twosome drove to the back of the apron, parked the cart, and walked onto the green for the tap-in formalities.

"It was indeed gratifying to make your esteemed acquaintance and to compete on such an altitudinous level," W. C. offered, tapping in for his par.

"I think I enjoyed this more than you'll ever know," Elliott said, nonchalantly tapping his three-inch putt backhanded.

To his dismay, the ball dribbled off the toe of his putter and nearly missed the hole, before barely catching the left corner of the cup and oozing in. He looked heavenward.

I know, I know. I should've taken my time. Every shot counts. Don't count your chickens. The Fat Lady . . .

With an enormous sense of relief, Elliott retrieved his ball from the cup, and when he straightened up and turned to bid a fond adieu to the Great Man, Fields looked back at him and, with a wry twinkle in his eye, tapped his top hat once, turned himself into a seagull, and winged his way gracefully into the wild blue yonder.

Elliott felt proud of himself as he walked to the third tee-box. By now, the bizarre disappearance of his opponent at the conclusion of the hole wasn't such a shock to his system.

The match was all square, thanks to his miraculous three-iron recovery. *Even-Stefano,* as Leonardo would have put it, and all because of traits he hadn't exhibited on the prior hole—planning, decisiveness, focus, clarity. True, he'd nearly blown all his good work on that idiotic backhanded putt, but the hole was in the record books now. He was still shaking his head at the very thought of meeting, chatting with, and competing against Leonardo and W. C. Fields, two of the greatest geniuses who ever walked the earth.

Elliott had no inkling, however, no earthly clue, not the vaguest premonition of what manner of worthy opponent God had waiting for him, armed with a propensity for witnessing miracles of otherworldly proportions and a golf game to match, at the third tee.

3

ALBATROSS

AND SO IT CAME TO PASS that on the third hole, God assigned to Elliott the mightiest of all His substitutes: shepherd, seer, sorceror, lawgiver, liberator, prophet, witnesser of miracles, author of the Torah, founder of Israel, orderer of the ten plagues, bearer of the ten commandments, leader of the Jews out of the desert. And God saw that it was good.

"Jesus H. Christ!" a surprised and awed Elliott blurted.

"No, Moses, actually," Moses corrected. "But you can call me Moshe."

The slender shard of optimism that Elliott had been grasping onto after his victory on the second hole vanished as he stood transfixed before this most venerable of personages.

So it's Moses, eh? Looks like God's taking out the big lumber, sending in the big guns. No more messing around with mere mortals. So what miracle worker's He gonna send down on the next hole? Harry Houdini? Aladdin's genie? Herb Brooks?

Moses flashed an avuncular smile, his thick, muscular beard and bulging biceps reminding Elliott of Michelangelo's impressive statue of him in Rome's San Pietro in Vincoli church. Except that now, instead of a tablet cradled in his right hand, Moses held a humongous Cleveland Launcher 460 driver and looked very much like he meant business.

Unsurprisingly, he wore a long, ankle-length robe and leather sandals. Surprisingly, he sported a white golf visor with "BBCC" scrawled across it, accompanied by a bizarre green, red, and yellow logo that looked to Elliott like a tiny floret of broccoli being consumed by a funky little flame.

Unsure of how to initiate a conversation with his new, intimidating opponent, Elliott pounced on the obvious.

"So, Moshe, what's the 'BBCC' stand for?"

"What, you never heard of it? *Gottenyu!* It stands for 'Burning Bush Country Club.' Been a member now since around 1500. I had just turned 2800, as I recall, and Leonardo had just invented the golf club. Golf caught on like wildfire then, and it sure beat heck out of playing pinochle every day! Then, a few years later, he also invented the Golf Club, and *melech ha'olom*, er, the Lord decided to build one up there," Moses answered, looking heavenward. "I was really flattered, since he sorta named it after me."

"Well," Elliott said, still in awe of playing with Moses but a bit surprised by the pronounced New York accent, "I guess I have the honor."

"Yeah, I know. I saw how you beat Fieldsie on the second. Nice going! Point of fact, I actually played up there with the *alter kocker* just yesterday and squeaked it out, two and one. And whaddya know if he didn't hit a seagull on the second hole against me, too!"

Elliott couldn't suppress a grin as he teed up his slightly scuffed Titleist and gazed out upon the sweeping, intimidating third fairway.

The third, a 514-yard par-5, is the first leg of a unique trifecta in the history of golf. Inwood is the only outstanding golf course in the world that can boast of having not just two, but *three* consecutive par-5's. In fact, just for fun, its maniacal designers—Edward Erickson, Herb Strong, and Jack Mackie—added two consecutive par-3's, the sixth and the seventh, right after. Consequently, the front nine has the outlandish configuration of 4-4-5-5-5-3-3-4-4.

Elliott stepped up to his ball, slightly unnerved by the prospect of having to play the monster third hole against the most famous Jew in history. He addressed it, did his waggle, and, adrenaline pumping through his entire body, hit it pure, right on the screws, a towering fade that landed dead center 270 yards from where he was now proudly posing.

"*Hoo-ha!*" Moses cheered magnanimously. "Some drive!"

Elliott felt gregarious and chatty. "Moshe, I can't help asking about your accent. I just thought—"

"I know, I know," the prophet interrupted. "Get asked about that all the time. Long story short, in the Torah, you know, my speech was sorta stilted and stiff. I wrote it myself, and God told me I should sound formal—authority figure to my people, bla bla bla. . . . And when God tells you to sound formal, you sound formal. So that's why all the *thee*s and *thou*s and *thy*s and *shalt*s. A real pain in the *tuchis*, if you want to know the truth! But outside of the Bible, I can relax and speak naturally, especially on the golf course, where everyone's a *mentsh*."

Moses stepped up to his ball and produced a shot the likes of which Elliott had never witnessed in his entire life. The Great Lawgiver took his driver back in a huge arc, way past parallel, and, using no lower body at all, no hip turn or leg drive whatsoever, made contact with the ball by using only his massive, Popeyesque forearms and super-supple wrists. He struck the ball with such brute force—the *tock!* of club against ball was accompanied by a staccato, stentorian *oy!*

belched out by the prophet at impact—that the tee itself, rudely dislodged from the ground, flew nearly fifty yards down the fairway. As for the ball, it was hooked slightly but landed an inconceivable 495 yards from the tee-box.

Elliott's mouth was frozen open. He had no idea how Moses had been able to produce such force and distance without using his lower body. It just wasn't possible; it defied the conventional physics of the golf swing. He had never seen a drive remotely this long, not by George Bayer, not by Tiger Woods, not by John Daly, not even by the brutish lugs in those long-driving contests.

"*Vey iz mir!*" Moses groaned. "Uncle-Charlied that one. Think I caught the trap."

Elliott was amazed that anyone, even Moses, could see that far down the fairway. As incredible as the mammoth drive was, he was still encouraged by the whole scenario. Despite the huge distance differential, his ball was sitting in the middle of the fairway, and Moses' was, apparently, lying in the deep, ominous bunker in front, and to the left, of the green.

Drive for show, putt for dough.

They clambered into the cart—Moses drove, natch—which carried in the back two identical Callaway bags with identical sets of pristine clubs. The bag on the left had a large "Moshe" scrawled (right to left) on the back. The one on the right, a much smaller and more orthodox (left to right) "Elliott." Elliott noticed that on the driver's side of the dash sat a tube of Ben-Gay and a squarish lump of something wrapped in silver foil.

"Open it," Moses said, peripherally noticing Elliott's curiosity.

Elliott obeyed with deference. Inside the package was a delicious-looking piece of noodle kugel, made with apricots and white raisins.

"Go ahead. Try it, you'll like it. Crispy on the outside, mushy on the inside. My wife, Tzipporah, she made it special for you. Got the recipe from Yocheved, my momma."

Again, Elliott obeyed and took a bite. Best he ever tasted. While Elliott munched, Moses drove and then spake.

"Elliott, you and I have something in common. Did you know that I am the only person in the Bible who was permitted to speak to God? Now you have spoken to Him, too. Doesn't happen every day. So I'll share something with you I haven't shared with a soul for all these years.

"I'm talking *justice*. Y'know, some people see my life as pretty exciting and special. The basket in the Nile, Pharaoh's daughter finding me and all, then the burning bush and the 'Let my people go' business, the plagues, the Golden Calf, writing the Torah, leading my people out of Egypt, then the forty years in the wilderness . . ."

Moses got a little *verklempt* at this point.

"And then . . . and then . . . that whole Canaan thing. I was so mad, I could *plotz*. I mean, just because I struck that rock with my rod instead of ordering it to yield water, I was punished? Because of *that*, I had to sit up there on Mt. Pisgah and watch my people enter Canaan, like a sub on the bench not being allowed to enter the game? You call that *fair*?"

Elliott was touched by this sad tale, but more by the fact that Moses was confiding in him so openly.

"I mean, I spent my whole life fighting for justice," the prophet continued. "I even smote that Egyptian overseer and defended those seven daughters of Jethro who were, well, let's say 'abused' by the Midianite shepherds! And what'd it get me? Nothing but heartache!

"Do you know what it's like not being able to attain your goal? Canaan was a real *simcha* for my people, but nothing but *tsores* for me. Plus it gave me plenty of *shpilkes*. As the years went by, I used to joke up there with Tzipporah that it was just a case of *introitus interruptus!* We'd laugh and laugh, but *in here*, Elliott, I still hurt."

Moses pointed to his heart and stopped speaking, overcome with emotion.

"That is so unfair, Moshe," Elliott consoled. "It's sort of like Bill Buckner having all those great years at bat and in the field, and then that one ball squirts through his legs at the end, and that's all he's remembered for."

Elliott was deeply affected by this whole discussion of how unfair life could be, and it made him think about the injustice of certain events in his own personal saga.

How his firstborn, Adam, had been suddenly stricken with acute epiglottitis at age eight and had perished in the hospital, a boy with so much talent, so much goodness, so much to offer the world. How he had played his best tennis ever in the biggest tournament of his life—his first event as a senior, just a week ago—only to lose in the finals because of that horrendous line call. How he had crumpled to the floor of Widener, the victim of an inexplicable heart attack, in the prime of his life . . .

The cart stopped at Elliott's ball, cutting short his daydream.

He couldn't believe his eyes.

What he had thought was a dream of a drive ended up being a nightmare. His ball had somehow nestled itself inside an ugly divot left by some unthinking *zhlob* who forgot to repair it. Talk about justice. What he'd thought would be a straightforward three-metal turned into a difficult three-iron challenge. Exchanging clubs, he returned to his ball and addressed it.

The image of poor Moses sitting helplessly on a basketball bench danced around in his head, followed by a cameo appearance of Themis—Lady Justice—and her sword and scales, but with one eye peering suspiciously out of her blindfold.

Setting his jaw in spite of these visions, Elliott drew back his three-iron and picked the ball perfectly, taking just the right amount of divot and propelling it hard and low into the tailwind. It ended up, incredibly, just a few yards in front of the apron.

Just as I thought. Golf is an *exceedingly* fair game!

"*Gott in himmel!*" Moses said, duly impressed. "Whatta shot!"

As the cart bumped its way down the rolling fairway, Moses turned to Elliott and asked, "Would you mind rubbing *ein bissel* Ben-Gay on my upper back? These muscles aren't getting any younger."

"My pleasure," Elliott answered, as he squirted a small blob of the balm on an area just below Moses' nape.

A few weeks ago, I was teaching a course called "The Bible as Literature," and now I'm rubbing Moses' back?

When they reached Elliott's ball, Moses dropped him off and said, "Thanks, Elliott. I'll take the cart behind the green and see what's doing with my ball in that bunker. Good luck, and *sei gesundt!*"

Elliott thought that was a bit curious, Moses wishing him good health and all, but perhaps the prophet was being courteous. At any rate, Elliott was feeling mighty good, with his ball there just off the apron, *in two!* Never mind that Moses was in the bunker in one. Elliott had never had such a feasible chance for eagle and certainly expected nothing worse than an up-and-down for birdie, while Moses, at best, would probably explode out and two-putt for birdie, as well.

At best. The Lawgiver could always leave the ball in the deep bunker or, with his massive might, hit it over the green and end up with a par, or worse.

Moses parked the cart, doubled back, and descended into the bunker, where his body, then his head slowly disappeared from view.

Elliott hit a few imaginary chips with his eight-iron as he waited, studying the two-tiered green, a compact, devilishly tough tester that sloped at about a twenty-degree angle, right to left and back to front. From where Moses lay in the bunker, it was almost impossible to explode out and hold the green below the hole. Even a great shot on the putting surface would leave him with a nearly impossible downhill putt.

Then, a dull thud as Moses' sand wedge made contact with sand and ball, the latter sailing straight up and high in the air before bouncing on the green once, twice . . .

The ball clanked sickeningly against the flagstick and dropped into the hole.

An albatross!

Elliott had never even heard of an albatross—a double-eagle—except for Gene Sarazen's famous two at the par-5 fifteenth during the final round of the '35 Masters.

Oh . . . my . . . God . . . I guess golf isn't so fair, after all. What the hell? I play my tush off, get ready to card my eagle or birdie, maybe go one up in the match, and now this?

Elliott waited for Moses to exit the trap so he could congratulate him, but what he saw instead coming out of the bunker was a swirling cyclone heading at breakneck speed toward the heavens. Moses had disappeared, miraculously, like the others. It was just Elliott Goodman there now, all alone, left standing once more to ponder.

Why was this happening to him? Was God playing with his head? Was He allowing him to play well and lose to a miracle shot, just to prove some point? Was *that* why He chose Moses? There was also the fact that both Moses and Elliott had spoken directly to God, and then, of course, the issue of justice, which so clearly marked Moses' life—and Elliott's, too? Was golf, or life, for that matter, fair? Was it even *supposed* to be? Was justice simply an illusion, a conceit based on expectations, realistic or otherwise—Moses' of reaching Canaan, Elliott's of winning the hole?

Elliott took a deep breath and listened to his heart, which, miraculously, sounded strong and healthy. He took in a large gulp of crisp Long Island air, admired a flock of Canadian geese that was gracefully winging its way to Miami, exhaled. As always with him, he wasn't able to escape the oncoming waves of thought that kept lapping up on the shores of his hyperkinetic brain.

Why was he feeling so weird? Was it the uncomfortable sensation of playing well and losing? This wasn't the first time he had encountered that paradox, but it felt especially unsettling now, in light of what was hanging in the balance. Which of the two feelings should he choose? Should he feel good about his playing so well, about being on the verge of chipping for eagle? Bad about losing the hole and again being one down in the match?

Was this all about the bigger issue of success and failure, of winning and losing, in his own life? Because he was such a jock—and a thinking jock, at that!—he had spent years and years struggling with this huge metaphor of winning and losing in sports, and in life. Had even given a semester course at Harvard, his most popular course ever and the academic culmination of his "thinking" life, titled "The Poetry of Triumph and Disaster." Fifteen weeks dedicated to winning and losing, featuring his favorite poets, one per week. Yeats and Rilke, Dickinson and Whitman, Eliot and Auden, Frost and Stevens, Lorca and Neruda, Thomas and Plath, Rimbaud and Mallarmé and Valéry. Liberally peppered, as he was wont to do, with quotes from the world of sports. His favorites were former Ohio State assistant football coach Lou Holtz's "The people of Columbus are great. They're behind you 100 percent, win or tie." And Boston Red Sox Johnny Pesky's "When you win, you eat better, you sleep better, and your beer tastes better. And your wife looks like Gina Lollabrigida."

Ah, the American way! Win or go home! But that wasn't his way really, and it wasn't what he'd taught Jake and Molly, either. He'd taught them to love the thrill of competition, win or lose, and had drummed into them that admittedly tiresome cliché, "it's not whether you win or lose, it's how you play the game."

All by himself on this windswept and challenging golf course, where winning or losing literally meant life or death, he felt his beloved philosophy of "how you play the game" begin to burst apart at the seams.

Elliott took another deep breath and walked down the cart path and up the hill toward the slightly elevated fourth tee. Again, the lapping of the cerebral waves.

I've gotta win. I've *got* to!, Elliott thought to himself, trying to pump himself up. I'm in the groove, hitting the ball on the screws, feeling *fine*. And that 3-iron from the divot! *Hoo-ha!*

I think I can, I think I can, I think I can, he repeated silently, invoking the mantra from the classic bedtime story he most loved reading to Jake and Molly decades ago, way before they got into GameBoys and iPods and PlayStation 2s and Xboxes and GameCubes and MP3 players.

Trying to focus, to concentrate on winning, he was aware of nothing but the pleasant click-clacking of his metal spikes against the asphalt of the path. The attempt was short-lived, as a quote popped into his mind, out of nowhere. This time from Ecclesiastes: "a time to seek, and a time to lose." Did he think of this one because he was still in a biblical frame of mind? Was it something more profound?

Is there *ever* a time to lose? Was there a reason for my loss? And . . . a time to seek? Am I supposed to be seeking something here? Is God asking me to look for something? It's been great so far, I'm playing well, and I've discussed with Leonardo,

MATCH MADE IN HEAVEN   55

bantered with Fields, and given Moses a back rub! But I'm losing, and when you're losing, who's got time to *look for stuff*?

Elliott passed the clubhouse on his left—like the golf course, it was deserted—and thought for a split second that he heard the unlikely sound of a loudspeaker emanating from the dining room area.

"Testing . . . one . . . two . . . three . . ."

He shrugged slightly and saw the outline of a figure awaiting him as he made his way up the slope toward the fourth tee.

Elliott felt the need to bounce back from his setback, unlike Moses, who in life never got the chance. He felt the need to show the old Goodmanian resilience. He felt the need for something good to happen, and right now.

Perhaps he even needed some outside . . .

4

HELP!

PRECISELY ON CUE, John Winston Lennon was crooning the first few lines of "Help!" and merrily strumming an air guitar as Elliott encountered him at the fourth tee-box.

Elliott was blown away by who his next opponent was to be. In his pantheon of writers, artists, musicians, athletes, and performers who had profoundly influenced his life—intellectually, aesthetically, and emotionally—this Fab One had no peer.

There he stood, not Lennon the moptop or Lennon the political activist, but John Lennon the boy genius of the Sgt. Pepper era. He was sporting his walrus mustache and wearing his getup from the *Sgt. Pepper* album cover, that brightly-colored, two-piece military uniform, chartreuse with red trim, cuffs, and epaulets. He also had on his round "rosy" spectacles and was barefoot.

Elliott was instantly imbued with a mixture of shock and pleasure at seeing and having to play against the icon. Not meaning to sound pious or melodramatic or fawning, but simply to state the facts, Elliott exclaimed, "I'm so happy that God has brought us together."

"I am you as we are He. . . ," John replied in his familiar mellifluent Liverpudlian monotone, his broad smile filling up the tee-box, his words instantly transporting Elliott back to a sacrosanct time in his own personal history.

It is January 1976, and Elliott's arms are around Joy Garb, his best friend, lover, and future wife. College seniors, they are dancing slowly, cheek-to-cheek, in his frat room, each holding a large plastic cup of keg beer, grooving on some primo bud, listening to the Magical Mystery Tour *LP. Life is good.*

Young Elliott is a huge Beatles fan, spending almost as much time listening to their albums as studying and playing sports. Throughout his adolescence, he has loved the anticipation of each new revolutionary LP, so vastly beyond its vinyl predecessor: Help!, Rubber Soul, Revolver, Sgt. Pepper, Magical Mystery Tour . . . *to what heights will the* next *one soar?*

Elliott and Joy, in their own little world, hold each other tight between hits and sips, oblivious to all but the music and themselves, swaying to the haunting strains of "I Am the Walrus." It is pitch black, except for the warm glow of a lava lamp. Ah, to be free and in college and in love during the mid-seventies!

Sex, drugs, and rock 'n' roll!

The fourth hole is a 539-yard par-5, where bogey is a respectable score. What throws you off is the diabolically designed tee-box, where the markers are actually pointing you to the right of the fairway and toward the third hole, creating a sort of directional optical illusion of disorientation. Putting the ball on the fairway with your drive is thus a challenge, as is the hole itself, which features a line of trees on both sides of a rolling fairway and, behind the small green, as with the second hole, the dreaded Bay.

Having the honor, John walked to the golf cart, on the back of which rested a single ratty-looking soft white canvas bag that contained only a three- and a five-iron, a pitching wedge, and a putter. He selected a five-iron and approached his already teed-up ball. Familiar with Lennon's general modus operandi, Elliott was expecting an unorthodox swing, but he had no inkling of what was to come.

John first stood a good twenty feet *behind* his ball, then ran up to it full throttle in the manner of a cricket bowler, kicked up his front leg—just like Mel Ott!—and, expressing air into his left cheek and out of a tiny opening on the side of his otherwise closed mouth to imitate the sound of a bugle playing one of those fanfares announcing a cavalry charge ("Da-de-la-DAH-da-DAH!"), he took a half-lunge, half-swipe at the ball and somehow made solid contact, sending it screaming in a boomeranglike arc toward the woods that lined the right edge of the fairway, as pure a "banana ball" as can be hit.

"Groovy," he exulted nonchalantly, ceding the tee to Elliott.

If he weren't playing to save his hide, Elliott would have simultaneously burst out laughing and peed in his pants.

Elliott plucked three-iron out of the bag, annoyed that, for some reason, God had narrowed his clubbing options so severely. He teed up his ball, addressed it earnestly, and cracked the ugliest, nastiest-looking shot of his golfing life, a dead pull hook that traveled a good distance but ended up hitting a huge sugar maple with a nauseating *thwack!* and dropping straight down into a large, lumpy bed of leaves.

Elliott felt sick to his stomach.

"Well, man, this is gonna be fun, y'know?" John said as they both hopped into the cart. Elliott noted how cheery John was, which made him think about the irony of the end of the Beatle's life.

How sad and unfair, he thought, with the issue of injustice still fresh in his mind from his encounter with Moses, that John's life was snuffed out at the age of forty by that deranged lunatic, Mark Chapman, while the equally brilliant and talented Paul went on to even greater fame, success, happiness, and knighthood and was still, at the age of sixty-four (and not even losing his hair), going strong.

How amazing that John remains so upbeat!

The steering wheel was on the right side, so John was the chauffeur by default. Elliott noticed, on the driver's side, a few drawing/writing pads, a fountain pen, an opened deluxe pack of Black Jack chewing gum, and, hanging on a hook, a French horn.

"Stick?" John asked.

"Huh?"

"Sticka gum, man?" John asked again, in an effort to clarify. "Always carry me gum when I'm playing—guitar, golf, possum . . ."

Elliott declined the Black Jack as John stuffed two sticks of gum into his own mouth. He was dying to ask John about the evolution, writing, and performing of all his favorite Beatles songs, like "Blackbird," "Penny Lane," "Eleanor Rigby," "Lady Madonna," "Lovely Rita," "Martha My Dear," "Maxwell's Silver Hammer," "Girl," "Paperback Writer," "Rocky Raccoon," "Day Tripper," "Norwegian Wood," "Strawberry Fields Forever," "Hey Jude," and "When I'm Sixty-Four." Assuming John would be annoyed at being asked for the zillionth time about his music, he opted for a topic the former Beatle had probably never discussed with any other mortal.

"John, tell me how you got into golf. I never knew—"

"Well, now," John interrupted, "when I got up there?"—he pointed skyward—"everybody and his uncle was, like, playing the game, 'cuz it was incredibly popular? I was mostly writing my music—been branching out a bit into reggae, grunge, and rap, y'know?—and I needed the exercise and something relaxing?

"So I said to meself, 'What the hell, I'll try golf.' And then being that I was able to play with the likes of, uh, Lewis Carroll and Elvis and Buddy Holly and Buddha, it was something I became keen on doing a lot?"

Elliott enjoyed being in John's company, not only because he was in awe of the man's talent, but also because his upbeat disposition was so contagious. It almost made him forget how annoyed he still was at hooking his drive and ending up in God knows what sort of trouble.

John stopped the cart in the middle of the fairway, 100 yards from where his ball had landed in the rough.

"Mind if I have me a bit of a tune?"

"By all means," Elliott answered, delighted at the chance to witness firsthand an impromptu performance.

John removed the French horn from the hook. "Didn't bring me guitar down, so you'll have to settle for this. It's the very same horn that I was carrying on the cover, y'know, of the *Sgt. Pepper* LP? Anyway, here's a tune I've always grooved on," he said, and played the first sixteen bars of "Norwegian Wood."

Elliott was stunned, since it was not only his favorite Beatles song, but also the one that was playing when he first laid eyes on Joy.

John put the horn back on the hook without finishing and then his foot on the accelerator, and Elliott gave him a respectful clap and continued his line of questioning.

"John, do you like the game because of who you play with?"

"Nah, it goes way beyond that? I mean, some people play golf 'cuz they wanna see how low they can shoot? And some play 'cuz they're outgoing or competitive? Me? I couldn't give a shit about the scoring. I play 'cuz it's fun!

"Hitting the ball from one spot to the next and just being

outdoors, y'know? And feeling free and looking at the trees and the grass and the birds and the clouds? Up there, the golf courses are gorgeous like you wouldn't believe. They're, like, my own private strawberry fields, real peaceful? But most of all, it's *fun*!"

Elliott was touched by John's eloquence and passion, but he had other fish to fry. Amid the excitement of playing with Lennon, he realized that he needed to start concentrating so that he could win the hole and square the match.

The surreal scene that followed had to be seen to be believed. Not only was John's jollity contagious, but so was the quality of his golf. Try as he might, Elliott was not able to get himself in the groove he seemed to be in on the previous hole. Partly because of John's carefree and unpolished shot-making, partly because every shot Elliott hit landed behind a root or in deep rough or at the base of a tree or partially buried in leaves, he never had the kind of lie that would allow him to take an unobstructed swing or drive the ball confidently down the fairway.

Because John's utter enjoyment of the game was expressed by his hopping from the cart, his skipping to the ball, his cockamamy cricketer's approach–*cum*–military trumpeter's fanfare, and his general smiling, chatting, animation, and good humor, Elliott, too, was sucked in to playing more quickly and frenetically than he was accustomed to, swinging with no rhythm at all and losing every bit of focus that he had succeeded in finding during the test against Moses.

To make matters worse, ever since he first saw and heard John at the tee-box, he had become obsessed—for some reason he was unable to fathom (was it a "clue" from above, like Moses' miracle shot?)—with the lyrics of "Help!" and couldn't get them out of his head, humming them to himself before, during, and after each shot.

As a result, the hole was played at a horrifyingly low level of execution, in a crazy "zigzag" way, with each player hitting each ball from the rough on the right to the rough on the left, or vice versa. So the cart—driven with abandon by the madcap member of the Lonely Hearts Club Band—seemed like an out-of-control toy car crisscrossing the fairway in a staccato, swerving, speeded-up pattern, as if it were in a fast-motion scene from *A Hard Day's Night*.

It went, and sounded, something like this:

JOHN: Da-de-la-DAH-da-DAH! *[Second shot lands in left woods. Drive across fairway to woods on left, to E's ball.]*

ELLIOTT: Help! *[Second shot lands in right woods. Drive to J's ball.]*

JOHN: Da-de-la-DAH-da-DAH! *[Third shot lands in right woods. Drive across fairway to woods on right, to E's ball.]*

ELLIOTT: Help! *[Third shot lands in left woods. Drive to J's ball.]*

JOHN: I know why they call it the rough, the rough, I know why they call it the rough! Da-de-la-DAH-da-DAH! *[Fourth shot lands in left woods. Drive across fairway to woods on left, to E's ball.]*

ELLIOTT: Help! *[Fourth shot lands in right woods. Drive to J's ball.]*

JOHN: Da-de-la-DAH-da-DAH! *[Fifth shot lands in right woods. Drive across fairway to woods on right, to E's ball.]*

ELLIOTT: Help! *[Fifth shot lands in left woods. Drive to J's ball.]*

JOHN: Da-de-la-DAH-da-DAH! *[Sixth shot lands in left woods. Drive across fairway to woods on left, to E's ball.]*

ELLIOTT: Help! *[Sixth shot lands in right woods. Drive to J's ball.]*

JOHN: Da–de–la–DAH–da–DAH! *[Seventh shot lands, merci-fully, on green. Drive across fairway to woods on right, to E's ball.]*
ELLIOT: Help! *[Seventh shot lands, mercifully, on green.]*

Elliott, exhausted, frazzled, and frustrated, hopped into the cart. John greeted him with a big, warm smile. "Bit of a struggle, that," John said cheerfully. Elliott was in no mood to be cajoled.

"Yep."

"But y'know?" John continued in his euphonious drone, "sometimes ya gotta just get up there an' *hit* the ball? That's all. It's like life, and it can be as simple as you wanna make it? Just smell the roses a wee bit, I say, then just *hit* the ball again."

John drove the cart behind the left side of the green, and the twosome hopped out. Elliott, who was away on the green, grabbed the putter violently.

He walked up to his twenty-five-footer, lined it up, took his usual two practice strokes, and hit a pretty cruddy putt that ended up three feet short. He lay eight.

Eight!

John also putted for an eight but came up eighteen inches short.

Then Elliott holed his putt for his nine, and John strolled up jauntily to his and . . . *missed his eighteen-incher!*

Elliott was in shock, and relieved. He couldn't believe that he had played so badly and still won the hole, a pathetic nine strokes to ten. He picked up his ball from the cup, basking in the knowledge that, after four holes, he had come from be-hind twice and was once again all square.

"God, I really *needed* that!" Elliott muttered under his breath, not suspecting anyone would hear.

But John, with his keen ear, did. Looking Elliott straight

in the eye, he said, with a knowing wink, "No, Elliott, all you need is *love!*"

And, with a smile and a snap of his fingers, he went up in a lovely pink puff of smoke.

Elliott was sad to see John go because he had really enjoyed his company. He was also glad to see him go because the golf had been so putrid. Still frustrated and annoyed that he had gone from being in the groove on the previous hole to not having a clue of what was happening to his swing, he walked toward the fifth tee, stopping at the little ball-washing machine.

You *turkey!* You let John bring you down. You let his crappy golf affect your game. You couldn't just pay attention to yourself, now *could* you?

Then the lightbulb above his head.

Of course! It wasn't about excellence. It wasn't even about winning and losing. It was about . . . *joy!* How happy John seemed on the golf course, hopping and skipping and humming and singing and smiling and laughing and loving every minute of it! What had escaped me during the heat of battle seems perfectly clear now. What joy John had exhibited! What carefree innocence! What unbridled happiness!

I've seen a few pro athletes show that same spirit, the one that embodies what sport at its best is meant to be. The sheer joy of competing and, like John, just enjoying the moment. Willie Mays, cap falling off every time he slid into a base: joy! Magic Johnson, with that sparkling smile and mirth on the court: joy! Shigeki Maruyama, even when he missed a putt: joy! Under duress and pressure—like *when your life is on the line!*—playing golf, like living life, should still give you . . . joy!

Then a second lightbulb.

Of course: *Joy!* It was right there under my very nose all

these years! Right there in my wife's very name! It was she alone who'd begged me to relax when the bills were piling up, or when I got too intense during a tennis match, or when I was giving the kids one of my semibombastic lectures. "Sweetie pie, smell the coffee," she'd say with her usual grace. "Just have fun!" I've gotta start doing that right now, putting some joy back in my life, before it's . . . too late!

Elliott said a silent prayer. Despite the growing pressure to perform, maybe he would start enjoying himself more and playing well again and maintain his momentum and win back-to-back holes and, for the first time, surge ahead in the match?

Maybe God in his mercy would now send down another duffer, someone who was *really* athletically challenged, some uncoordinated egghead who was mentally fragile and physically weak, and whose mind and body would crumble under the intense pressure of competition?

5

GOOD SECHS

ELLIOTT'S PRAYERS WERE ANSWERED. Standing before him at the fifth tee was a bespectacled, slightly slumped-over sesqui-centenarian with a neatly manicured gray beard, thinning hair, and a large, wrinkled forehead—the least athletic-looking person one could possibly imagine.

Decked out in a three-piece tweed suit—from the vest pocket of which hung an impressive silver watch fob—a starched shirt, a cravat, and a pair of polished black boots, he looked as if the last place on the planet where he would feel comfortable would assuredly be a golf course.

He was a man who possessed great analytical powers, ambition, and intellect, qualities that might easily be inappropriate for the proper playing of golf. He held a large, foul-looking cigar in his right hand, and his name was Sigismund Schlomo Freud.

Freud!

Elliott greeted the eminent doctor with respect, although instinctively he felt uncomfortable in the presence of the father of psychoanalysis. Freud sensed this and sought to break the tension.

"*Guten Morgen!* So, then, how is your sex drive?"

"Excuse me?" Elliott answered, puzzled at Freud's blunt and unannounced interest in his concupiscence.

"Sorry, just kidding," the therapist said, chuckling. "I meant, to shoot a *sechs* on this hole, you need a good *drive!* Parapraxis!"

"Huh?"

"Freudian slip," Freud explained in his heavy Viennese accent. "Haven't you read my essay on the theory of sexuality, jokes, and their relation to the unconscious?"

"Afraid not," Elliott said, anxious to get back to business, to get his game back on track. "I believe I have the honor," he added curtly.

The 512-yard fifth hole, a gentle dogleg right, is the shortest, flattest, easiest, and last of the three consecutive par-5's. A dense fog, not an unusual morning phenomenon at Inwood, had begun to drift in from the Bay behind them and to permeate the fairway, making the hole less than visible and endowing it with an eerie, dreamlike quality.

Elliott chose driver from the bag, then stepped up to the tee-box briskly, brimming with confidence. He stuck the red tee with his Titleist on it into the ground, stepped up, took his stance, addressed the ball, did his brief waggle, stopped his clubhead, locked his wrists and forearms—all done seemingly in one motion, crisply and with purpose—and, without hesitating, creamed the ball 255 yards right down the middle of the fairway.

Yes!

Three-metal in hand, Freud shuffled slowly to the tee-box. The old man bent down with great effort into an awkward-looking squat, placed his tee methodically in the ground, raised it up a half-inch, then back down a half-inch, then finally up a quarter-inch, meticulously balanced his old Acushnet ball on top of it, straightened up slowly, stretched his legs—first the right one, then the left—and, after blowing a carefully conceived smoke ring, put his lit cigar in his mouth and, without taking it out, took a puff, blew out a prodigious cloud of billowing smoke, and set his feet.

Elliott fidgeted with impatience. Unfortunately for him, he had until now only seen the tip of the Freudian iceberg.

Cigar still in mouth (he had been playing like this long before Larry Laoretti or even Charlie Sifford), the Austrian physician addressed his ball, paused to pick a minute particle of lint off his vest, then went back to his address, then adjusted his spectacles, then the address again, then scratched an itch, address, shooed a fly, address, cleared his throat, address.

This was all taking place in Super Slo-Mo, as if a movie camera were overcranked at 256 frames per second, making a snail or a large tortoise seem, by comparison, like Jesse Owens in his prime.

Finally, at long last, the waggle.

Freud's waggle wasn't just your average, run-of-the-mill, two-to-three-part waggle with alternating wrist fidgeting, leg rocking, and fairway gazing. No, this was the waggle of waggles, the mother lode of waggles, the Taj Mahal, Rolls-Royce, Hope Diamond, Dom Perignon, Kobe steak, bagel-with-the-works, waggliest waggle of all time. Lasting just under two minutes, and including virtually every part of the psychoanalyst's anatomy, it was the most idiosyncratic, facial-tic-filled, anal-retentive, repression-infested, denial-covered, defense-mechanism-slathered, ass-wiggling waggle ever witnessed by man or beast.

And now by poor Elliott, who, toward the end, was fantasizing about dumping Freud and hooking up with some great, *really fast* player like Julie Boros or Lee Trevino or Tom Watson or Jim Thorpe or Nick Price . . .

Snapping back to reality, Elliott watched the doctor complete his preparations and bring his clubhead to a grinding halt behind the ball.

After a healthy pause to make sure that all was perfect, Freud took his club back to the top of his swing, not quite parallel, and . . . *held it there for a good ten seconds!* Like an orgasm building up to its apogee, the swing was held there erect, building . . . building . . . until it could be held there no longer, at which point arms, wrists, and club all came crashing down heavily, exploding at contact—*yes!*—and releasing the white projectile down . . . down . . . down the fairway.

Ahhhhh . . .

But it was Elliott, not Freud, who was spent at this point, fit to be tied from all the waiting, and mentally exhausted.

"Hop in, I'll drive," Freud said. "I always like to be in control."

Elliott noticed on the driver's side of the dash a small vial with some fine white powder in it, a copy of *The Interpretation of Dreams*, and a videotape (*Debbie Does Dallas*).

"Elliott," the psychotherapist began, "tell me about this heart attack, will you?"

Elliott was surprised that of all his opponents so far, Freud was the only one who had taken an interest in his recent harrowing experience.

"Well," he answered, "I don't remember very much, just collapsing in Widener, then the gurney and the doctors, and then God—"

"*Nein, nein,*" Freud interrupted, "I mean, tell me what you imagine to have been the reason *behind* the heart attack."

Elliott hemmed and hawed. "Well, I'm not really certain. I guess I was under some stress, and my father had a history—"

"*Nein, nein, mein Kind,*" Freud interrupted again. "I'll *tell* you why. It was because in your unconscious, there was a basic conflict, probably begun in early childhood, between your id—that is, your libido, impulses, pleasure, desires—and your superego—that is, your limits, rules, parents, teachers, authority figures in general, and also society.

"And this superego was all the time trying to control this id, sometimes in dreams, sometimes in symbols, all the time in conflict. Until one day, *BOOM!*—the heart attack!

"And tell me about your dreams. Did you ever have dreams of a . . . *sexual* nature?"

"Well, lemme see. There was one where this drop-dead gorgeous—"

"Oops, sorry," Freud cut in, "but your time is up."

The cart had, in fact, reached Freud's ball. The therapist got out, selected three-metal again, and, after his two-minute ordeal of a waggle, hit the ball—as most 150-year-old golfers do—not too far but straight down the middle. He now lay two, still 250 yards from the pin, and only five yards or so ahead of Elliott, who lay one.

"Well now," he said, as he stepped gingerly back into the cart and began the drive toward Elliott's ball, "let's do a little free association, shall we? I'll say to you a word, and then you will tell me what it makes you think of. Ready? Okay, here we go.

"Breast?"

Elliott thought this was all a joke, but he saw from Freud's look that the shrink was dead serious.

"*Breast?*" Freud repeated sternly.

"Milk," Elliott answered begrudgingly, still annoyed at the pace of the golf action, but acquiescing to the exercise.

"Good," Freud said. "And milk?"

"Cow," Elliott answered.

"And cow?" Freud continued.

"Moo."

"And moo?"

"-shu pork."

"Pork?"

"Bacon."

"Bacon?"

"Eggs."

"Eggs?"

"Chicken."

"Chicken?"

"Afraid."

"Afraid?"

"Authority."

"Authority?"

"Stress."

"Stress?"

"Heart attack."

"*Aha!*" Freud concluded, as he stopped the cart at Elliott's ball.

Elliott jumped out, pulled three-metal out of his bag, and strode briskly to his ball. He addressed it, took a quick look at the flagstick through the now-thickening fog, looked down again at his ball, and froze.

Time stood still, and although what happened next only took thirty seconds, it seemed like forever to Elliott.

In his head, a daydream of spectacular theatrical and choreographic proportions is transpiring. The background theme is somewhere between the "Ballet" scene from *Carousel* and "Tevye's Dream" from *Fiddler on the Roof.* At times, they can be heard in stereo. Scenes from childhood to the present form themselves and then dissolve, weaving in and out of view in kaleidoscopic fashion, ebbing and flowing, advancing and receding.

There's little "Ell" sitting at the dinner table in front of a plate of brussels sprouts, with his mother, played by Margaret Hamilton as Miss Gulch in Oz, cackling from behind him, "Eat up, my pret-ty!" . . .

And look! There's little Ell in school, so proud of the little tree he's creating by his own rules, with its crazy branches and its blue-and-purple leaves, while his art teacher—a female version of Hitler, mustache, uniform, and all—stands behind him (shot with a fish-eye lens), wagging her finger and ordering him to start over and draw one of those round, puffy trees with green leaves and a brown trunk. . . .

And there's Elliott Goodman in college, his heart open to the world, and he's reading a book at a large, round table in the library and learning how cruel that world can be, with its rules and controls clashing with the desires of the individual. . . .

And out of the book emerge and come to life a whole procession of characters. Oedipus ripping his eyes out of his head and Romeo and Juliet at the balcony, played by Richard Beymer and Natalie Wood, and old Don Quixote on his nag and Julien Sorel and Emma Bovary and Hester Prynne and David Copperfield being yelled at by Mr. Murdstone and Joseph K. and Holden Caulfield, and then a quote from Dickens ("The law is a ass!") floats out of the book, its letters soon dissolving into the smoky library air, followed by another one, this time from Sartre ("Hell is other people") . . . .

And now, replacing the library scene, are young Elliott and young Joy, so much in love and at odds with conventional wisdom, and they're running away and eloping, armed to fight the world with nothing but their backpacks full of clothes, and their love. . . . [Music builds, and the scenes appear with greater frequency and intensity.]

And there's Professor Elliott Goodman fighting the good fight for his best friend, Ron, who's being denied tenure at Harvard, and they're in a courtroom and Elliott is Ron's lawyer, standing up against the entire department and their politics and their prejudice, and suddenly the scene turns ugly and becomes the trial in Alice in Wonderland, *then segues into the one in Kafka's novel.* . . .

And there's Elliott playing in his first seniors tennis tournament, and he's about to win, and then that terrible line call, and the linesman who perpetrates the vile act is none other than Freud himself, with his three-piece suit and cigar in mouth and laughing his ass off. . . .

And there's Professor Goodman in the bowels of Widener Library, book in hand, suddenly clutching his chest and dropping to his knees in a heap and pleading to God. . . . [Music reaches crescendo.]

And there are the scales of Lady Justice, and on one scale is God, smiling in all His glory, weighing down His scale so that it is much lower than the other one, and on the upper scale is poor Elliott Goodman, naked and supine and alone on the operating table, his heart bravely pumping inside his chest, pumping . . .

Elliott snapped out of it, his brow covered with tiny beads of sweat. He tried to loosen his grip, but his tight hands were locked in, as if they'd been epoxied, bonded together by the twin resins of impatience with Freud's waggles and resentment at all the conflict and struggle that had been building up in his life during the past five decades.

His mind racing and his heart thumping, he took his club back—glued hands and all—and, venting all his anger and all his frustration, buried his three-metal deep into the turf three inches behind the ball, taking a divot of gargantuan proportions and leaving the ball untouched and lying precisely where it had lain prior to his swing.

There is nothing more mortifying for a golfer, at any skill level, than a whiff. It is the equivalent, in emotional impact, to no other phenomenon known to the human species. The only reaction possible from its author is an immediate and overpowering urge to bury his or her head, ostrichlike, in the gaping hole made by the club and cover it up tight with the divot. Under the circumstances, this particular option was not available to Elliott.

He took a deep breath and gathered himself. His pride still stinging from the non-shot—especially as he was a 10-handicap and had never experienced such humility—he now lay two, and, to his profound embarrassment, it was still his turn to hit.

He spotted Freud out of the corner of his eye, sitting in the cart with a smirk pasted on his face, accompanied by a vague look of transferred mortification. He gripped his club, still tightly, and this time he made solid contact, whacking it a good 220 yards but pulling it into the sycamores to the left of the green.

Freud again performed his painfully intricate waggle and hit the ball another 130 yards straight down the fairway. He resumed his place in the driver's seat, but this time neither player—and that included Freud—had any desire to talk.

The drive to the therapist's ball was marked by stony silence.

Any vestige of the competitive fire that usually burned inside Elliott had been snuffed out, and he was trying desperately to refocus, to rediscover his swing, and to empty his mind of the clutter of psychological baggage that Freud had (consciously? subconsciously?) deposited there. But to no avail.

While Freud slowly but surely lollygagged his way to the green in five—another down-the-middle fairway metal, a chip to fifteen feet of the cup—Elliott struggled mightily with mind and body, first hacking out of the trees into a greenside bunker, then exploding onto the green, twenty-two feet from the hole. He, like Freud, lay five.

Elliott putted first, his grip still pathologically tight, and pulled the ball badly, leaving it a foot to the left of the hole. He tapped in for his double-bogey seven.

Freud lined up his putt, set up, took an inordinate but not

surprising amount of time analyzing both speed and direction, and finally drew his putter back and rammed his ball confidently into the hole for his bogey six.

"Who's yo' *momma*?" Freud squealed, unable to contain his glee.

Crap! One down again!

After the two exchanged handshakes, Freud looked at Elliott and said wryly, "Well, what can I say, *mein Kind*? I guess I had good *sechs* today . . . compared, that is, to your *sieben*!"

Unable to leave well enough alone, he added, "As I always say, '*Das Leben ist wie eine Hühnerleiter: kurz und beschissen!*'— 'Life is like a chicken-ladder: short and shitty!'"

Leaving Elliott to chew on that for a while, he took one final puff on his cigar and, behind the smoke screen, evanesced, ever so slowly and methodically, into the fog.

Elliott was numb. He remained on the green, leaning on his putter, assessing the situation.

He was emotionally drained and needed to refuel. Not only had he just gone through the first four holes of tough competition—with his life in the balance—and in so doing met, spoke with, got to know, and learned from the likes of Leonardo, Fields, Moses, and Lennon, but now he had just struggled through what seemed like an hour of grueling therapy, in addition to enduring the Freud Waggle and a whiff, and, in the end, had come up empty.

In truth, the hole had been a disaster, beginning with the sobering fact that he had *lost*. And not to a peer, but to a frail, old, slumped, slow, obsessive-compulsive fuddy-duddy. Forget about the superego. What an insult to his *male* ego!

So I lost the hole? No biggie. That's why they make eighteen of them, as the great Hogan would say. One down again, for the third time in five holes. *Damn!*

The good news is that I keep coming back, and that's

what I have to do once again. The bad news is that I not only butchered the hole and lost it, but I forgot to do a bunch of things I'd promised myself to do during the first four holes. Never underestimate an opponent. Never overthink. Focus. Find joy in the playing of the game. Pay attention to your own game and not to your opponent's.

Funny, but I used to teach Jake and Molly the lesson of *"facta non verba,"* "deeds not words" . . . Missouri's "Show Me!" . . . Nike's "Just Do It!" How Joy would laugh at my Latin and my pomposity! But in my heart, I believe deeply in this wise aphorism, and now, I'm guilty of being deaf to my own lectures!

Why Freud? Was the therapist sent by God to annoy me, to put me through the psychological ringer, to subject me to an embarrassing loss? Was there a reason for all that? Didn't Freud actually help me clarify something about my life . . . and my heart? Didn't he get me to think about the issues of conflict and control and authority and rules and my relationship to the world at large? Or was it just a clever ruse to make me take my eye off the ball?

Elliott had to put the fifth hole, with the loss to Freud, behind him, and *pronto.* He had to get his act together and steady the ship.

So whom, he asked himself, in an attempt to put the recent past behind him, would he face next, following this truly terrifying tale of horror?

6

NEVERMORE

HE WAS DRESSED ALL IN BLACK—black, I say!—*yes, black!*, and nothing more or less than the blackest of blacks—*'tis true!*: black shirt, black necktie, black frock coat, black trousers, black socks, black boots—no, I would not, *could* not lie to you! Even his hair and eyebrows and mustache were the pitchest of *black*. And his eyes. Ah, his *eyes!* You cannot imagine how black his eyes were—*alas!*, will you not *believe* me?—and so sad and soulful a black, you could not, even if you were the strongest and most virile of men, stop yourself from shedding a slow—ah, how *slow!*—and mournful tear at the very sight of them!

Awaiting Elliott at the sixth tee, in the fog and the gloom, was the man whose gripping stories he had fallen in love with at first read at the tender age of nine. A brilliant and magical writer, who plumbed the terrifying depths of the human psyche as no one had before or since. A man who was one of the chosen few to be selected for the cover of the *Sgt. Pepper* album.

Edgar Allan Poe!

"I believe I have the honor, sir," the Southern gentleman

said, his delicate, lilting voice oozing Virginia charm. "And 'tis indeed an honor to play with you—Elliott, is it not, if I recall aright?"

You could have knocked Elliott over with a quill pen.

He had not only fallen in love with Poe's stories as a youth, but he had also taught—just fall term of last year—a graduate seminar devoted entirely to Poe and the French poet Charles Baudelaire. Now he was about to trade middle-iron for middle-iron with the great writer on the deceptively treacherous sixth hole.

Said sixth is a 171-yard par-3, with a gloomy, heath-like marsh between tee and severely undulating green, behind which is some terrifying OB swampland. The flagstick, tucked in a depression, is virtually hidden from the golfer standing at the tee-box. Today the swirling wind and thickening fog were of no help.

"Begging your pardon, sir," the author of "The Raven" and *Ligeia* drawled, grabbing three-iron from his bag, "but I couldn't help but notice the hospital shirt you are wearing. You must have, as the great Charles Dickens might have put it, been through some hard times."

Struck by Poe's caring, Elliott answered, "Well, to be honest, I don't remember very much. It all happened so quickly, and then . . . the pain . . . and then God . . . and, well, here I am!"

"I can truly commiserate. Suffering and I are old bed-fellows," Poe replied dolefully. "Seems like we used to find ourselves together with some reg-u-la-ri-ty. First my momma and papa separating when I was but a boy of two, leaving me an orphan. Then the death of my blessed momma, God rest her soul! And then my unhappy childhood. And later meeting the adorable Sarah Elmira Royster, only to have her parents break up our engagement. And then the death of my foster momma, Mrs. Frances Allan. And of course my expulsion from West Point. And finally my darling wife, my beloved, Miss Virginia Clemm, flew up to be with the angels."

The author of *The Murders in the Rue Morgue* and *The Fall of the House of Usher* teed up his ball and continued somberly, "Not to mention my constant and loyal companions—illness, poverty, unemployment, calumny, and, shall we say, *excess!*"

Elliott listened, enraptured by this anguished tale of woe—it occurred to him how ironic it was that *woe* just happened to rhyme with the poet's surname—and the elegance and pathos with which it was spun. He noted the sharp contrast between this measured, poignant voice, so gentle and vulnerable and with its charming twang, and the darkly deranged and manic one Poe used as the narrator of his tales. He was particularly struck by the look of unshakable melancholy that covered the writer's face like a shroud.

Poe addressed his ball, then looked up at Elliott and said, "Good luck to you, sir, and may the best man win!" He took his club back—his swing was beautifully balanced and athletic—and hit a stinger, a low, sharply struck ball that, cutting right through the fog, made a beeline for the green.

It was hit too hot and ended up hopping in front of the green, bouncing once on the putting surface, shooting past the flagstick, and heading toward the swampland behind.

"Just my luck!" the author of *William Wilson* and *The Masque of the Red Death* moaned as he bequeathed the tee-box to his opponent.

Elliott grabbed four-iron, then made as good a swing as he had all day, striking his Titleist crisply and propelling it into the fog at just the right trajectory and altitude. The result, as with Poe's drive, was a bit unfortunate, as the strong right-to-left wind, which Elliott had accounted for but had slightly underestimated, grabbed the ball in its treacherous teeth and spit it out unceremoniously into the bunker to the left of the green.

"Mind if I drive?" Elliott asked, feeling confident and, for the first time all morning, in control.

"By all means, sir," Poe answered, settling himself in the passenger seat. "Mind if I indulge?" the author of *The Tell-Tale Heart* and *The Cask of Amontillado* queried, pointing to a bottle of Kentucky bourbon that had been conveniently provided for him on the dash. "It's the wind that's agetting inside my bones. . . ."

The question was rhetorical. Not waiting for an answer from Elliott, Poe took a swig and, emboldened by the rotgut whiskey, continued to address his interlocutor. "Well, sir, of all my misfortunes and regrets, can you guess which one I feel most deeply about?"

"I can't presume to know the answer to that," Elliott answered, curious, nonetheless, to discover it.

"It's the one thing precious to a Southern gentleman, above all else. Rep-u-ta-tion," Poe enunciated pointedly. "And without his reputation, sir, a gentleman is worth nothing. In my life, and well after, I have seen my reputation sullied and the facts of my existence distorted.

"Sir, I have always attempted to follow my heart and to do what I thought was honorable. I have had great loves. I have, in my poetry and my prose, produced, in my humble opinion, some measure of beauty. I have been responsible for inventing and perfecting the short story and the detective thriller and for taking literary criticism and theory to another level.

"But what am I remembered for, I ask y'all? My heart is heavy when I but think of it. Marrying my cousin with dishonorable intentions when she was but a lass of thirteen! Being a negligent journalist! Getting disinherited! Wasting my life away due to my gambling and my drinking and my carousing and my drugging! Appearing to be the mirror image, in life, of the twisted and unstable characters I have created! *Lies! Lies! Lies, every one*, I tell y'all! . . . ," he trailed off hysterically, in mock imitation of one of his deranged protagonists.

The author of "Annabel Lee" and *The Black Cat* leaned back, exhausted and distraught. Elliott was at a loss for words.

How sad the life of this genius was! How sad that his reputation was so shamefully tarnished, and that so few people in America know him for his good heart and the beauty and power of his writing! Sadder still to think that this poor wretch cares so much about his reputation and what people thought of him during his life, and then after he died! I wish I could do something to take away his anguish, but what? He seems so decent, so engaging, such a good guy. I feel like I've known him my whole life, which I sort of have, ever since I first picked up his short stories as a kid. I just wish there were something I could do to make him feel better. . . .

Elliott parked the cart behind and to the left of the green, and they both hopped out. As they went their separate ways—Poe toward the swampland, Elliott toward the bunker—the author of "The Bells" and *The Pit and the Pendulum* looked at Elliott with those soulful black eyes of his and said balefully, "Wheresoever you have ended up, sir, I am quite certain you are better off than I am."

And he walked off, pitching wedge in hand, and disappeared into the fog.

Elliott was away, so he entered the bunker to assess the damage. It was considerable. His ball was buried deep in the sand, as nasty a fried egg as you would ever want to see, and, to boot, just below the lip of the bunker. The shot was nearly impossible, requiring an explosion that had to be high enough to clear the lip, low enough to avoid the tree ahead, and far enough to reach the difficult and undulating green.

Still preoccupied with thoughts of the despairing Poe, but mindful of the challenge at hand, Elliott dug his spikes into the sand, steadied himself, and did everything right. Steep take-back, early cock of the wrists, slight hip turn, hitting of sand an inch behind ball, head down, acceleration through contact, short follow-through.

Sand flew into his face, and the ball went flying in the direction of the green. The shot felt good, it looked good, and it sounded good, too, especially that dull, sweet thud of ball on green. Followed by another, unexpected sound, a quick, popping sound, like that of a . . . *pistol!*

Elliott took a split second to admire his shot, then instinctively realized that the second sound was, in fact, a "shot" of a different kind.

Could it be?

Fearing the worst, Elliott tossed his sand wedge into the bunker and started running as fast as his short, muscular legs could carry him. As he raced toward the fallen writer, his eyes confirmed what his ears had feared.

There, ahead of him, lying prostrate on the green, was the author of *The Gold-Bug* and *The Purloined Letter*, a pistol in his right hand and a bullethole in his right temple.

Edgar Allan Poe had taken his own life!

Beside himself, Elliott knelt down to verify that Poe was dead. He was. Elliott was paralyzed with grief, but before he could mourn in a proper and respectful manner, Poe's motionless body was inexplicably stripped of its skin, muscle, and organs, leaving nothing but a skeleton, which, bones tinkling, was wafted away and out of sight by a swirling gust of wind.

Huh? What was *that* all about? Was this another game God was playing with his head? A clue he was supposed to be paying attention to? A sick joke with a bad punch line? What, if anything, did Poe's suicide mean? Was this really happening, or was it a nightmare?

Recovering from the initial shock, Elliott realized that, out of all this chaos and grief, there was a silver lining. He had, by default and pursuant to an obscure and newly added edict, in fact won the hole!

Rule 10-1.d of *The USGA Rules of Golf:* "If a player shall take his or her own life while playing a *hole* and thus not be able to continue play, he or she shall be deemed disqualified from said *hole* and shall forfeit the *hole* to his or her opponent . . . ."

For a third consecutive time, he had fought back from a deficit to square the match.

Elliott's body was filled with adrenaline, and his heart was beating nearly out of his chest.

Was it the euphoria of winning the hole and squaring the match? The grief of witnessing in person the great writer's self-destruction? The sudden and intense awareness that what had happened to Poe was a grippingly graphic metaphor for the life-and-death consequences of this golf match? A myocardial infarction? All of the above?

Once again, Elliott stood alone in the middle of the green, deep in thought. As he walked toward the seventh tee, he wished he had someone else to talk to about the devastating ordeal he had just endured. Someone with a sympathetic ear, and with whom he could have a meaningful dialogue . . .

7

GOLF LESSONS

PERSONS OF THE DIALOGUE
SOCRATES.   GOODMAN.
SCENE: The seventh hole at Inwood.

Socrates. So, then, Goodman, I see that you are coming from the sixth hole with a heavy heart.

Goodman. Yes, Socrates, I have just experienced the terrible waste of a beautiful life. Poe has killed himself!

Soc. That is indeed very terrible. But let me ask you this: Do you know if he suffered much?

Good. I cannot tell, as I did not actually witness the end.

Soc. But is it not true, Goodman, that Poe was already dead and, in fact, was sent here to this place from above, where all the souls who reside there are deceased?

Good. That, Socrates, is true. I had not thought of it until now.

Soc. So it is safe to say that it was not Poe who suffered, but you, in your grief at his "demise"?

Good. Yes, that is clearly true.

Soc. Would you not agree, then, that you were filled with

suffering because you felt compassion for this man whom you so admired?

Good. Yes, I would agree.

Soc. And would you not also say that the game of golf has brought out of your already sensitive nature an added feeling of empathy for this fellowman, whom you reckoned to have taken his own life?

Good. Exactly true. It appears that I have learned something new about myself.

Soc. And do you not see that your compassion was selfless, in that even though you knew tossing your sand wedge into the bunker would cost you a penalty stroke and quite possibly the hole, you still attempted to run to Poe's rescue without a thought of yourself?

Good. Quite so.

Soc. And do you not find it a coincidence that both *compassion* and *empathy* share a common etymology—the Greek *pathein* or the Latin *pati,* "to suffer"?

Good. I had not thought of that until you mentioned it.

Soc. Would you agree, then, Goodman, that it was not Poe's death, but the game of golf, that has evoked the feeling of suffering that you are presently experiencing?

Good. Yes, it does seem so.

Soc. Well, then, pursuing this line of reasoning, how would you describe your deepest feeling for the game?

Good. I suppose I would say I feel a certain *passion* for it.

Soc. And what word would you use to characterize your second shot against Freud?

Good. I would call that shot *pathetic.*

Soc. And what quality did you sadly lack while you were waiting during the slow-as-molasses pre-swing antics of Freud?

Good. I would most assuredly say *patience.*

Soc. And were you proactive when you struck that wishy-washy eight-iron on number one?

Good. No, Socrates, I must admit that I was *passive*.

Soc. Now do you not find it revealing that *compassion, empathy, passion, pathetic, patience, passive*—the very words we can use to describe what the game of golf can teach or inspire in you—all spring forth from the same word, which means "to suffer"?

Good. I suppose that is true, now that I think of it.

Soc. It brings to my mind the poignant words of a fellow Greek, the great tragedian Aeschylus. "*Pathema mathema*," or "lessons through suffering."

Good. I believe that was from *Agamemnon*, lines 177 through 178?

Soc. You are *good*, Goodman. You have done your homework. My point is that when one plays golf, one suffers considerably, but one also can learn from this grief.

Good. To be sure, Socrates. It is quite a paradox.

Soc. My thought precisely. For is it not that sweet paradox, among many others, that makes the game so extraordinary and so mysterious? You have already experienced a number of them, Goodman. Thought and non-thought. Struggle and joy. Control and letting go. Surprise and disappointment. Failure and success. These contradictions explain why golf is a perfect game for us humans, who are flawed and fallible and always trying to improve. And why God, who is perfect, never plays but is content to be a spectator. Oh, and I forgot my favorite paradox. Do you not, Goodman, play to win?

Good. Certainly, Socrates.

Soc. And do you not also play to enjoy yourself and to attain excellence?

Good. Yes, that is true, too.

Soc. Yet can you not attain one goal and fail at the other, and vice versa? You played very well against Moses, for example, and lost the hole, and then you played like an absolute dunce against Lennon and still won. Does that seem fair to you?

Good. Not at all, Socrates, and I have often wondered about that.

Soc. That is a good word to use, since it is with wonder that we should view golf's justice. It is not our justice, but the special justice of the golfing gods, who, you may not have realized, reside in a special clubhouse on Mount Olympus and look down upon us mortals. So we do the best we can, and the rest is up to them. It is indeed a humbling game. Which brings me to the issue of humility.

Good. Yes, that is one I am always working on.

Soc. I see by your round so far that this is true. Humbled by Leonardo's putter-from-the-bunker shot on one, by your dunderheaded putt on two, by Moses' miracle on three, by the miserable play on four, by the lack of concentration on five, by the suicide on six. Sometimes, Goodman, the game can humble us mightily, make us feel like the lowliest of worms. Is it no wonder, then, that the word *humble* comes from the Latin *humus,* "earth"? But there is one saving grace to being a worm.

Good. And what might that be?

Soc. Worms have low centers of gravity. This is important, for keeping to the center is the key to playing golf.

Good. How so, Socrates?

Soc. Well, let me ask you this: Which part of the fairway gives you the greatest feeling of comfort and well-being?

Good. The center, I suppose.

Soc. And which part of the green?

Good. The center, as well.

Soc. And toward which part of the cup do you aim all your putts?

Good. The center, of course. I should have seen that coming.

Soc. Focus, and keep to the center, as any worm would know! But this brings to mind yet another curious paradox.

Good. And what could that possibly be?

Soc. This "center" business doesn't always work. For example, did you notice that you hit the center of the fairway on all the odd holes?

Good. No, I didn't notice. I was too busy playing to save my life!

Soc. Well, it is so. And did you win any of those holes?

Good. Let's see: one . . . three . . . five . . . No, actually, I lost them all.

Soc. And did you notice that you missed the fairway *completely* on all the even holes?

Good. No, but thanks a bunch for reminding me.

Soc. That is not a problem.

Good. Yes, you are correct, now that I think about it: I missed the fairway *completely* on two, four, and six.

Soc. And did you lose any of these holes?

Good. Let me think. No, actually, I won them all.

Soc. The golfing gods, once again. It means that the center of the fairway is sometimes important and sometimes not. But there is one center that is always constant.

Good. And what is that?

Soc. The center of *you*. It is the only thing you can depend on, when all is said and done. You cannot depend on justice to prevail, or luck, or good bounces, or mistakes from your opponent. Golf is ruthless and contradictory and inscrutable and mysterious and unforgiving.

Good. Just like God, I suppose. And I suppose that's why he chose golf as—

Soc. And all you have on your side of the ledger, Goodman, is you and your center. It is worth getting to know that center, do you not agree? As my fellow Greek, the great Menander, once said, "*Lupes iatros estin anthropos logos,*" "For man, knowledge is the physician of grief." And the greatest kind of knowledge is knowledge of the self. Do you remember the two golden rules of the Delphic Oracle, Goodman?

Good. Is that the same Delphic Oracle, Socrates, who once said that you were the wisest man in Greece?

Soc. The same. You are most kind to mention it. It is funny, though. I have often said that I know nothing and that I have gained no wisdom, despite what the Oracle said. But after many centuries of playing the game of golf, and listening to it speak to me, and asking questions of it, I shall let you in on a little secret: I must finally admit that I know a thing or two! But I digress. The two rules of the Oracle . . .

Good. Let me see. . . . One of them was *meden agan.*

Soc. Yes, "nothing in excess." That was a good one. And the other?

Good. That would be *gnothi seauton.*

Soc. Very good, Goodman. "Know thyself": This is the one I always keep in my heart when I play golf. And today, I think that you have been doing some of that yourself.

Good. How so?

Soc. First, you learned about focus on the first hole and applied it to number two. Then, you questioned the issue of justice and the meaning of competition, and what they mean to your center, at number three. Then, your inner self learned the lesson of joy at number four. And came face-to-face with humility on five. And on number six, you got to know your compassionate self. *Gnothi seauton*: Yes, there is much wisdom in that. Which brings me to my final question, Goodman, after which we shall, at long last, play this excellent and demanding seventh hole. I know you are anxious to get started. . . .

Good. Yes I am, but I have been enjoying our dialogue very much indeed. So your final question, what would that be?

Soc. Ah, yes: Why do you think God has chosen this format of having you play all these different dead people, one per hole?

Good. Well, as you have said, He, being perfect and all, doesn't play Himself. And, besides, I guess He thought I'd find pleasure in being with and speaking to them.

Soc. Yes, that is all true. But since match play is usually one player against another for the full eighteen holes, why did He choose to send down from heaven a different opponent for each hole?

Good. If you put it that way, I am not certain why.

Soc. Well, how many of them will you be playing against today?

Good. Eighteen, presumably, if the match goes that far.

Soc. And are these players not different, one from another?

Good. Undoubtedly.

Soc. And do they not represent different personalities and different points of view?

Good. And how!

Soc. And is each hole, too, not different, one from another, with changing layouts and shot situations and challenges?

Good. Of course.

Soc. And if all these different players and different holes are constantly changing and variable, what then remains as the one unchanging and constant presence upon which you can rely, depend, and count on?

Good. Well, that would be me.

Soc. Very good, Goodman. And while we're on the subject of you, do you recall the song Lennon, and then you, were singing at the fourth hole? What was it about?

Good. Well, it was about somebody helping me. . . .

Soc. And this help that you need, do you not now see that this "somebody" who could give it to you is none other than . . .

Good. My body! I am, ultimately, the only "body" who can help myself, truly. Me, Elliott Goodman—

Soc. That is excellent, Goodman. I have often said, "The unexamined life is not worth living." And I believe that, under these most difficult of circumstances, you are beginning to examine yourself and your life. If you will forgive me one final thought to leave you with . . .

Good. How could I deny you this, Socrates?

Soc. Thanks. This thought is not even mine, actually. It was inspired by one of my brilliant compatriots, Thales.

Good. Thales of Miletus, the first great philosopher?

Soc. One and the same. Do you know, Goodman, how golf is a game of fundamentals?

Good. Yes, I have been playing for long enough to know that.

Soc. Well, Thales was always interested in studying the four elements and in examining their crucial importance as the fundamental pillars of life. Can you see how that could relate to golf?

Good. I can see that earth is a big part of golf. Dirt and rocks and grass and sand and trees and divots and hills and hardpan and heather . . .

Soc. Good. And air?

Good. Well, the wind is very important, I would say. Definitely. Little breezes and gusts of wind that swirl and change direction. And also the intimate sound of your breathing when you are playing.

Soc. Yes, and what about water?

Good. That's easy. There's rain sometimes, and then casual water on the course, and also man-made ponds, lakes, creeks, sounds, bays, seas, oceans . . .

Soc. And, finally, fire?

Good. Umm . . . er . . . There *is* no fire on a golf course.

Soc. You are mistaken, Goodman. Yet another paradox: The most important fundamental element in golf is not even visible. It is *here*. [*Points to stomach.*] In your belly. This fire is there with you, Goodman, all the time, and it is on *that* that you will have to rely. It will sometimes flicker or even seem like it is being extinguished, but it is up to you to blow on it even in the darkest of times and keep it burning.

Good. Thank you, Socrates, for that wonderful insight. You are a great teacher.

Soc. No, Goodman, you are once again mistaken. It is *golf* that is the great teacher.

On that note, the Dialogue with Socrates was officially over, and Elliott enjoyed a sudden burst of strength and confidence. He was pumped, and ready to rock 'n' roll.

The fog had by now rolled in from the Bay considerably, and, teeing up his Titleist, Elliott could barely see the green from the tee-box.

The seventh hole is a 219-yard par-3, a straight and wide affair with a fence to the right of the green—OB if you flew it—and a green, guarded by traps on both sides, that tilts slightly from back to front. With the wind at his back and his adrenaline flowing, Elliott figured he could reach it with three-iron.

His swing felt easy and uncomplicated, his mind uncluttered and free. Clubhead made contact with ball, picking it crisp and clean and perfect. Elliott lost sight of the ball after it had traveled only fifty yards from the tee-box, but it didn't matter. He knew he had hit a great shot and wasn't concerned in the least about the result.

Fee fi fo fum! I smell the blood of a Greekishmun! I, Elliott Goodman, with the pressure on, am about to take charge of this match and go one up!

As Socrates took his place at the tee, Elliott was finally far enough away to get a more objective look at the great philosopher. An imposing figure with the gentlest and most gracious of smiles, Socrates was wearing only a very old, wrinkled toga and worn sandals.

It was toward his face that Elliott's gaze gravitated.

The philosopher's reputation as an uncommonly unattractive man was certainly well deserved. Elliott was struck by how large Socrates' head was. Was it an extra large simply to house his amazing and voluminous brain? Elliott perused his face, top to bottom. The disheveled hair. The half-bald pate. The deep furrows along the length of the forehead. The sunken and caring eyes. The jug ears. The nose not quite decided on whether to be puckish or aquiline. The badly chapped lips. The curly, bushy beard. The yellow, decaying teeth. The oversize Adam's apple.

Socrates placed his ball on top of a white tee and addressed it thoughtfully. Elliott noted that the ball was very old and grayish, its surface was completely covered with nicks and scuffs, and it sported a red ZEUS 1 logo.

Socrates' setup was strange. He was bent over, half-crouched, half-squatting, pigeon-toed, and knock-kneed, a bit like a young Arnold Palmer putting. His take-back was stranger still, with the clubhead, at its zenith, only reaching parallel—*on the way back!*—and his wrists not even half cocked.

From this awkward position, the great philosopher paused slightly, and, in a violent and frenetic fit of fury, he gyrated his hips forward, then his lower legs, and, with phenomenal hands-and-wrists action, beat down hard on the ball, actually burying his clubhead into the ground at the precise point where the tee was poking out. His club broke the tee in two and propelled the ball, which never reached a height of more than three feet, straight down the fairway and in the general direction of the green. The ball bounced on a spot a mere sixty yards from the tee and disappeared from view into the now nearly opaque fog.

Socrates drove the cart. The conversation, suffering from post-Dialogue letdown, consisted of meaningless pleasantries.

When they reached the green, the fog was less thick than it had been on the fairway. Elliott walked toward his ball—which was resting a mere four inches from the cup!—and marked it with an old dime he'd removed from his right pants pocket. He sported the barely concealed smile of a Persian cat who had just caught and swallowed an unsuspecting sparrow.

"Wonder where my ball landed," Socrates said with some concern as he scoured the areas beyond and to both sides of the green, then the bunkers, and then beyond the cart path and toward the ninth green, where he stood now, scratching his head in bewilderment.

Elliott responded, "Never saw it land. Wait, I'll help you look."

As he was about to leave the area around the flagstick, he happened to look down and spied something actually sitting at the bottom of the cup. Moving closer for a better look, he recognized, to his horror and disgust, a small, dimpled object, gray in coloration and with . . . *a red "ZEUS 1" written on it!*

For chrissakes! I hit a gorgeous, perfectly struck shot to within four inches, and he hits this ugly, crazy, cockamamy drive that bounces probably ten times and rolls into the cup for a hole-in-one?

Elliott joined up with Socrates behind the green, bearing tidings of the philosopher's great stroke of fortune. In response, the wise old man gave Elliott a heartfelt look of compassion, sighed, "*Pathema mathema!*" and melted away, leaving nothing but his wrinkled toga and battered sandals in a heap on the cart path.

Elliott stood, alone and dazed, under a canopy of trees. His initial reaction was one of disappointment at losing the hole after such a magnificent drive. Then, anger and frustration at what had taken place.

Was Socrates sandbagging him? All that talk about leaving justice to the golfing gods, and then he just happens to clank his drive in for a goddam ace?

Magically, Elliott's grumpy mood evaporated, replaced by a feeling of lightness and grace, an unexpected sensation of being illuminated internally by a warm, satisfying glow. His new mood was fortified by his recollection of various snippets of the Dialogue he had had with Socrates, which were just sinking in.

Yep, I did everything I had to do, and the rest was left to the golfing gods! They turned out not to be merciful on this hole, but things will turn around, I know it. I'm feeling good about my swing, my competitive spirit, and I'm going to keep fighting no matter what else is about to happen, holes-in-one or whatever.

Keep to the center! *Pathema mathema*, baby!

Elliott wended his way to the other side of the cart path and toward the eighth tee, situated just adjacent to Inwood's entry gate. Although he was one down in the match yet again, he felt a renewed optimism and was determined to face with grit and valor whomever God had in store for him now.

Let's get *rea-dy* to *rum-ble*!, he said to himself peppily, set-ting his jaw and looking skyward.

I don't care if, for the eighth hole, you've sent down the biggest, the strongest, the fiercest, the meanest, the cruelest, or the nastiest macho man you've got up there. Goliath? Genghis Khan? Sonny Liston? It doesn't matter to me . . . just *bring him on!*

8

A Lot at Stake

IT WAS NOT GOLIATH, Genghis, or Sonny who was taking practice swings at the eighth tee, but rather a slender, boyishly attractive seventeen-year-old girl, whom Elliott recognized immediately, both by her dress and her bearing.

It was Jehanne la Pucelle . . . *Joan of Arc!*

Elliott's testosterone level, which had shot sky-high at the very thought of doing battle against a behemoth, a beast, or a brute, plummeted at the sight of the slight maiden.

His first, male-ego-driven thought was how bitter a defeat to a woman would taste. Then, realizing that Mlle Darc was barely a woman, he thought how bitter the taste would be to lose to a girl.

Abandoning such negativity, he summoned up from somewhere deep in his hippocampus the bare essentials of her biography that he had learned way back in Frank Exline's eighth-grade history class. *Born in French village of Domremy in 1412 . . . begins to hear "voices" at twelve . . . on mission from God . . . drives British out of Orléans . . . helps Charles VII become King of France . . . captured at Compiègne . . . condemned by*

Church as witch and heretic . . . burned at stake in Rouen in 1431 at the age of nineteen . . . becomes Saint Joan in 1920.

What an impressive, extraordinary, brave, single-minded, determined, all-too-short life! Dedicated to the sole end of serving God and France, on her Great Mission . . .

"I am on a *Great Mission,*" Joan said, interrupting his thought midstream, "to win this hole, *pour Dieu et pour la France.*

"I will beat your brains in, if I must," she continued, in her thick, northern French peasant accent. "I will take no prisoners. I will fight to the death if that is what is required of me. I will *die* on this hole if that is what God wills. *Je suis cy envoiée de par Dieu!*"

If Elliott was ready to rumble, so was the Maid of Orléans. As she finished her practice swings and addressed her ball, she cut an imposing figure, belying her youth and slightness of stature.

Her hair was cut short, like a boy's, and she was wearing a one-piece, tight-fitting catsuit made of a closely woven, lightweight, pewter-colored nylon mesh—complete with sewn-in simulated pallettes, breastplate, brassards, skirt of tasses, tuilles, cuisses, knee pieces, and jambeaux—the closest facsimile to a suit of armor that synthetic fiber could offer.

On her right breast was a fleur-de-lis, and on her left a Nike swoosh with NIKE AIR: MAIL inscribed below. A hand-painted, gold-and-black sword-in-scabbard affair ran down the length of her left side, from waist to ankle. A pair of matching pewter-colored pointed-toe spikes that resembled sollerets—the suit-of-armor footwear—complemented her outfit.

She could neither read nor write.

Ah, but her swing! It was long, loose, flexible, graceful, quick, and powerful, as La Pucelle demonstrated, taking her

Grande Berthe 480Z back effortlessly and absolutely *waxing* her drive. Against a nasty headwind, her ball traveled an impressive distance but just caught one of the bunkers on the right side of the fairway.

"*Par mon martin!*" Jeanne muttered, angrily picking up her undisturbed tricolored tee and taking her place beside the cart.

His psychological momentum thwarted by Saint Joan's surprising physical prowess, Elliott stepped up, teed up, and looked up.

The eighth, with the headwind, was playing tough today, tough and long. It is a shortish, 415-yard par-4, four yards shorter than its twin brother, the ninth, which, on its left, runs parallel to it. Bordered by a fence and private residences on its right (OB) and trees down the length of its left side, the eighth hole is punctuated by a menacing, two-tiered green that today, with the wind drying it out, read about an 18 on the Stimpmeter.

His competitive juices flowing full tilt as a result of the mammoth drive struck by France's patron saint, Elliott swung hard and flushed his drive, way out there, but a slight hook pulled his ball, which had started its flight right down the heart of the fairway, toward the tree line on the left.

The two scrambled into the cart. Elliott drove.

"Mademoiselle," Elliott began his query to the rebellious teenager, "I'd love to know where you got that swing. It's pretty sweet."

"*Merci mille fois.* Oh, sorry about what I said about your brains on the tee. It can get a little intense when you are on the Great Mission, *non*? My swing? Well, you know, after Léonard has invented the game, for a longtime, the women, we were not allowed to be the members of the golf clubs. Then I have heard voices that told me to go on a Great

Mission to give the women the right to play golf up there. And with God by my side, I *did* it! At first, the women, they did not come. But then, little by little, they *all* come and play!

"First, all the great queens—Hatchepsout, Néfertiti, Sammuramat, Cléopâtre, Éléonore d'Aquitaine, Isabelle I, Marie-Antoinette, Élisabeth I, Mbanda Nzinga, Catherine la Grande, Victoria, Liliuokalani . . . And then came Sappho and Émilie Dickinson, then Jeanne Austen, *les soeurs* Brontë, Marie Shelley, George Sand, George Eliot, Virginie Woolf, Gertrude Stein, Simone de Beauvoir, and then Marie Curie and Florence Nightingale, then Amélie Earhart and Sarah Bernhardt, and Joséphine Baker and Coco Chanel—she has designed this outfit!—then Suzanne Lenglen, Hélène Keller, Anne Frank, Harriet Tubman, Éléonore Roosevelt, Golda Meir, Indira Gandhi . . .

"Oh, the swing! Sorry, but I get—*comment dirais-je?*— 'carried away' talking about all the great women! Well, I learn the swing from the Lord, who has told to me the basics when I hear the voices in my head, you know, 'Keep the head down, Joan! Turn the hips, Joan!' And then, I practice very, very much, and once in a while I get the tips from the different peoples, like van Gogh, Einstein, and Buffalo William. . . . But, in the end, the swing, she is *mine!*"

Not expecting such a meandering answer, Elliott still found Jehanne gregarious, entertaining, and spunky—strangely enough, she reminded him of his daughter, Molly—and, before he knew it, they had arrived at his ball, which, to his embarrassment, was away.

Elliott's drive had landed only a few feet from an imposing sugar maple, but the lie was clean, and he definitely had a line to the pin. Because he was so close to the tree, however, his stance was restricted, and, with the headwind, he'd be lucky to land anywhere near the green.

Let's see . . . about 180 . . . usually a three-iron, but with the wind . . . let's try the five-metal. . . .

Elliott selected five-metal from the bag and, feeling a kind of paternal rush as he passed the cart, gave Jeanne an affectionate wink. As he addressed his ball, he recalled, and drew strength from, the discussion he'd had with Socrates concerning self-knowledge. He'd hit the five-metal in this situation a bunch of times, and he knew he could pull the shot off.

Gnothi seauton . . . gnothi seauton, he mantraed to himself as he addressed his ball and then . . . absolutely *cranked* it.

Maple leaves flew, and the ball, oblivious of the head-wind, traveled straight and high and true and toward the flag. But it veered, at the very end—he'd turned it over a smidge, as he'd done with his drive—and landed in a greenside bunker on the left.

It's okay. In the bunker? No biggie . . . *pathema mathema*, baby! It'll be up and down from there for my sweet little par, and the rest is up to the golfing gods!

Elliott drove to the maiden's ball, and she hopped out briskly to assess the damage.

"*En nom Dieu!*" she shrieked upon discovering her ball leaning up against two humongous pinecones in the center of the bunker. "*Saperlipopette!* I have not the smallest idea how to hit this!"

Choosing five-iron from the bag, she returned to her ball in the bunker and, her brow riddled with wrinkles of uncertainty, dug her pointed spikes deep into the sand.

You'll need some aid for that one, my dear!, Elliott opined silently, singing the opening lines of "Help!" to himself.

Jehanne la Pucelle suddenly cocked her head to the side as if she were a marionette manipulated by an invisible string. After listening intently to something—Elliott was clueless as to what, since the golf course was as quiet as a tomb—she said, in a half-whisper and looking straight up, "*Oui, Sire Pere, roy du ciel . . . oui . . . soit faite votre volonte. . . .*"

With purpose, she walked out of the bunker, back to the cart, and exchanged the five-iron for . . . a seven metal!

Back in the bunker, she took her stance, closed her eyes, and, with a heavenly admixture of power, speed, grace, fluidity, and balance, picked the ball cleanly, pulverizing both pinecones in the process and sending it just barely over the lip of the bunker and straight at the flag.

The shot was struck so well that the ball hit the apron on the fly and, following the natural flow of the terrain, bounced twice and bounded into the greenside bunker on the right.

Elliott had never before witnessed such a wonderful shot from such a horrific lie. As Joan entered the cart, he smiled with fatherly approval and began the drive greenward.

Wait just a second . . . hold your horses! Great shot, yes, but did I detect some hanky-panky? I mean, yeah, I guess she hears voices all the time, but . . . *during my match?* According to Leonardo, God didn't come down to play me Himself because it'd be unfair. Okay, no problem with that, but doesn't that include aiding and abetting any of His subs?

Elliott was getting steamed. He smiled politely at Joan, then sank back into his reverie.

So that's how He wants to play this hole? He sees I'm getting into a groove, and He can't take the heat? Little Miss Darc with the picture-perfect swing can't beat me fair and square, so she needs her Heavenly Daddy to give her a little friendly coaching? Okay, that's how it's gonna be, I guess, but you know what? I'm gonna win this hole anyway. Golfing gods, shmolfing gods. I'm gonna take this big ol' bull by the horns and ride him to victory!

Thinking he'd gotten the anger out of his system, Elliott engaged the maid once again in conversation.

"That was a real beauty. *Bien joué!*"

But he still apparently harbored some residual annoyance at that "illegal use of voices" business, and he surrendered to a sudden, uncharacteristically mean-spirited urge to give Joan the needle.

"Hey, how'd it feel to be . . . *burned at the stake*, huh?"

After three seconds of uncomfortable silence, Joan—armed with a ready wit, a feisty nature, and enough colloquial English to defend herself ably—responded, with a wry smile, "Well, it did not feel . . . too *hot!*"

At which point, the two, in exact unison, went into an uncontrollable fit of uproarious, gut-busting, side-splitting, knee-slapping laughter, rocking back and forth, then side to side, in the cart.

After another hiatus of three seconds, a second simultaneous paroxysm had them both, in turn, guffawing, giggling, groaning, snickering, sniggering, snorting, shrieking, roaring, tittering, wheezing, huzzahing, convulsing, cackling, chuckling, chortling, and cachinnating.

When they recovered, Elliott was filled with an uncomfortable ambivalence. On the one hand, he had grown quite fond of Jehanne, partly because she was such a sweet kid, whose charm and sense of humor endowed his history-book learning of her sketchy bio with warmth and humanity, and partly because she reminded him so much of his darling Molly.

On the other hand, with the crucial third shots coming up and already one down in the match, he desperately needed to win the hole and couldn't dare allow himself to give in to these paternal feelings when there was still such serious work to be done.

Elliott hit a magnificent explosion out of the bunker, but his ball just nicked a hanging tree branch and fell short of the green, into a gnarly patch of grass.

Now it was the Maid of Orléans's turn. She grabbed a sand wedge and set up for her shot in the right bunker. To Elliott, it looked like one of the most difficult bunker shots imaginable, and not because of the half-buried lie. No, it was the *green* that was the problem. Since the pin placement was, diabolically, at the very crest of the green's top tier and her ball was exactly pin-high, Joan had to choose between two equally unappetizing courses of action.

She could explode the ball onto the top tier, but not too close to the hole—in which case, no matter where it landed, she would actually have to hole her putt, or else the ball would slide past the hole and roll precipitously down the incline, onto the lower tier, and, picking up speed, most probably off the green.

Or she could explode onto the bottom tier, in which case she'd have an easier putt but would also run the risk of either (a) not hitting it hard enough—the ball would then roll back down to where she was in the first place (like one of those miniature golf shots where you have a windmill, a tunnel, a bridge, a clown's mouth, or some other annoying obstacle to negotiate, without the slightest guarantee of not having the ball keep returning to your feet, ad infinitum, for your remaining time on the planet)—or (b) hitting it too hard— she'd then end up on the top tier and putting toward the precipitous incline: See Unappetizing Course of Action Number One.

Faced with this quandary, Joan took a deep breath, then, as in the previous bunker, and to Elliott's dismay, performed the same routine—the cocking of the head, the rapt listening, the half-whispered, skyward-looking response: "*Oui, Sire Pere . . . [yada yada yada] . . .*"

With a finesse and a touch that would have seemed unimaginable in a maid so young, she exploded out of the trap, a gentle spray of fine sand forming a perfect rooster tail and accompanying her ball onto the top tier, where the ball hit ten feet from the cup and, with the slightest amount of sidespin, rolled gently toward it, not picking up any appreciable speed. As it slid by the cup by an inch or so, it rolled slowly down the incline and landed just where the incline ended, only four feet from the hole.

That shot was impossible!, Elliott marveled silently, not knowing whether to applaud Jehanne's wonderful effort or demand that she be retried and reburned at the stake for witchcraft and heresy.

Faced with the daunting task of holing his own impossibly difficult chip from the furze, in the event that Joan drained her putt for par, *just to halve the hole,* Elliott gritted his teeth and paused.

You can do this. I know you can. Maybe she'll miss the putt, and you can up-and-down it. Nah, she'll make hers . . . you gotta make yours. *Gnothi seauton.* Keep to your center.

Elliott set himself and, dedicating the shot to Molly and digging deep into his very core to summon up the best he could offer, executed a creatively conceived, absolutely Mickelsonian flop shot from the thick growth that exploded his Titleist out of the gorse, shot it straight up twenty-five feet in the air, and bounced it softly on the upper tier, where it spun back toward the hole and finally settled an eighth of an inch from the cup.

Elliott was filled with pride and satisfaction. He'd done what he'd set out to do, in spades. He tapped in for, under the circumstances, an amazing bogey five.

Joan lay three. She stepped up and, this time not needing a voice from somewhere up there, knocked her putt in, front door. Wham, bam, *merci, Madame.*

Elliott's heart was broken.

He had battled so hard, so valiantly, *without help from else-where!* The sad fact remained that he was now two down, for the first time in the match, and was feeling, also for the first time, that things were beginning to slip away.

Fighting through the heartbreak, Elliott Goodman was still a gentleman and a strict observer of golf etiquette. He walked toward Jehanne to shake . . . no, to greet her with a warm hug and congratulate her for her brilliant play and hard-earned victory.

Then he remembered the scenario of what had happened previously to everyone else at the conclusion of the holes— the disappearing into thin air, the flying and the swirling away, the vanishing, the evanescing, the skeletonizing, the melting—and just as he reached her, to his horror, he witnessed his sprightly new friend, who had been so full of life, suddenly burst into flames, her ashes spread hither and yon by the headwind that had been such a major participant in the golfing drama that just unfolded.

Elliott rued his loss, not only of the hole, but of having lost it to a female. To boot, he also lost a person he was terribly fond of.

Where could he go from here but up? If only he could get another chance on the next hole, this time, perhaps, against an ordinary woman with ordinary talent, a woman who was human and flawed, a woman with no "special connections" and against whom he could go *mano a womano* and beat fair and square.

9

RINGER

THE GOOD NEWS WAS that a woman was waiting for Elliot at the ninth tee. The bad news was that this was no ordinary woman.

Not by a long shot.

Elliott found himself looking at—according to the incomparable sportswriter Grantland Rice—"the most flawless section of muscle harmony, of complete mental and physical coordination, that the world of sport has ever seen."

She was the holder of more medals and records in more sports than anyone else, man or woman, on the planet . . . *ever.* Was a world-class champion performer in four major sports. Held multiple records in track and field, basketball, swimming, skiing, horseback riding, and rifle shooting. Possessed incredible skill at billiards, skating, cycling, handball, lacrosse, tennis, boxing, bowling, and fencing. Won two world-record-setting Olympic gold medals. And, for good measure, in baseball, had struck out Ruth and Gehrig, and . . . *DiMag on three pitches!*

She could type eighty-six words a minute.

It was the "other" Babe—Mildred Ella "Babe" Didrikson Zaharias.

Elliott's initial reaction when he first laid eyes on her was one of anger. *Ringer!,* he whined to himself, as if he were a Little League batter who had just stepped up to the plate to face a twenty-three-year-old pitcher with a beard.

So it's not enough to send down special, extraordinary, one-of-a-kind people? Now I gotta deal not only with one of those, but with a pro athlete, not only with a pro athlete, but with a pro golfer, not only with a pro golfer, but with one of the greatest ever, a woman who once won thirteen consecutive titles and seventeen of eighteen, the trailblazing co-founder of the LPGA, who won both the U.S. National Open and the All-American Open—after cancer surgery!—and not only that, but the cockiest, most arrogant and boastful and intense and tenacious and aggressive and overbearing and viciously competitive prima donna who ever stalked the fairways?

Give . . . me . . . a . . . *break!*

Ever since Socrates, Elliott had been working on trying to control his passion and channel it into his golfing effort, so he tried to let his anger go. Now that he thought about it, he felt honored to be playing against the feisty Babe.

Jock and sports addict that he was, underneath his professorial persona, Elliott had, over the years, preoccupied himself with ranking all the great athletes (his six criteria were impact, dominance, versatility, competitive intensity, records, and longevity). Contrary to most of the pundits, he had always ended up placing her—and *not* Jim Thorpe or Jim Brown—at the very top of the list. Since she was a little girl, she'd always wanted to be the greatest athlete, man or woman, who ever lived, and Elliott, for one, believed she'd accomplished that.

"Howdy, now how're they hanging?" the cheeky Babe

inquired, speaking slightly out of the side of her mouth, her twangy Texas drawl greeting Elliott with a wry and deceptive solicitude.

"Good, thanks, and yours?"

"Fine. *Real* fine," she said, smiling. "But enough of the sweet talk, brother. Better hold on to those pants, 'cuz I'm gonna beat them off of you!"

Elliott smiled an internal smile, noting how this intimidating greeting was reminiscent of Joan of Arc's.

The ninth hole at Inwood is a 419-yard par-4, featuring a fairway trap and an imposing row of sugar maples and native locusts to the right of the fairway, trees lining the left side, and, behind the green, the ominous and ubiquitous cart path that could come into play if the second shot were hit too aggressively.

"May the best man win," the Texas Tornado quipped with a wink as she teed up her ball.

She was five-foot-five and wore a wide-brimmed hat, longish skirt, shirt, and golf sweater, all charcoal gray, all business. You couldn't see her muscles, but, by her bearing and her movements, you could tell they were there in force, built up through years of working out with her homemade backyard weights made of broomsticks and her momma's flatirons. Her hair was plastered back, her face was weather-beaten, and her leathery hands were gnarled, like a boxer's, from the millions of balls she had hit in practice sessions, which had made them bleed and require bandages.

She wore no lipstick.

"Well, as I always say, to drive the ball way down there, you gotta loosen your girdle and let 'er rip!" she exclaimed, and proceeded to do just that. With a powerfully athletic swing and revved-up hip action, she powdered the ball 260 down the middle of the fairway.

"Mercy!" Belting Babe bellowed. "Now you try and catch *that* one, brother!"

Refusing to be bullied by the Terrific Tomboy's bravado, Elliott cranked a beaut of his own, one of his trademark fades that kept carrying and landed five yards past her ball, center cut.

He gave Babe one of those "put-*that*-in-your-pipe-and-smoke-it!" looks, and she came right back at him with one of those "oh-*yeah*?-one-of-us-is-gonna-lose-this-hole-an'-it-ain't-me!" scowls, and they both jumped in the cart, with Whatta-Gal-Didrikson in the driver's seat, and headed down the fairway.

Barely after they left the tee-box, Elliott went into brain-lock. He had been competing hard for over an hour and a half, digging deep inside himself and trying to play well and find joy in the game and correct his mistakes and learn from his amazing opponents—*and save his life!*—and he had never once allowed himself to lose contact with the moment. Ninety minutes of grinding, and the pressure and the intensity of the experience got to him at last. He lost all sense of where he was and what he was doing, and his mind wandered aimlessly.

Was this golf match really happening, or was he dreaming? It seemed so real, so palpable, but . . . how could all these deceased icons possibly have been resuscitated? Were they really living a second life up there in heaven, and . . . playing golf?

Was God indeed omnipotent, capable of this elaborate arrangement? Or was Elliott playing this golf match only in his mind, deep inside his cerebral fissures, even as his real body, lying defenselessly on the operating table, was being opened up, kept alive by a machine, and subjected to all the insults of a major rerouting procedure?

Was it possible to be sent down from heaven to perform acts like playing golf against someone whose life was at stake? Could you also descend, like Billy Bigelow in *Carousel*, to see how your family was doing down here? Why did God choose these particular icons for him to compete against?

Screeching to a halt, the cart was the key that unlocked Elliott's brain.

"Well, sir, you sure make snappy patter!" the Amazing Amazon said sarcastically. "Looks sorta like you were out for lunch just now. That's okey-dokey by me. That's the kind of opponent I love to play. Yessirree, if you're not concentrating one hundred and ten percent, I'm gonna eat you for breakfast, lunch, and dinner every time!"

Elliott was embarrassed and a bit put off by her cocky remark, but she was right.

I gotta get back in the saddle, get back my focus. I gotta compete like hell now. I gotta *beat her!*

The gal from Port Arthur hopped out and grabbed her six-iron. Elliott had always been blown away by the stupendous coincidence that this small East Texas town had spawned both the greatest athlete ever, man or woman—Babe—and the greatest rock singer ever, male or female—Janis Joplin!

Mildred Ella was 160 from the pin and was planning to cozy an easy little six right up there. She set up, fixed her steely gaze upon the ball, then at the flagstick, then back at the ball. She took her strong, controlled backswing and hit down sharply and fiercely, catching the ball perfectly and taking a huge divot in the process.

Her eyes followed the flight of her ball, willing it to direct itself toward the pin. It bounced once on the apron, then on the green, and struck the flagstick with a glancing blow, ending up ten feet away, to the right and pin-high.

"Lawdy! Dumb luck!" she squawked with fire in her eyes,

meaning not that she was fortunate to hit the stick, but that she was unlucky that the ball didn't go in the hole. "Dad-gummit! Thought for sure the eagle had landed!"

That shot was *unreal*! This is one tough cookie I'm playing here, everything I expected her to be.

Elliott selected six-iron, too. He was concentrating on his center by the time he addressed the ball, trying to relax and stay calm.

"Two down, you turkey! You're falling apart, and you know it!" razzed the devil—dressed in that silly red Dr. Denton outfit, complete with horns and a tail, and holding a pitchfork—who was sitting on his left shoulder.

"No way! You've flushed this shot hundreds of times, and when—*not if*—you win this hole, you'll only be one down and right back in it!" cooed the angel—bedecked in robe, wings, and halo—sitting on his right one.

Elliott dismissed these distractions, relaxed his hands, and, pronating his wrists hard and moving his hips and left side into the swing with every ounce of energy and effort in his body, flushed his ball perfect, sending it high and true. It landed softly on the green, bounced twice more, and ended up pin-high, eight feet to the right of the flag. And inside Babe's ball.

Yes! Elliott hissed to himself.

He had often thought that golf is a particularly glorious game, not just for all the obvious reasons, but for one in particular. Of all the major sports, it is the only one where, if you're "in the zone," you can perform, at any given moment, on any given day, just as well as, and probably better than, anyone on the face of the earth who ever played the game!

If he canned this putt for his birdie, for instance, no one in the world—unless an unthinkable, million-to-one eagle were shot—could beat *him*, Elliott Goodman, here and now, on this ninth hole at Inwood Country Club. Not Vardon or Jones or Sarazen or Hagen or Nelson or Snead or Hogan or Palmer or Player or Nicklaus or Trevino or Watson or Vijay or Tiger . . .

Was Babe pissed! Losing was never an option for her— not now, not ever—but she was, as always, the consummate professional and had to give credit where it was due.

"Heck of a shot, brother!" she said to Elliott as she pressed her foot on the accelerator and motored toward the green. "Man, that ball cozied right up there nice and tight, like a young buck sidling up to his honey on a front-porch swing on a cool summer night in Beaumont with a full moon in the sky, a gleam in his eye, and two Dr. Peppers in his hand!"

Elliott smiled at Babe's homespun and charming, if slightly prolix, simile. He also appreciated her sportsmanship and her acknowledgment of the brilliance of his pitch. It's not every day that the great Babe Didrikson looks you in the eye and gives you a nice compliment in the heat of battle.

"Tell me, Babe," Elliott began, now feeling chipper and loquacious, "how do you think you'd do against the women on today's LPGA Tour?" Ever the sports nut, he was dying to get her take on the matter.

"Well, sir," she drawled, not mincing her words, "there are some real good gals out there, far as I can tell. But between you and I? I'd eat 'em up and spit 'em out. Still, I reckon there are a lot more great players now than there were when I was playing. I think Annika's a crackerjack. Like a dadgum machine, that one. And I love to watch Inkster and Pepper! Real tigers. Sort of remind me of me, but with less pepper! [*She laughs.*] And there are some great strikers of the ball, that's for darn sure. Davies, Webb, Mallon, Pak, Park, Ochoa, Pressel, Creamer, Wie . . .

"But if I had to put money on any one of 'em against me? No contest, brother! If we all used today's equipment? Heck, even if they did, and I used hickory shafts and the ol' dead ball. Would've loved to play today, though, with all that money on the line, y'know?"

She licked her chops in mock hunger, then smiled forlornly. "But those're the breaks, I guess. Like the cancer I got toward the end. Sometimes you got to play life from the rough, as I used to say."

Elliott could feel a lump form in his throat as they approached the green. He remembered, when he was just a kid, hearing the story of her tragic death at forty-five. And thinking, through the years, about how courageous she was and how she had fought cancer till the end, just like she fought all her other demons during her hardscrabble life—all those golfing opponents, all those ignorant homophobes, all those folks who thought that a gal should stay at home and cook and sew and take care of her hubby.

But this was no time for sentimentality. He was two down and now had a great shot at cutting the deficit in half.

Mildred Ella parked the cart behind the green, grabbed her putter, and walked briskly to her ball.

As she lined up the putt, her eyes, as always, told the story. They stared at—no, they stared *down!*—the hole, heartlessly, as if to anthropomorphize this mere opening in the ground, as if to tell it—*person to person!*—that she was, in no uncertain terms, about to violate its vulnerability, to take advantage of its openness, to start her ball rolling inexorably toward its very core, to drive it into its heart like a stake, to show it who's boss.

Plop!

Elliott was up against it now. His eight-foot birdie putt, which had, seconds before, seemed like a virtual gimme, was now looking like a twenty-footer. The Babe's bravura performance had cruelly transformed his confidence into self-doubt. Here he was, in the presence of this *force*, this winning machine, on the verge of beating her and teaching her a lesson, and now this.

Right to left, about two inches if you hit it firm. You know the line. *Gnothi seauton.*

This time, the mantra didn't work. With the pressure of possibly going three down—*three down!*—and Babe standing there watching, his hands turned to jelly, and he pushed the putt weakly. Not even close. An inch to the right of the cup, and short, no less.

As John Lennon might have put it, *this bird has flown.* Now Elliott was in profound caca.

He picked up his ball in disgust, and when he looked up, there was no one else on the green with him. On closer inspection, Elliott spied Babe's hat on the ground at the far edge of the green. Above his head, skywriting formed the large, bold letters NOT IN *MY* HOUSE!

Elliott felt like he had just snatched defeat from the jaws of victory and felt sick to his stomach. Maybe he just needed to put something *in* it?

He headed dejectedly toward the Halfway House, a small structure beyond the cart path between the ninth green and the tenth tee, where, after your front nine, you could go for refreshments and refuel before tackling the final nine holes.

Elliott, a deeply thoughtful person, was once again deep in thought.

Crunch time! Man, how'd this happen? I was just all square on number-seven tee, and before I know it—*bam . . . bam . . . bam*—three down! Socrates with his ace, Joan with her voices and magic shots, now Babe with her nerves of steel. I played great, and still I go *three down?*

God, Babe was good! Like she just refused to lose! That's how I was, too, but when it came down to it, she makes her putt, I miss mine. Funny how humility works. First I figure how no one in the world could possibly beat me after my pitch, then somebody does! Sometimes, no matter how good you think you are, how well you play, how hard you try, there's always someone out there a little better than you.

It was the *hubris* that did it. The same affliction that did Oedipus in, just like I taught in class. Thought I could beat Babe, then look what happened. Reminds me of that great old English proverb, "When they came to shoe the horses, the beetle stretched out his leg." *Ha!* The ol' beetle! I can just see him now. . . .

I remember, after losing to Jehanne, how I wished for an opponent who was "human" and "flawed." Well, guess what. That was *me*! Yep, human and flawed, that's me, all right. Okay, fine. That's who I am, and if my opponents are gonna make all their goddam putts and chip in from bunkers and profit from divine guidance, what can I do? Not my problem. Just gotta keep grinding. Never give up. So maybe there *is* a justice somewhere, where everything balances out in the end? Maybe someone's gonna miss a putt or make a bad play, and then I'll be ready. Maybe the golfing gods will reward me for hanging in there.

As Elliott approached the Halfway House door, the rekindled fire in his belly was doused by a dark thought. He was feeling terribly alone—he, the human and flawed Elliott Goodman—and not just because the course was deserted or, hole after hole, his opponents kept vanishing on him. The match was quickly going south now, and a strong, visceral storm of panic was beginning to gather itself somewhere deep inside him.

Three down, and only nine holes separating me from the ol' Reaper? So who's gonna care if I lose . . . if I fail . . . if I . . . *die*?

To make matters worse, his mind wandered to W. H. Auden's *"Musée des Beaux Arts,"* a magnificent poem he had taught many times, and one of his favorites. Its main theme—how people always seem to die alone, while others around them go about their humdrum business—is brilliantly reflected in the mythic figure of Icarus, who, having flown too close to the sun with his waxen wings, plummets to a watery grave, virtually unnoticed by anyone.

If I go on and lose this match, would my demise be . . . unnoticed by anyone? Would my life be a meaningless statistic? Perhaps a tiny notice on the obit page? I can see it now: "Elliott Goodman, 50, Harvard professor, passed away yesterday . . . *because the poor bastard couldn't win a goddam golf match!"*

Elliott opened the door and sat down on a stool in the Halfway House, trying to rehabilitate himself. Behind the counter was an old guy with a full white beard and deep facial wrinkles.

"So what'll it be, sonny?" he asked.

"Oh, I guess I'll have a pack of peanut-butter cheese crackers and a small black coffee to go," Elliott said.

"Coming right up."

Elliott took a closer look at the old codger.

Funny, but I could swear I know this guy from somewhere. Can't quite put my finger on it, but don't I know that face? Nah, no way . . . been over thirty years since I was last here.

"Here ya go, buddy-boy. One pack of crackers, one java, and it's on the house," the old guy said. "How's the golf going?"

"Thanks. Oh, it's—" Elliott began.

"Say, mind if I give you a tip, from an old codger who's been around the block a few times?"

Elliott nodded yes.

The codger looked Elliott straight in the eye and said, solemnly, "Whatever happens out there . . . *don't take any wooden nickels!*" He followed this profound pearl of wisdom with a hearty, boisterous belly laugh.

Elliott took his snack and container of coffee and thanked the old guy for his service and his helpful advice.

Crazy old coot!

Elliott left the Halfway House, chomping and sipping his way to the tenth tee. En route, he had one of his epiphanies.

What kinda jerk am I, huh? Somebody in this world *does* care. *Joy and Jake and Molly!* How I miss them! How I want to see them again! To put my arms around them and smother them with hugs and kisses! Then there's all my close friends and relatives. . . . I know I'm gonna die sometime, but . . . I will *not* go unnoticed by anyone!

With renewed strength and resolve, Elliott took the last chomp of cracker and the last sip of joe and walked past the small man-made pond on his right, across the cart path, and up the grade leading to the slightly elevated tenth tee-box.

He was determined to turn the match around, determined more than ever that nothing—*nothing!*—would intimidate him or sidetrack him or distract him from his goal of winning this golf match and reclaiming his life.

BACK NINE

10

SIREN

n [ME, fr. MF & L; MF *sereine*, fr. LL *sirena*, fr. L *siren*, fr. Gk *seirēn*] . . . any of a group of female and partly human creatures in Greek mythology that lured mariners to destruction by their singing . . . a device often electrically operated for producing a penetrating warning sound . . .

THERE SHE STOOD, her pouty lips quivering slightly, her delicate white golf skirt blowing in the breeze, her platinum bangs dancing to and fro on her pale forehead, her ample chest heaving softly under her pink cashmere sweater, her voluptuous and vulnerable persona piercing brilliantly through the foggy gloom, beckoning . . .

Marilyn!

"Happy birthday!" she said, in her trademark whispery voice. It was not the first time, Elliott was quick to note, that she'd uttered these two words so breathlessly.

You cannot be *serious*! First, it looks like it's three women in a row! And right in the middle, the heart of the order, the 3-4-5 slots in the lineup! Then I go from playing a saint to a golf goddess, and now . . . a *real* goddess! Can you believe it?

Marilyn Monroe! The very first crush I ever had, ever since I saw *Some Like It Hot* when I was five or something! And, icing on the cake, she just happens to know it's my birthday today?

Today was, in fact, Elliott's fiftieth.

Fifty years old! My God!

Elliott's initial frustrations evaporated, and he was suddenly filled with a terrible sadness.

I'm fifty! And what am I doing on my fiftieth birthday? Spending time with my wife and kids? Celebrating with a few close friends? No, I go get myself a heart attack, and then I'm out here all alone, playing golf! If things don't turn around somehow here, those fifty years are gonna go right down the toilet. To cap it all, I meet up with the first woman I ever had eyes for while Joy's probably at home wondering where the hell I am and what the hell I'm doing!

He became sadder still when he gazed up at Norma Jeane Mortenson taking her practice swings on the tee. Norma Jeane, who had died so young, at thirty-six, with her whole life ahead of her.

What a waste! She had everything but I guess was just overwhelmed by it all. Funny how a person can get overwhelmed by it all. I know how complicated my own life can get, with publishing pressures and deadlines, preparing lectures, grading papers, seeing students and discussing their ideas and their problems, not to mention all those committees to serve on, writing papers, and going to conferences and shmoozing with colleagues. And then there's maintaining friendships and maintaining the house and maintaining the marriage and doing stuff with the kids and paying the bills and paying the bills. . . .

Elliott was feeling overwhelmed now, and it wasn't just by the thought of how overwhelming his life could get. It was by everything he'd been through on the front nine—all the characters he'd met and the discussions he'd had and the golf he'd played and the things he'd learned and not learned—and now, after all that, he's three down with time running out and faced with holding his feelings and libido in check and playing against this screen idol.

"Well, hello there," MM purred warmly as Elliott stepped up to the tee-box at number ten. "How very nice to meet you."

"Likewise, I'm sure," Elliott answered.

Likewise, I'm sure? What pure, unadulterated bulldung!

He was, on the contrary, not wanting to be polite and formal with the actress but instead entertained indecent, even nasty thoughts concerning her. Thoughts that had something to do with the stereotypical golf pro standing behind the drop-dead gorgeous beginner and teaching her a thing or two about the rhythm of the swing and the turning of the hips . . .

To make matters worse, Elliott continued, "You look great! Nice outfit."

This dilly, he realized, was almost as lame an icebreaker as the brilliant "Nice clubs!" conversation opener he'd employed with Leonardo on number one. He also knew from the look she flashed him that he'd hit a nerve.

"You know," Marilyn responded, "that's been the trouble all my life. People seem to be interested only in my looks and my body and my clothes and my outside. But I wish they'd care a little more about what's *inside* me."

After a pause, she added, "Dr. Goodman—can I call you Elliott?—you know all about books, being a professor and all . . . so you should know as much as anyone else that you can't *really* judge a book by its cover."

Elliott was blown away by the simplicity and profundity

of Marilyn's seemingly innocent remark. It summed up, in an uncomplicated, if overused, metaphor, what her entire existence on earth had been. What her feelings about herself and others were. What, in essence, most people feel inside about the disparity that exists between them and the outside world.

She might look like an empty-headed starlet, but here was a real philosopher.

By now, Elliott's anger and sadness had melted away. All he felt was a warm, empathetic fondness.

Okay, let's cut the crap! This is a real slippery slope, y'know. Better watch out for your emotions, or you'll lose all your focus. Remember what happened with Freud? And besides, you made yourself a promise that you wouldn't get distracted, and, whaddyaknow, here's the granddaddy of all distractions staring you right in the puss—*et ne nos inducas in tentationem sed libera nos a malo.* Just like Applegate sent ol' Lola to tempt young Joe Hardy, now it's you and Marilyn. . . .

Be strong!

With this final word, a feeling of towering strength filled Elliott. He got his mind back on his golf, and he felt a rush of power—a combination of testosterone and adrenaline—suffuse his body, from the crown of his head to the tips of his toes. He was *strong* now, and he would win the hole against this beautiful, warm, sensitive, but, ultimately, fragile woman.

It was the Big Bad Wolf against Little Blond Riding Hood.

The tenth hole is a very short, 106-yard par-3, with virtually nothing between the slightly elevated tee and the slightly elevated green but a pretty, round, man-made pond. Obviously, you can't be short, but you can't be long, either. Behind the green are nasty rough, a bunch of trees, and, back right, a bunker you really don't want to mess with.

Marilyn smiled at Elliott and whispered, "Well, I guess it's my turn!"

She grabbed an old, banged-up seven-wood from the bag and returned to the tee. She waggled (boy, did she waggle!), addressed the ball as if it were the first time she'd ever done it—turning the clubface toward, then away from, the ball a few times with a slow, tantric movement of her delicate wrists—took her club back gently and awkwardly, and, in unison with a meek little whimper of a grunt that exited her luscious mouth, the very bottom of her club barely made contact with the tippy, tippy top of the ball and sent it skimming, with overspin, along the grass in front of the tee, down the mound of the tee-box, bouncing once on the cart path, then through some short grass, and—*ker-plop!*—into the pond.

A stunned Elliott felt an unfamiliar tingle run down the length of his spine. For the first time in the entire match, the proverbial door had been opened wide, offering him a Golden Opportunity on a Silver Platter.

"Oh dear," Little Blond Riding Hood squealed. "I think I have to hit another one, don't I, Elliott?"

Big Bad Wolf nodded in assent, barely containing his glee at the plight of his weak, innocent adversary. He also felt bad for Marilyn, since he really did like and admire this complex and surprisingly substantial woman. But since he had his game face on and dared not let his good feelings for her dilute his strength, the glee prevailed.

He felt in his heart that nothing could stop him from winning this hole and narrowing the margin to two. Not with him playing well, and now Marilyn, the rank amateur with the laughable swing and the nonchalant attitude toward athletic competition, already screwing up and lying two, with, it seemed to him, no chance to make solid contact with the ball. Unless she somehow figured out (and real quick) how to negotiate the dreaded water.

Norma Jeane set up a second time, biting her upper lip

with determination. She was hitting three and wanted desperately to avoid embarrassing herself again. She took her club back, this time with a little more confidence, and made good contact. The ball rose delicately into the air, negotiated the pond, and landed gingerly on the green, fifteen feet left of the hole.

"Yay!" MM gushed, jumping up and down with mirth and relief.

Elliott, not the least bit concerned with the ultimate outcome, clapped a polite clap and walked toward the tee-box, pitching wedge in hand. As he passed Marilyn, he took in a huge whiff of the powerful, alluring fumes of the *My Sin* she'd dabbed on generously behind her ears and on her nape before coming down for the golf game.

It is 1962, and Elliott Goodman has just turned six. What a joyous time to be alive! JFK is in office, and hope is in the air. Even at his young age, the precocious Elliott is hungry, for knowledge and for pleasure, and can sense that life is pretty special. Everything he experiences has magic dust sprinkled all over it.

Hessing's Luncheonette, with its Topps baseball cards and bubble-gum boards, its Mary Janes and Mason Black Crows and Beemans pepsin gum and BB Bats. His little saddle shoes he helped his mom paint first black, then white, with those wands with the round thingy-doos at the end. His little pompadour and that wax in the applicator that made it stand up.

The Jints and Bums had skipped town, but how 'bout them amazing, amazing, amazing, amazing, amazing Mets? Nathan's hot dogs and sour pickles and Othellos and blackout cakes. Little Lulu, and Nancy and Sluggo, and Archie (he preferred Betty to Veronica).

His mom's canasta and mah-jongg games. His parents' rhumba lessons in the basement. Murray the K and Cousin Brucie. His beloved Spaldeen in the driveway, and his Duncan yo-yo ("Around the World," "The Windmill"). Riding the phony horse in the barber shop, and trips with his mom to the "beauty poller." Cool cars with fins.

His first crush . . . on Marilyn! To him, she was the most beautiful girl in the world. Then, so soon after he first laid eyes on her and felt his heart beat fast for probably the very first time, on that night in early August, the night when the papers said she took her own life . . . a little of that magic was gone, forever. . . .

"Hey!" Marilyn called out, nudging Elliott gently on the shoulder. "You okay?"

Elliott returned from his little mental voyage, thanked MM for caring, and stepped up to the tee. He shook off the cobwebs and stared at his ball. He once again felt the sensations of strength and power fill his body. He felt the adrenaline/testosterone mixture kick in again as he addressed his ball and took a final glance at the flagstick.

He pictured, in his mind's eye, Charles Atlas, the guy on the back of the comic books who had had sand thrown in his face because he was a "ninety-pound weakling," then built himself up to be a gorgeous muscleman. He pictured himself *as* Charles Atlas, all bronzed and shiny, with his muscles popping out, and he'd get that girl and show that bully.

While Elliott did his waggle, this incredible power coursed through his veins and into his arms and hands and wrists.

Then . . . *ka-blooey!*

Elliott had never hit a golf ball with such ferocity, such violence. He figured it was the combination of wanting for sure to clear the water and his feeling of supreme confidence and strength against a weaker opponent. The good news was that he had never struck a wedge this solid or this flush.

The bad news was that he airmailed the green and landed in that nasty bunker behind it. But he was still one in the trap, and Marilyn was lying three up there, fifteen feet away from the stick on a tricky, undulating, hard-to-read sonuvabitch of a green.

They drove around the pond and up to the green, and the cat was definitely getting the better of Elliott's tongue. Of all the incredible characters he'd met so far, all the brilliant and creative and profound and entertaining and charismatic personalities he'd rubbed shoulders with, Marilyn was the one who fascinated him most, who had this special, ineffable aura about her that rendered him completely and uncharacteristically speechless.

Elliott ventured into the bunker with his sand wedge.

Okay, down to business. Let's figure she's good for five— maybe four, if she pulls a Moses—so it's just a question of blasting this anywhere on the putting surface, two-putting for my bogey, and getting outta Dodge. Gotta be careful, though, to take plenty of sand, or else I'll fly it over the green and into the pond.

The adrenaline had subsided somewhat after his colossal drive, and Elliott was feeling loosey-goosey.

Okay, she's outta the hole. Just take plenty of sand.

Elliott took plenty of sand. In fact, he took more than he had bargained for. He hit about four inches behind the ball, and his Titleist moved six inches forward and remained there in the bunker. Just for good measure, the ball had relocated itself in a fried-egg lie and was half-buried.

Now he lay two and had a *really* tough explosion shot, with the pond becoming even more menacing.

What in tarnation is going on here?, he whined as he dug his spikes into the sand and prepared to take another whack.

This time, he hit a beauty, eight feet below the cup. This was now a real horse race, with both players lying three on the green.

MM was away, with a slippery fifteen-footer and the putting skills of a bad miniature-golf player.

"My turn?" Marilyn asked.

"Yep," Elliott answered in a monotone, a great deal more interested in his putt than hers.

"Elliott, I'm not sure where to hit the ball. Could you help me?" she queried meekly.

Don't go there. Don't you *dare* go there!

"Why, sure," he said amicably, and stood behind her to help her read the putt.

Et ne nos inducas in tentationem sed libera nos a malo. . . .

"This green sure is hilly!" she remarked.

Ever the gentleman, Elliott stood behind the luscious, irresistible woman, took another whiff of the *My Sin*, bit his lower lip so hard that it bled slightly, and read her putt correctly. Pretty severe left-to-right, slightly uphill slider. Never up, never in.

"Just hit the ball four inches to the left of the hole, pretty firm, and I think you'll be okay. And keep your head down!"

"Thanks, Elliott. You are *so* nice!"

Yep, that's me, nice ol' Elliott. But you know what Leo the Lip said about nice guys. . . .

Marilyn took her stance, looked once at the hole, and stroked her putt exactly as Elliott had instructed her to. The ball responded by curling left to right, exactly four inches and toward the center of the cup, and stopped two inches short.

"Aww, too bad!" he said, in mock empathy.

"So what'd I make on this hole?" she asked innocently as she tapped in.

"You had a five. But that was *very* good, considering the first shot."

Elliott read his own putt now, a simple eight-footer, uphill all the way and no break, as far as he could see. He conferred with his imaginary caddie.

Eight-footer. I love this distance. Make these putts with my eyes closed. No break, just ram it in the front door.

Hypertestosteronal Elliott rammed it, all right, *way* too hard, and his ball flew right over the hole, smashing violently into the flagstick, popping up, and rolling three feet past the cup.

Elliott could easily have panicked. He now lay four—after having been in the bunker in *one*—and he had to drain the three-footer to halve the hole with Marilyn, who had driven in the water and had been hitting three off the tee without a clue.

Elliott stepped up and canned his putt, to his great relief. He picked up his ball and spun around quickly, wanting to get a last glance at his first crush.

As in her life, Norma Jeane made her exit too soon, leaving behind only the scent of her *My Sin* and the sweet memory of her presence.

Man, did you butcher that hole! What were you *thinking*? What a wuss! Couldn't even beat Marilyn Monroe, a rank beginner!

Walking to the eleventh tee, Elliott had some second thoughts.

So I blew it, but let's look at the bright side. I didn't lose the hole. I ended the little losing-to-women streak. I stopped the bleeding with the halve. I learned something again that I should've remembered after I underestimated "old man" Leonardo on the first hole and then "fuddy-duddy" Freud on the fifth. As MM said so eloquently, "Don't judge a book by its cover."

I thought she was gonna be a pushover and that I could just put myself on cruise control. There's that pesky hubris again! But there was more substance to her than met the eye, I must admit. She did pretty well for herself, actually, recovering from her first shot like that and nearly draining the putt for bogey. Should've let her fend for herself and worried more about taking care of my own business.

Still, the naked truth of it was that Elliott had pretty much butchered the tenth hole against a—presumably, he'd learned the hard way—weaker opponent. As he walked hopefully to the eleventh tee, he resolved to play the next hole more artfully.

11

GREEN PERIOD

HE WAS LIKE NO ONE ELSE, before or since. He wore old tan cargo shorts, a pair of funky, weather-beaten leather sandals, and nothing else. His bare barrel-chest was swarming with curly gray hairs. His head was tanned and smooth and bald, except for a patch of gray on both sides. He sported an elfin smile. He was an authentic masterpiece.

¡Pablo Ruiz y Picasso!

"*¡Hola! ¿Qué tal?*" the artist said with brio. "*¡Encantado,* how nice to make your acquaintance!"

Elliott couldn't believe he was now meeting, and about to play against, the great Picasso, who was—along with Rembrandt, Blake, and Goya—one of his all-time favorite artists. He noticed with some surprise that Pablo spoke not with his adopted French accent, but with a peculiar Castilian lisp, perhaps the linguistic vestige of his Iberian youth?

"It's a real honor to meet you, too!" Elliott enthused, like a schoolboy about to ask for an autograph. "I had no idea you played golf!"

"*¡Cómo no!* I have been playing for about a century now," Pablo said, never shy about telling stories.

"*¿*Did I ever tell you the story of how I started playing? Well, señor, it was between my Blue Period and my Rose Period. I called it my Green Period. I took off a year from my art and did nothing but play golf, at a little course outside of Paris. ¡No one knew about this at the time, but it is true!"

"Wow . . . I . . . didn't know!" Elliott stammered, at a loss for words. "I think you have the honor. . . ."

"Yes, you are right. ¿But did I ever tell you the story of my theory of golf? *Lo siento,* but I must. You see, *mi amigo,* what is *not* real is what is out *there* [*points to fairway*], and what *is* real is what is in *here* [*points to forehead*]. It is our mind, not our eye, that creates the only true reality. Take this hole, *por ejemplo.* ¡It is not what it appears to be!"

The eleventh hole is a 433-yard par-4 tester, a slight dogleg left (amazingly, the only one at Inwood) with huge sugar maples bordering the left side of the fairway. For the average right-handed player who can't hit a draw, it is a challenge getting the drive past the over-sixty-feet-tall trees and down the fairway. You have to hit either a low three-iron stinger or a high fade that clears all the trees.

"It seems to be a dogleg left," the artist continued, "and that is how most people look at it. For me, it is a succession of geometric angles—modularities—that combine to make the hole. ¡That is to say, the parts are the sum of the hole! [*He giggles.*]"

Then he stopped, took a napkin and a drawing pen out of the left pocket of his shorts, and, placing the napkin against his knee, drew a quick sketch of the eleventh hole as he saw it:

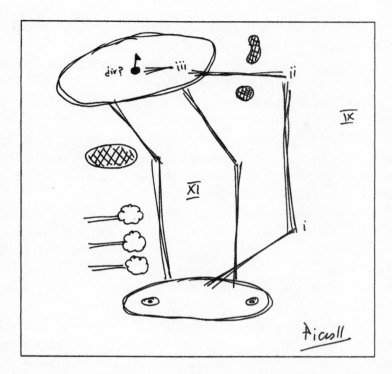

"I will not play it like everybody else. I will hit the drive onto the ninth fairway, then the second down the ninth fairway, then the third over the bunkers and onto the green ¿The putt? ¡Well, we will see about that!"

What a genius! He may well be right about how to play this hole, who knows? I've always had trouble putting my drive on the fairway, so we'll see. Actually, Pablo's theory reminds me of that wonderful quote of his about the creative ability of the mind to go beyond accepted wisdom: "When we love a woman, we don't start measuring her limbs."

Pablo stepped up between the markers, teed up his *pelota*, set up facing right, and, with a tempo roughly three times faster than that of Nick Price's frenetic swing, swatted the ball straight and true, through the eleventh fairway and into the exact middle of the ninth fairway.

"*¡Bien jugado!*" Pablo cheered in self-adulation. "¡You know, you should try this route yourself!"

Elliott smiled his approval and walked with his driver to the tee-box, deep in thought.

This cockamamy theory, it's pretty tempting. Seems to work for him. But I'm gonna stick to my guns. Always liked the challenge of this drive, and I'm gonna do it my way. Just have to get my legs into the swing.

Which he did. He absolutely *smoked* his drive, a towering fade with a glorious left-to-right arc that easily cleared the row of maples and landed way down the fairway, 255 yards from the tee.

The two climbed into the cart. Elliott drove; Pablo sketched.

On the dashboard, on the passenger's side, lay an opened pack of Gauloises cigarettes—the *papier maïs* kind, favored by workers, that last longer because they stop burning every ten seconds—a green Bic lighter, a tube of SPF5 Bain de Soleil suntan lotion, a wheel of stinky Camembert, and a well-chilled bottle of 1904 Sancerre.

Picasso took a bite out of the cheese, a few swigs of the wine, and a puff of the cigarette, sketching furiously and chattering at the same time.

"¿Did I ever tell you the story of the different Periods of my golf game? Well, señor, there were many. Just like I always wanted to try new things in my art—Blue, Rose, Cubism, Neoclassicism, Surrealism, Symbolism—it was the same with golf. Breakahundredism, Breakninetyism, Driveism, Chipism, and Puttism. I liked to try things that were new and different."

As the cart reached Picasso's ball, The Master paused to

chomp on some cheese, took a quick swig from the wine bottle and a quick puff from the cigarette, hopped out with his three-metal, quickly hit his second shot and then watched it bound down the ninth fairway and stop, just as he had planned, pin-high and fifty yards right of the flag.

"*¡Bien jugado!*" Pablo cheered in self-adulation.

When they reached Elliott's ball, he handed the napkin on which he'd been sketching to Elliott. It was a signed drawing of Elliott hitting his drive:

"This is *so* cool!" chortled the devil with the red suit, horns, tail, and pitchfork sitting on Elliott's left shoulder. "My good buddy, you are now holding in your hand a napkin worth, oh, shall we say . . . *twenty million or so!*"

The angel with the robe, wings, and halo sitting on his right shoulder disagreed vehemently. "Listen, Elliott. Put that silly napkin in your pocket, grab your four-iron, and get back to business. You're down three, and you're running out of holes!"

Obeying the angel, he stuffed the priceless napkin into his pocket, grabbed four-iron, and took his setup.

Okay. Stick to your guns. I hit a great drive, and I don't care how Picasso plays this hole or what his theory of angles is. Maybe it works for him, but I'm playing it my way. I can't get distracted, like I did against Leonardo, John, Freud, and Marilyn. Okey-dokey. I'm 170 to the apron. Pretty good tailwind. Just gotta hit it solid.

Elliott hit the four-iron of his life, as he watched his Titleist soar, bounce, then land eight feet right of the flagstick. He was feeling mighty pleased with himself, but not cocky. How could he forget what had happened after his great shots on numbers three, seven, and nine?

He took the steering wheel and drove toward Picasso's ball.

Pablo was again sketching at breakneck speed and lit up his third Gauloise of the hole. He drew in a wad of smoke and somehow exhaled it in the shape of his painting *Les Demoiselles d'Avignon*. Magically, the aroma transported Elliott to Paris in another Proustian olfactory moment similar to the one he'd savored at the first hole, where the mere scent of Leonardo had miraculously whisked him off to *L'Italia*.

It is June 1991, and Associate Professor Elliott Goodman is in his beloved Paris, researching a book he is writing titled Picasso, T. S. Eliot, and the Language of Collage. *How he loves the routine of his days, filled with the satisfying rhythm of toil and pleasure!*

The cute little apartment he's rented in the Marais, on the rue de Sévigné . . . the early morning strolls to his favorite pâtisserie—*ah, the smell!*—*where he buys a baguette and brings it back to his flat and makes* café filtre, *which he drinks with baguette slices he's topped with apricot preserves . . . walking to the rue de Richelieu and working all morning at the Bibliothèque Nationale . . . taking lunch at "Le Grand Colbert" on the rue Vivienne . . . working all day at the BN . . . then strolling toward the 3e and spending a few hours at the Musée Picasso, his favorite museum ever, better than*

MOMA, better than Moderna Museet, better than Het Rembrand-
thuis, better than the Musée Rodin or the Centre Pompidou.

How he loves the compactness of the museum, the incredible en-
ergy of Picasso, and his eclecticism, and the variety of stuff to see—the
photos and synopses of his life, the paintings, sculptures, lithos,
sketches, ceramics, illustrations . . . then, tearing himself away, finally,
to have an Oban (rocks, twist) at "Ma Bourgogne" on the Place des
Vosges.

And, to top off the day, dinner at one of his very favorite restaus
in the whole city, "Bayou la Seine," on the rue Saint-Paul, with its
Cajun specialties, its charming décor, including posters of New Orleans
concerts, its scrumptious dishes like the crawfish pie and the pirogue,
and especially his stimulating after-dinner chats about cooking and
life with the delightful owners, Judith and Frédéric . . .

Pablo interrupted his sketch, and Elliott's reverie, to hit
his third shot. He had to fly a pitching wedge between two
bunkers that stood between his ball and the green and bounce
it softly on the apron. With the frenetic movement of a fright-
ened Arctic hare, he set up, addressed his ball, looked once at
the flag, swung, and lofted a gorgeous pitch, which bisected the
bunkers, landed softly on the apron, and rolled to within fifteen feet of the cup. Just as he'd planned it.

"*¡Bien jugado!*" Pablo cheered in self-adulation.

Now it was down to the Battle of the Putters.

Elliott had the inside edge, though. He lay two, with a
pretty simple uphill eight-footer, while Pablo lay three, with a
downhill putt nearly twice as long.

Pablo took one last swig of the Sancerre, one final bite of
the Camembert, one terminal, lung-filling puff from his *mégot*,
and deposited one ultimate penstroke to the most recent of his
chefs d'oeuvre.

Lining up the putt with his patented pendulum, plumb-
bobbing, four-dimensional, nonperspective, eyeball-distorted

method, he quipped, "Putting is like art. It is all about the instinct. Señor, I have the *feeling* that this putt . . ." He barely hit the putt, coaxing the ball ever so gently, with an amazingly delicate touch, toward the hole. It headed down the hill, closer . . . "Is going to go . . ." And closer . . . "*¡In!*"

Upon which, his ball tumbled into the center of the hole. "*¡Bien jugado!*" Pablo cheered in self-adulation.

Pablo was now in for his par, and Elliott had a great chance to cut his deficit to two down by dropping the birdie putt. It was his third consecutive eight-footer, his previous two having missed badly.

He put a perfect stroke on the ball, had the perfect line and the perfect speed. It was, simply put, a perfect putt.

Simply put, his ball ran out of steam a half-inch short of the hole.

Despite yet another maddening miss at this distance, Elliott had every reason to be content.

You played the hole perfectly. Perfect drive, perfect pitch, perfect putt. It would've been a great bird, but as it is, it was a damn good par. Best of all, you weren't sucked into Pablo's way of playing. Who knows what you would've done going down the ninth fairway? You believed in your way, executed it your way, and came up a tiny bit short.

Another quote came to him, this time from Emerson's essay on self-reliance: "To believe your own thought, to believe that what is true for you in your private heart is true for all men—that is genius."

Elliott knew, in his heart, that he had played the hole well, had halved it and nearly beaten the amazing Picasso, had steadied the ship by not losing another hole, and was now in the groove again. More important, he knew in his heart that he had trusted his course management, had believed in and relied on himself, had become, at least for the moment, the "somebody" who could help him, as Socrates had pointed out. If *that* made him a "genius" in the Emersonian sense, well, that was fine by him.

Funny how I played so well on numbers three, seven, and nine and lost all three of those holes. And now, finally, I played well again and at least came away with a halve. I just gotta keep playing well, and we'll see what happens. . . .

Elliott tapped in for his par, and, when he looked up to pay his respects to Pablo, he was amazed to see the wise old genius smile at him wryly and then, artfully, fragment his body into a thousand little modular pieces that, one by one and in rapid succession, dematerialized.

As Elliot walked toward the twelfth hole, he had one final, encouraging thought:

What a genius Picasso was, and *is*! I saw this—after having admired him for much of my adult life—in person, and on the golf course, no less! It's inspiring how he viewed the world in his own unique way, using his personal perspective, breaking rules, following "the road not taken," in art as in golf as in life. Now that I think of it . . . so did *I*!

I mean, like him—*like Pablo Picasso!*—I did try things in my life that were different. I did sometimes buck the powers that be. I did live by the passion of my convictions. I did see things as only I, the one and only Elliott Goodman, could see them!

Picasso may have been a true genius, and so may all the other "subs" have been, in the peculiar and special ways in which they carved out their own paths: Leonardo, Fields, Moses, John, Freud, Poe, Socrates, Joan of Arc, Babe, Marilyn. For that matter, whomever else God wants to send down here to play against me and test me, but, y'know what? In my own way . . . *so am I*! In my own way, I possess a special genius not owned by anyone else on earth. Maybe it's Emerson's definition of genius, or maybe it's my own. But isn't that the whole point? Maybe *that's* the reason Pablo was sent down to play against me.

Elliott was now in high spirits, feeling, in a very deep place, what he had sometimes felt during his life but was beginning to see in a different way after playing golf with Picasso—his worth and meaning as a person of special importance, a person who made a difference by his uniqueness in the world.

His mind back on his golf and on the upcoming hole, he began to talk to himself in order to pump himself up for yet another golfing challenge.

Okay, the eleventh was a good hole for my self-confidence. I'm in the groove. Still three down, but I think I can start my big comeback now. I think there's hope for me yet. I'm gonna *do* this!

Honestly . . .

12

HONEST?

THE LEATHERY SKIN, the massive forehead, the large jug ears, the bushy eyebrows, the piercing gray eyes, the high cheekbones, the sunken cheeks, the deep furrows beneath the cheeks punctuated by the mole on the right side, the prominent nose, the pursed lips, the scraggly mustacheless beard, the coarse, jet-black, well-parted head of hair . . .

Who could ever mistake this face? The face that all red-blooded American first-graders are introduced to, the memory of which they will take to the grave. The face on the penny, the five-dollar bill, Mount Rushmore. The face that belongs to the sixteenth president of the United States of America, the honorable . . .

Mr. Abraham Lincoln!

The hulking, rawboned, gangly, 180-pound, 6'4" man with the huge hands and the huge heart and the trademark bow tie and stovepipe hat was waiting patiently at eleven tee for Elliott to finish up his battle with Picasso.

"Some battle that just was, sir," he said, with his painfully thoughtful Kentucky drawl. "Sort of recalls me of the one at Antietam. Yes sir, those were powerful perilous times, they were, and I reckon, Dr. Goodman, that these are powerful perilous times for you, too."

Elliott smiled internally at the thought that Honest Abe's voice sounded exactly like Henry Fonda's. Or was it Raymond Massey's? He wasn't sure of what to say in response. What *do* you say to the greatest president America has ever produced?

"Well," he stumbled, "that was a little before my time, but I sure had myself a pretty good battle there with Picasso. What a genius!"

"Yup," the Great Emancipator agreed. "I reckon he sure saw things different from most of us humble folks. As I said in my Lyceum Address, eight score and eight years ago, 'Towering genius disdains a beaten path. It seeks regions hitherto unexplored.'"

Never heard that one. Nice. Have to quote it in my lecture on Joyce . . .

Elliott realized, with some sadness and not a little panic, that if he didn't get on his horse and start winning a few holes ASAP, there might not ever *be* a lecture on Joyce.

"I'm curious, Abe, how'd you first get into golf?"

"Well sir," Honest Abe answered, "didn't have much spare time while I was alive. Couldn't pay no nevermind to anything but writing speeches and dealing with The War and slavery and Mary and the boys, dontcha know? Nope, 'twasn't till I passed on to my Maker that I had all the time in the world and took up this glorious and honorable game.

"I find golf enriching, sir, and very much suited to my particular temperament. All my years of hard labor and splitting rails and educating myself. I think that's what I enjoy most about playing. You put the work in, you get rewarded. But, you know, 'tis not an easy game. Sorta recalls me of trying to catch yourself a slippery Kentucky sow in the mud with your bare hands. You think you got her real good in your arms, and as soon as you think you got her, she slips away."

The twelfth hole at Inwood had always been one of Elliott's favorites, a long, majestic 456-yard par-4 with an OB fence running down the right side, a pretty straight hole but with a slight dogleg right that favors a nice, easy fade off the tee.

As Elliott had halved the last two holes since the loss to Babe on number nine, Honest Abe still had the honor.

"I believe I still have the honor, sir," Lincoln said as he ambled with large strides to tee up his ball, "and honor is in-dis-pu-ta-bly something I like to have!

"I'd like to wish you the very best of luck. 'Tis a mighty large burden that has been bestowed upon you this day, and you shall not take what is about to transpire lightly. As I said in my Gettysburg Address, seven score and three years ago, 'The world will little note, nor long remember what we say here; while it can never forget what we *do* here!'"

Elliott noticed that the driver Lincoln held in his mammoth hands was, to say the least, peculiar. Its shaft was attached not to the end of the clubhead, but to its *middle*, giving the club the appearance of a croquet mallet!

To Elliott's astonishment, our sixteenth president took his setup . . . *behind the ball, backward, with his back facing the fairway!* As Abe gripped the driver tightly with a baseball-bat grip, he noticed, peripherally, that Elliott was staring at him, his mouth agape.

"Oh, that?" Lincoln said. "Don't fret, son. I taught this here swing to myself when I commenced to playing the game. Figured out that I couldn't hit the ball worth a lick with this swing nor with that swing nor with the other swing, so I decided to use all my rail-splitting muscles and know-how and hit it . . . the only way I *knew* how. As I sorta said in my house-divided speech, seven score and eight years ago, 'A swing divided against itself cannot stand.'"

To Elliott's continued astonishment, Abe took back his driver, with his powerful arms strangling the grip, straight up over his head—his gangly elbows and his face pointing heavenward, his back arched to the limit, and his clubhead touching his butt—and then down again violently toward the ball, and—*between his legs!*—struck it a mighty blow, sure and confident and with pinpoint accuracy, as if he were splitting a log with his ax.

Thwack!—280, center cut!

Elliott stepped up to the tee and, somewhat shaken by Lincoln's outlandish drive, hit a so-so one of his own, pretty long, but his fade, like his drive on number two, didn't fade, and the ball went dead straight and through the fairway and into a nasty bit of rough on the left.

The two hopped into the cart, with the Great Emancipator taking the wheel. Elliott couldn't take his eyes off Lincoln. Of all the icons he'd met during the match so far, Abe was the one who'd been etched in his mind from his earliest age.

"Now, class, who chopped down the cherry tree and said, 'I did it!' and then became the father of our country?" Mrs. Fishkin asked hopefully. "George Washington!" the class of first-graders screamed, in unison and pridefully, back to their teacher. "And which great president of the United States was called 'Honest Abe'?" "Abraham Lincoln!" Edith Fishkin's lesson may have been rote and automated, but it was one that stuck in the mind of six-year-old Ell Goodman, one that would remain there during his entire life.

Time and again, the thorny issue of honesty and integrity—so simply posited in that class with the blackboard and the Palmer-method penmanship cards above it and the American flag and the ancient wooden desks with the names carved into them and the inkwells—would resurface in Elliott's life. Being truthful and direct, meaning what you say, following through on promises, maintaining high moral standards, a man's word is his bond . . .

Time and again, he would come to the same depressing conclusion—people are disappointing! They just are. And absolutely consistent in their behavior. Broken promises, fibs, cut corners, weaselly cover-ups, speaking out of both sides of their mouths . . .

The one thing he'd never been able to figure out was whether this disappointment, this general moral disparity between him and other people, was the result of his high expectations of decency or their low ones. Which was why he so deeply appreciated the handful of people in his life who did possess the rare qualities of honesty and integrity. A few close friends and, of course, Joy and the twins . . .

The cart stopped at Elliott's ball, which, as luck would have it, was buried in deep cabbage. The best he could do, alas, was to hack it out with a nine-iron about sixty yards down the fairway and take his medicine. A hard pill to swallow, considering he was only a foot from having a superb lie in the short grass with clear sailing to the green, but swallow it he had to, compliments of those venerable apothecaries, the golfing gods!

Abe, on the other hand, had a perfect lie 175 from the pin. As he had done at the tee, he lifted his croquet-mallet seven-metal way up into the air, his back toward the green, and—*chop!*—swung between his legs and smacked the ball senseless. It started out toward the green, but, as the wind had just started to pick up and howl, it was tugged way to the right and seemed to land perilously close to the fence that stood between the rough and disaster.

"Didn't reckon the wind could blow so fierce in these here parts," Honest Abe said as he rejoined Elliott in the cart and pressed one of his size-eighteens on the accelerator pedal.

He didn't have far to drive before they reached Elliott's ball. With five-iron in hand and a firm resolve, Elliott set up, addressed, waggled, and paused.

Okay, about 150, lots of wind . . . gotta bump-and-run it Scottish-style and bounce it up there and maybe get lucky.

He swung and nipped it just right, knifing his ball through the gale and, as he had hoped, bouncing it onto the green, where it stopped twenty feet left of the pin.

"Mighty nice shot!" Lincoln said graciously, and they headed toward the green.

"Y'know," Abe began, "I never lived to see the seventies. I mean to say, the 1870s. Well sir, one day a while back, maybe two or three score and twelve or thirteen years ago, I'm writing this speech up there in the Great Beyond for the retirement ceremony of Marco Polo, the distinguished outgoing president of the DGA. That's the Dead Golfers' Association.

"And I'm thinking to myself, Abraham, you may never have lived to see the seventies, but maybe you can talk about the seven −ty's. You know, those seven moral pillars that hold up the game of golf and also the game of life—Equali-ty, Equanimi-ty, Humani-ty, Sinceri-ty, Chari-ty, Integri-ty, and Hones-ty. 'Twas one of the greatest speeches I ever did pen, son, one of the greatest. . . ."

Lincoln parked the cart behind the twelfth green, about thirty yards from where his ball lay. He left the cart, grabbed a pitching wedge, and walked toward the fence. Elliott felt strong and hopeful.

I really hit that five-iron on the screws. Good news is I'm lying three and in great shape for a par putt. Bad news is . . . well, there is no bad news. Putt looks to be about fifteen feet. Twenty tops. And ol' Abe is probably screwed! Probably up against the fence. May even have to take an unplayable, so he'll most likely be hitting four and will need a miracle to get up and down for his bog—

Elliott's thought came to a screeching halt. What he saw at that exact moment was so far beyond the pale of plausibility, of credulity, that thinking, much less breathing or any other human activity, was rendered irrelevant.

In a nutshell, he saw Honest Abe go down into a hollow and toward the fence, stop just short of the fence, look around furtively, and . . . *actually kick his ball away from the unplayable edge of the fence and into an area of light, playable rough!*

As he laid eyes on this preposterous act, those very eyes felt as if they were popping completely out of his head, like in a cartoon, attached to his face by long Slinkylike springs and accompanied by that "DOI-OI-OING!" sound effect. Were these same eyes deceiving him? *No*: Without a shadow of a doubt, Elliott was positive that he had actually witnessed Abraham Lincoln, this Great Symbol of Honesty . . . *cheat!*

Elliott's motor skills were paralyzed. He remained in the cart while Lincoln looked at his new and improved lie and pondered his "third" shot. In Elliott's stunned mind, all hell broke loose, as if a Pandora's box of sinister ruminations had suddenly been unleashed.

Does God exist? How *can* He, when someone like Abe Lincoln cheats? Was Nietzsche right after all about His death? I *did* see Him in person in the OR, but now, after what I've just witnessed, was that just a figment of my imagination?

Isn't Lincoln's cheating like any other iconoclastic act that would destroy the fabric of an extreme paradigm? It's like Mother Teresa cursing or Santa Claus molesting a child or . . . William Safire omitting a comma! Why did Abe do it? Did he, perchance, not know the rules? Or maybe he is, just like the rest of us . . . *human?*

Elliott paused during his rant to flip mentally through the pages of *The USGA Rules of Golf,* which he had committed to memory years ago, to make sure he'd got it right. Yep, Rule 13: Ball Played as It Lies. Then, paragraph 13-2: Improving Lie, Area of Intended Stance or Swing, or Line of Play. A player must not improve or allow to be improved: the position or lie of his ball . . .

Play the ball as it lies—one of golf's great life-lessons! Every one of us gets dealt rotten cards at some point—my heart attack, your diabetes, her breast cancer—but in life, as in golf, we gotta play the hand the best we can, play it as it lies . . . . I've been challenged by some really tough lies today—the branches on 2, the divot on 3, the bunker on 6, the second shot on 12—but none was as tough a challenge as *Abe's* lie just now!

Omygod. Should I report "Honest Abe"—*now a common felon!*—to the proper authorities, whoever they are, and probably win the hole, with my life at stake? Should I stand up for my rights *and tattle*, or should I keep my big trap shut, out of respect for the Great Emancipator, and keep the transgression to myself, at the risk of losing this crucial hole?

Should I choose to follow the Great and Mighty Rules of Golf—the special, ironclad etiquette all golfers respect—or should I challenge their authority and opt instead for the integrity of a different order, the one that respects the reputation of others and their ability to make their own calls, as well as the noble concept of "to err is human; to forgive divine"?

Then again, am I such a bastion of honesty and integrity, am I so self-righteous as to be in the position to sit in judgment of someone else, and especially . . . of Abe Lincoln? What about that time when I was eight, when I went into Hessing's Luncheonette and paid for ten packs of baseball cards and left with eleven, and ol' Mr. Hessing never called me on it and just gave me a wise old wink? Maybe this new secret of mine finally balances out the one kept by Hessing, lo, those many years ago? Even-Stefano!

Nope, no way I call Abe on his kick. Never saw it. *Rules of Golf* or not, high stakes or not, this is the right thing to do. Now if I had to call myself on something *I* did—

A Canadian goose honked, terminating Elliott's internal monologue.

Honest Abe took his stance, facing the fence and his back toward the green, then—*chop!*—twelve feet from the cup.

They met on the green, Elliott throwing Abe a disappointed glance and Abe tossing Elliott back a sheepish one.

Elliott lined up his putt, took his stance, and addressed the ball, resting his flat stick gently on the putting surface behind the ball. To his horror, just before he took his putter back . . . *the ball moved!*

It moved barely, not even one-thousandth of an inch, hardly at all, scarcely a jot or a speck or a hair or a tad or a bit or a skosh or a smidgen or an iota or a whit or a particle or a trace or a touch or a dash or a molecule or an atom.

But move it did.

Elliott was aghast. Not once, but twice this hole did he have a Ruling to make! For the second time in not even five minutes, he flipped in his brain through *The USGA Rules of Golf*, and, sure enough, there it was. Rule 18-2.b, under Ball at Rest Moved—Ball Moving After Address: If a player's *ball in play moves* after he has *addressed* it (other than as a result of a stroke), the player is deemed to have *moved* the ball and *incurs a penalty of one stroke.*

This time, there was no agonizing, no head-scratching. Because this was a call against himself and not his opponent, it was less a question of morals than of basic decency and etiquette. Elliott knew instinctively what he had to do. In this situation, the *Rules of Golf* had to prevail.

"I hate to say it, Abe, but I'm sure my ball moved, and it looks like I lie four, not three."

"I'm mighty sorry, sir," Lincoln answered, "but a rule's a rule, I reckon."

Another disappointed look from Elliott, followed by a second sheepish one in response.

Elliott gathered himself, took a deep breath, and rammed in his twenty-footer for a "fake five."

Abe responded by pouring in his twelve-footer for a "fake four."

It had all happened so fast, it seemed to Elliott, and so strangely. This hole could easily have been Goodman: 4, Lincoln: 5 in a heartbeat, if he'd decided to make the two decisions differently.

Disconsolate and in shock, Elliott closed his eyes as Lincoln strode toward the hole to pick up his ball. It seemed like a few seconds, but he actually kept them closed for more than a minute.

When he opened them, Abe Lincoln was nowhere to be found. All that remained of him was his stovepipe hat on the apron and, behind the green, attached to a tree with an ax holding it in place, a note:

Dear Sir, I could never abide penalty strokes. Along with Mary's apple pie, it has long been one of my great weaknesses. But I am fixing to keep working on it. With my deepest apologies, A. Lincoln.

So Abraham Lincoln cheated! That is the world's greatest oxymoron ever! At least he apologized, I'll give him that, but cheating at golf, a *weakness?* Man, it really makes you think. . . .

And think he did, while he ambled over to thirteen tee.

He thought about one of his favorite paradoxes, one about which he'd lectured many times—perception and reality. The amazing relationship between what seems to be and what is. The ideal and the real.

He thought about witnessing Abe's transgression and wondering if, ultimately, history distorts what our icons are really like.

He thought once again about Mrs. Fishkin's class and how Americans are conditioned at such an early age to view certain figures as heroes and put them on pedestals, all those pols and athletes and actors and God knows who else, and about how he'd witnessed, firsthand, that they might not be all they appear to be.

He thought about the fact that Lincoln the icon and Lincoln the person were two different animals, and that the "real" Honest Abe was basically like all of us—flawed and human.

He thought about how the glorious game of golf exposes our human frailties and challenges us to face and improve on them.

He thought of a quote, the ending of T. S. Eliot's "The Love Song of J. Alfred Prufrock," that sums up tidily this whole issue of how our ideal perceptions, our romantic illusions, can turn brutally into cold, stark reality:

We have lingered in the chambers of the sea
By sea-girls wreathed with seaweed red and brown
Till human voices wake us, and we drown.

Speaking of reality, Elliott crashed back to it when it dawned on him again that he'd just lost the twelfth hole.

Yikes!

Before the actual panic came the anger at Lincoln—how dare he cheat and flout the Rules of Golf? Then the anger at himself—you wuss! You should've tattled on him and stood up for yourself!

And *then* the panic.

He was now *four down with only six to play!* Talk about pressure. If Elliott should happen to lose the next hole, the Almighty would be dormie in the match—five up with five to play—and Elliott would have to win every single one of the final five holes just to force a sudden-death playoff.

As Moses might have said, *Oy!*

Elliott gritted his teeth, fighting back feelings of self-doubt. He was a fighter and knew deep down that he'd never, *ever* give up, but things, he had to admit, were looking mighty bad.

Would he be able to crawl out from this humongous hole he'd dug for himself? What could he clutch at to give himself hope, to lift his flagging spirits yet one more time?

Thanks to his well-developed survival instincts, Elliott did manage to grab on to the one positive aspect of the past hole, despite its terrifying outcome.

Integrity!

He had lost the hole, sure, and this was about saving his own hide and winning, but wasn't there more to it than that? He was playing his hardest, playing by the rules of golf. But he was also playing by the rules of his heart. Doing what he thought was the right thing against Abe Lincoln had to count for something in the Grand Scheme of Things.

What an amazing game golf is, the only game where you can, no, where you are *obliged to* call yourself on a ruling. The only game where, at every turn, not only are your physical and mental abilities being tested, but your character, as well.

Just as, on the previous hole, the game of golf had confirmed his self-reliance, with Picasso playing Virgil to his Dante, so, on this hole, had the game of golf confirmed his fundamental personal integrity, with Lincoln as his guide.

Elliott was over the initial panic and determined to concentrate on the positive, and this last compelling thought, the one about integrity, left him feeling a whole lot better about the dire state of things.

In some place deep within him, it struck a chord. . . .

13

TAKING THE FIFTH

Ludwig van Beethoven, now dead nearly 180 years, was still stone-cold deaf. The implacable infirmity, which had haunted the great composer for most of his adult life on earth and which had precipitated the strong desire for suicide, as passionately expressed in the *Heiligenstadt Testament* of 1802, was still bedeviling him even in his celestial body.

Consequently, he spoke only rarely and even then could not utilize words for fear of appearing anything less than perfect. So when he did speak, as he did now at the conclusion of a mighty practice swing with his two-iron, all that came out of him were musical notes—the only form of communication of which he had complete and utter mastery.

For Elliott Goodman, veteran sports fan and aficionado of the arts, Beethoven had always been the Willie Mays of music. These two Giants had not only served as early models of exuberant achievement for him, but also shared similar Promethean niches in their respective fields.

Willie might not have been the pure hitter Ted Williams was or the power hitter Hank Aaron was or have had the early Mickey Mantle's speed afoot, yet he was greater than them all in his peerless brilliance in all aspects of the game, his unparalleled charisma, and his boundless and profound passion for playing baseball.

Likewise, Beethoven might not have approached the complex craftsmanship of Bach or the sublime perfection of Mozart or the ability to construct melodies as euphonious as Schubert's, yet he surpassed the lot of them in regard to his verve and symphonic ebullience and his boundless and profound passion for writing music.

Elliott stared at Beethoven as the latter continued taking practice swings, oblivious to his opponent's appearance and deeply into his private preliminary routine.

The great Beethoven! Look at those eyes! That concentration! You can actually *feel* his intensity, his aura, his passion, almost palpably. That same intensity that moves me to tears every time I listen to his Fifth or his Ninth or any of his late string quartets!

At last, the great composer acknowledged Elliott's presence behind him on the tee. Not with a friendly salutation or a handshake, but with a twisted grimace, a brusque shrug, and a begrudging grunt of a chord:

At the precise instant the grunt was emitted, the energy emanating from Beethoven literally charged the atmosphere surrounding the two golfers. The wind, already appreciable, began to whip and swirl. The skies blackened as ominous, foreboding storm clouds gathered. A bloodcurdling clap of thunder pierced the silence. An eerie sense emerged that lightning wasn't far behind. It was, apparently, the perfect time for the man who had ignited the world of music, and who was later to become Schroeder's hero, to hit away.

Ludwig wore a silk beige-and-black ascot, a burnt siena hair shirt, a dark brown waistcoat, and tan corduroys, all carelessly thrown on his body, as well as a brand new pair of brown leather golf shoes, on the bottoms of which were affixed the most scientifically advanced Kevlar spikes, courtesy of the latest Teutonic technological advances.

He was short and stocky, in the manner of an Ian Woosnam or a Craig Parry, and possessed powerful biceps and forearms. His face featured pockmarks and a sneer produced by a serious, tight-lipped mouth that had been, it appeared, curved downward since birth. His most prominent physical feature, however, was his hair—light gray, voluminous, tousled, flying all over the place.

Beethoven took his stance and addressed his ball. His every quick movement, every cock of the wrists, every tilt of the head reflected the impatience and impulsiveness that were at his very core. Method was in his madness, too, and Elliott had the feeling that even in golf, the musical genius had to be the Master, the one in control, that even his slightest twitch had a purpose, and that that intractable purpose ultimately was to stamp out mediocrity and to execute his drive in a "my-way-or-the-highway" manner that was pure, well, Beethoven.

The Maestro took his two-iron back—his locks of disheveled hair blowing furiously in the wind—and exploded into the drive, with the brute, compact, nervous force of a Gary Player on six cups of coffee. At impact, he let out a violent, joyous, and triumphant paroxysm of notes:

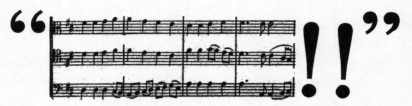

The golf ball, as if shot from a cannon, took off into the furious gale, a clap of thunder punctuating the blow, and headed straight down the gut of the fairway.

Then—*crack!*—a thin bolt of lightning, with pinpoint accuracy, struck it flush and turned it into a pile of steaming, smoking ash, 240 yards from the tee-box.

To punctuate this most bizarre and wondrous of drives, Beethoven pumped his fist toward the heavens in defiance.

Like his opponent, Elliott was struck speechless.

His first thought, like any golfer's, was that since there was lightning on the course, the prudent thing to do, with metal clubs daring the electrical particles to descend and be conducted, was run like a bandit to the nearest sheltered spot.

On second thought, having learned from his experience with Poe, Elliot had to take into consideration the fact that Beethoven was already dead and that he himself was, in reality, on his proverbial deathbed and had much to gain by proceeding with the match.

The thirteenth hole is a cute little 341-yard par-4, tilted slightly left to right and perfect for Elliott's fade. In spite of the current elements, it is eminently parable.

Elliott stepped up to his ball and tried to relax and forget about Beethoven's recent pyrotechnics. Then a funny thing happened.

The figurative electricity of the composer's aura, combined with the literal electricity in the atmosphere, became contagious. The passion and energy exuded by Beethoven were transferred directly and galvanically into Elliott's body in a modern-day version of the Frankenstein phenomenon.

Elliott was jacked up and ready to go. He stepped up to his ball confidently, addressed it, and pasted it with his three-metal. His Titleist landed three yards past Beethoven's heap of smoldering ashes.

Elliott drove the cart, with Beethoven riding shotgun. The Maestro, making no eye contact, grabbed a composition book and quill pen from the dash and scribbled furiously, totally engrossed in his musical annotation.

Elliott took a sideways peek at him, and the composer returned the glance, raised his right eyebrow, formed a stealthy sneer with cheek and lips, and, putting his pen aside, held up all ten fingers in a gesture of crazed, triumphant showmanship. Elliott knew immediately what the crazed gesture meant. *Ludwig was working on his Tenth Symphony!*

After resuming his scribbling, Beethoven barked once more, in a fit of crazed passion:

The cart stopped at Beethoven's mound of smoking ashes, and the Mad Scribbler bounded out, grabbed a pitching wedge, and assessed the damage. Elliott flipped through the *Rules of Golf* in his head but could nowhere find an official ruling concerning the proper play of a cooked and powdery golf ball. Beethoven took it upon his blustery self to make the call. He reached into his golf bag, pulled out a brand-new Top-Flite, and teed it up, right on top of the heap of ashes. Stepping up to his ball, he did one intense waggle and punched it violently into the gale, grunting in mad ecstasy:

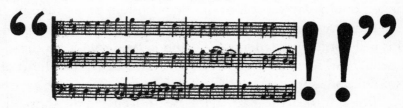

The ball landed on the green and rolled to within twelve feet of the cup. Ludwig van punched his fist in defiance toward the sky:

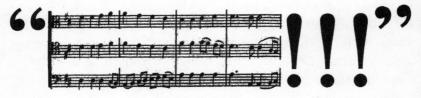

As Elliott took his setup, the same phenomenon that had occurred on the tee happened again. As if he had received a transfusion of electricity from Beethoven's body, he felt newly energized, omnipotent, raring to go.

Then—*whap!*—wedge and Titleist connected, the latter cutting through the wind, landing on the apron, and rolling six inches inside of Beethoven's Top-Flite.

Elliott was flying. He had never in his life felt such power inside him, such electricity. As he drove the cart toward the green, with Beethoven resuming his mad scribbling, his thoughts wandered to a series of mad, passionate moments in his life— all things he had experienced for the first time—during which he had felt a similar jolt of energy and excitement.

Entering Amiens cathedral. Seeing Gaudí's "Parque Güell" and Le Corbusier's chapel of Notre-Dame-du-Haut at Ronchamp. Viewing the Goyas in the Prado. Giving his first public lecture. Reading Crime and Punishment. *Witnessing certain movie performances—Brando in* Streetcar, *Raf Vallone in* A View from the Bridge, *Loren in* Two Women. *And certain theater performances—Brynner in* The King and I, *Olivier in* Hamlet, *Robards in* Long Day's Journey into Night. *Watching Willie slide, Sayers juke, Gretzky rag, Maravich pass. Making love to Joy. Hitting a diving backhand drop volley. Eating Indonesian food. Drinking single-malt Scotch. Listening to Beethoven's Ninth,* Sgt. Pepper, *and Cocker's first album. Visiting San Francisco, Paris, and Rio. Sledding down the hill with the kids at breakneck speed . . .*

Elliott parked the cart behind the thirteenth green. The wind was whipping, the clouds were more ominous than ever, and the thunder clapped at regular intervals of fifteen seconds. His mind had abandoned the passionate thoughts of his lifetime and had returned to the field of battle and to the task at hand—*winning the hole at any cost!*

Ludwig lined up his putt first, a quick, sidehill, twelve-foot snake that required the touch of a cat burglar. He took his stance and stroked it with a delicacy that hardly seemed possible in view of his enormous passion. It slid gently toward the hole and stopped a half-inch short:

Then he tapped in for his par:

Elliott's fate was in his own hands. If he could just can this putt, he'd crawl to within three down with five to go and maintain his flickering chances of survival.

Just this once . . .

Elliott was fortunate that his putt was on the same line as Beethoven's. The only decision he had to make was the speed. If he hit it too soft, it would suffer the same "short" fate as the composer's. Too firm, and it would trickle by the hole and end up three feet past it.

Still feeling the energy he had stolen from Beethoven's aura and always a believer in the "never up, never in" aphorism, Elliott opted for the latter, more aggressive strategy.

He struck the ball with the same finesse as Beethoven had exhibited, only a touch firmer, and it wended its way across the rise and down toward the hole, then . . . *plop!*

The relief Elliott felt upon winning his first hole since the sixth was ineffable. It overpowered all the other emotions he was feeling now, including joy, elation, happiness, delight, exuberance, rapture, bliss, ecstasy, and beatitude.

Elliott walked to the cup, retrieved his ball, and, when he looked up to bid farewell to the Maestro, he saw Beethoven shaking his fist defiantly at the heavens and shrieking at the top of his lungs:

The heavens responded in kind by sending down a bolt of lightning, which struck Beethoven's putter, traveled through his body, and delivered to him the very same fate his Top-Flite had suffered.

All that remained of the creator of "An die Freude," the "Ode to Joy," was a joyless mound of ashes, instantly dissipated by the howling wind. As soon as the ashes disappeared, the thunder and lightning ceased, and the clouds became white and puffy.

By this time in the match, Elliott was no longer awed or shocked by anything he witnessed at a hole's conclusion, so, without dwelling on the composer's electrifying demise, he left the green and began the short walk to the fourteenth tee, his mind racing.

He'd beaten the great Beethoven, and not a moment too soon. He was running out of holes and needed desperately to stop the bleeding. The nicest things about winning this one were, one, winning the hole, period; two, winning the hole by playing at a high level, pushed by a highly intense opponent; three, winning the hole by playing with lots of passion, focus, and commitment; and, four, winning the hole, period.

It was also the first time since the fourth hole, against Lennon, that he had been aware of the lesson of playing with joy and passion, thanks to Beethoven's example. A swift, sorely needed kick in the butt by the great composer! He had played the hole better than virtually anyone on the planet could have, but this time, as opposed to the ninth hole, against Babe, he had actually won!

Elliott was on a roll, albeit a little one. At last, he had some momentum to build on, between the victory just earned and the high quality of golf played.

The bottom line was that he was still in the golf match and still scratching and clawing to save himself.

He felt the urge to put his feelings into words, to affirm to himself what he was experiencing as a human being, to articulate what was in his heart, to verbalize the depths of his emotions. If only he could find the words to express his relief and joy. . . .

14

The Tempest, Part II

DRAMATIS PERSONAE

SHAKESPEARE, *the Bard of Avon*
ELLIOTT, *a professor still in deep caca*

Act I

SCENE I. *Inwood. Hole the XIVth, a 142-meter par-III.*

[SHAKESPEARE *at tee, waiting in a howling gale.*]

SHAK.   Relief and Joy! O twin embodiments
Of human suff'ring ne'er to return!
Each with its own sweet smell of recompense
And, smelling sweet, doth let sweet Ell'iott learn.
The one twin inner turmoil doth release,
And by releasing doth itself erase.
Th'other, younger brother, lives in peace
Which of itself doth justify its place.
Yet o'er thy life thou hast engaged both twins,
Sweet Ell'iott, and so doing thou canst choose
'Twixt sweet Relief, which comes perchance with wins,
And sweeter Joy, which comes when thou don't lose.
If this be wrong, myself I do resolve:

I ne'er writ, nor no man e'er playèd golf.
[*Aside.*] But soft, what noise? Methinks 'tis sweet Ell'iott!

[*Enter* ELLIOTT.]

ELL.   Ah, yes, it's me, kind sir, thanks for the poem!

SHAK.   'Tis nought, and yet I must admit a rust
          That eats away, like maggots at a corpse,
          My poetry; 'tis o'er four hundred years
          That last I penned a sonnet, and it showeth.
          But let us not waste time on sonneting.
          Instead, come hither, sir, as I would fain
          Talk trippingly—

ELL.   Of golf? Oh, I would, too!
          I'm so excited to be playing you. . . .
          Darn! That's a rhyme, and rhymes are not allowed
          In blank verse.

SHAK.   Tut, kind sir, I shall allow
          Whate'er thou dost desire to do herein,
          Since it is not thy habit to speak thus,
          So speak with loosèd tongue, in rhyme or no—

ELL.   Thanks, William, oh, and may I call you Will?

SHAK.   But, sir, please call me simply as thou will,
          For Will's mine name, and Will will be the name
          Which will be mine, and now Will will be yours.

ELL.   Hey! Being forced to speak this way is fun!
          Though, as you say, it's not my normal mode.
          But since I'm stuck inside this little play
          And since I'm playing Will, I think I will
          Attempt to be iambically correct.

And I can even think pentameters!
So this won't simply be a dialogue,
But I'll have thoughts between the repartee.
(I think I'm getting pretty good at this!)

SHAK. But hark, dost thou not feel yon howling wind?
            [*Wind howls.*]
 Blow, blow, thou winter wind! And do not cease
 Until the hounds of hell bark ne'er again,
 Until the crimson rose doth smell no more,
 Until the sun doth tumble from the sky.
 The air bites shrewdly. It is very cold.

ELL. It is, sweet Will, much colder than I thought.
 I wish I'd brought a jacket or a coat:
 It's not as if I really had a choice,
 Since I was whisked away to play this round
 Directly from the Operating Room!
 But cold it is, with nothing but short sleeves!
 In fact, it's colder than a witch's—

SHAK.   Sire!
 Do not forget this is a gentle play,
 So choose thy words a bit more carefully.

ELL. Your pardon, sire, but let us talk of golf!
 What brought you first to this amazing game?
 And did you play while you were still alive,
 Or, rather, did you take it up in heaven?

SHAK. O golf! The very name evokes a feeling,
 And no terrestrial words could well describe
 The ecstasy that cometh from its playing;
 No syllables could near approach its grandeur.
 I know whereof I speak, wherefore I say this,
 For many years of play have bless'd mine life.

O golf! Thou dost imbue mine life with meaning
And givest me a purpose to trudge on!
Thou showest me mine frailties today,
Then showest me anew, quite on the morrow,
And makest me relate to mine own flaws
And human peccadilloes of mine doing;
Just as I have revealed in others' lives
The sins and imperfections of a Man,
So hast thou shown in me that vanity,
That greed, that lust for pow'r, that blind ambition,
That madness born of rage, that indecision,
That green-eyed monster envy, which inhabit
Yet every pore and wrinkle of mine being!
O golf! Now I beseech thee to forthwith
Bless both of us this day with all your bounty,
That we may struggle through this wretched wind
And profit from thy treasures, as, in May,
The gentle hummingbird doth suck, with joy,
The sweet, sweet nectar of the flow'r's blossoms.
And as for where I first took up the game,
'Twas when I shuffled off that mortal coil
And found myself above, at heav'n's gates.
And, as I had more time at mine disposal
(For tragedies were not in great demand),
I learned to play, taught by that old Chris Marlowe
(Who ne'er wrote a solitary word
Of any of mine plays or other writings!).
And play I did, of course: "The play's the thing!"
And it did catch mine conscience from the start.

ELL.   Well said, my liege, I couldn't say it better!
        (Of course not, dummy! He's the Bard of Avon!
        Not you, nor anybody on the planet
        Could e'er, er, ever say it quite like that!)
        And now, I think that I do have the honor—

SHAK.   Not so, thou errant knave; methinks the honour
         Is mine.

ELL.   But I beat Ludwig—

SHAK.   Yes, thou hast,
         But pow'rs in the heavens have decreed
         That, for some unknown reason, I should go
         Ahead of thee. Do not protest too much,
         Sweet boy, and nothing ill will come of it.

SCENE II: *The same.* SHAKESPEARE *is hitting away.*

SHAK.   A fie on thee, damn'd wind, thy wretched bluster
         Doth make me bilious and perchance uncertain
         Of which metallic instrument to choose
         In order to best strike mine whey-faced ball.
         Methinks the III-ir'n is the best solution,
         Considering the howling, blust'ry wind
         Which, left to right and into mine own count'nance,
         Is whipping.
                        [*Wind whips into his count'nance.*]
                        Now to work.
                                        [*Wind whips again.*]
                        [*Aside.*] O cursèd wind!
         'Tis sweet revenge for you, is't not? For just
         As I used thee to vent thy wrath on Lear,
         So, aptly, hast thou vented thine on me!
         [SHAKESPEARE *drives ball into wind, which dumps ball
                        into Bay.*]
                        'Sblood! 'Zounds! O wind, I curse thee once again,
         Because of thee, and thee alone, mine ball
         Hath flown amiss and found a wat'ry grave.
         And all its yesterdays and frolicking
         Amidst the grasses tall, and sandy beach,
         Have giv'n up their place to dusty death.

[SHAKESPEARE *tees up again, addresses new ball.*]
Foh! Let a plague accurse thy family's house,
O tempest black and foul. Avaunt! Be gone!
[*Wind keeps blowing.*]
How now! I prithee cease and let me play—
[SHAKESPEARE *drives second ball into wind: Ker-plunk!*]
O Spartan dog! O wretched wind, 'tis two
That now thou hast deliver'd in the drink!
I now lie IV and will not let thee spoil
Mine next attempt to hit one on the green.
[*Wind keeps howling.*]
[SHAKESPEARE *tees up yet again, addresses third ball.*]
Pish! I shall hit this third ball on the green!
And if I fail, let ravens come and pluck
Mine eyeballs out. 'Sblood! 'Sblood! A fie on thee!
Accursèd wind! O diable! I hit it—
[SHAKESPEARE *hits third ball, this time onto green!*]
thus!
O joyous day! O blessèd game of golf,
Which mixeth suff'ring with eternal bliss!
I prithee, wind, forgive me for mine wrath.
All's surely well that ends well.
[*To* ELLIOTT.] Now to thee—

SCENE III. *The same.* ELLIOTT's *turn to drive.*

ELL.   *So he lies five, about ten feet away?*
And even if he holes the putt, that's six.
The wind, it sure is blowing left to right:
Not great for my ol' fade, I must admit.
So I should hit it twenty-five yards left.
(This goddam wind is getting on my nerves.)
[ELLIOTT *driveth ball, but wind is stronger than he thinketh:*
PLOP!]
Aw, crap! The wind is stronger than I thought!
I'm so disgusted now that I could puke—

SHAK.   [*Aside.*] And "puke," good sir, is yet another word
          That good Will Shakespeare coinèd in his day,
          Along with "alligator" and "eyeball,"
          "Assassination," "leap frog," not to mention
          "Zany," and "transcendence"—

ELL.   Yes, I know,
          Sweet Will, you've given so much to our tongue!
          But I must concentrate on my next shot.

SHAK.   O prithee pardon me, I didn't mean
          To break thy concentration. Carry on—

ELL.   Thanks, Will. *Now let me see, what shall I do?*
          He's five upon the green, and all I need
          To do is knock the ball along the ground
          And roll it up, avoiding any wind,
          And easily make six from where I lie.
          But that would be a sissy thing to do,
          Avoiding this great challenge that the wind
          Is giving me to overcome its strength
          With guile and perseverance and my—

SHAK.   [*Aside.*] 'Zounds!
          Methinks young Ell'iott falls into the trap
          Of hubris! Thinking he is better than
          This mighty game of golf which humbleth us!
          He thinketh he shall drive the ball again
          And thus defy the game with his persistence,
          Yet shall he suffer now that selfsame fate
          That my dark Moor and Scottish king both suffer'd!

ELL.   Okay, I'm ready now with my six-iron:
          I'll aim it even farther to the left
          And thus avoid another Out of Bounds

And show this mighty wind who's boss out here!
[ELLIOTT *hitteth second drive, which again findeth the drink!*]

SHAK.   [*Aside.*] Aha! I told thee so! Am I not clever?

ELL.   Oh man, I really need to win this hole!
         But wishing isn't gonna make it so.
         I've gotta use my noggin, so, let's see:
         The wind is not relenting one damn bit—
             [*Wind howleth relentlessly.*]
         I think I've gotta hit a bump-and-run—

SHAK.   Ah, "bump" is yet another word I coinèd!
         Oops, sorry, sire, I prithee carry on—

ELL.   That's quite all right. So I'll just bump it up,
         And play a little quaint "St. Andrew's" shot
         Like I was in the country of Macbeth!
[ELLIOTT *hitteth third drive . . . low and onto green and just
             outside of* SHAKESPEARE's *ball.*]
         At last! We both lie five now. So I still
         Have got a fighting chance to win the hole!
         And so, kind sir, let's bound into the cart
         And see just who's the mouse—

SHAK.   And who's the man!

SCENE IV. *A ride in the cart.*

ELL.   The one thing I'm now wondering, kind sir,
         Is how a common person such as I
         Now finds himself the hero in a play
         Conceived and written by the Bard himself,
         As if he were the equal of the Dane
         Or Lear or King Macbeth or, yes, the Moor?

SHAK.   A fair and honest question thou hast ask'd,
              And answer it I shall, the best I can.
              To start, I should not call myself a hero
              If I were you—until you win the hole!
              That we shall see anon. But as to how
              A person of your ilk can find himself
              Included in a play Shakespearean,
              The answer is quite simple, my sweet sir:
              Thou canst not claim to be of noble birth,
              As many of my personages can,
              Yet thou dost share one thing with all of them
              Which, o'er the rest, reflects the best in Man.
              Thou art a human being! Of flesh and blood,
              And this means that thou hast enormous pow'r
              To do both good and evil through thine acts.
              Ah, human! I salute thee in this play!
              Because thou art a Man and thus art flawed!
              And, e'en flawed, thou canst withal realize
              The greatness of thy essence, warts and all!

ELL.   But why golf? What is in this simple game
              That lets you write of all these noble things?

SHAK.   How now! Thou hitst the nail upon the head!
              'Tis golf, this simple sport, which doth bring out
              The nobleness of spir't whereof I spake!
              Just look at what thou didst upon the tee
              In actions subsequent to thy first shot:
              Thou hast decided to repeat thy drive,
              Because, in verity, thou thoughtst thou couldst.
              How noble! How divine! Yet still thy hubris
              Didst make thy ball go *plop!* into the drink.
              In doing thus, thy nature was both noble
              And doom'd to fail, both in the selfsame breath.
              (Aye, fools rush in where angels fear to tread!)
              And then, thou hast rethought thy strategy

(Thy creativity hath prov'd a boon!)
And altered thy original first plan
To overcome the wind (that Spartan dog!!!).
And so, for all of this, I have included
The likes of thee, sweet Ell'iott, in my play.
Though Hamlet thou art not, thou art *thyself*,
And that might be the noblest thing of all.

ELL.   Well said, sweet Will, I do appreciate
            The thought, but we've arrived at yonder green,
            And I must park the cart, and we must act in
            The final scene—the dénouement—The End!

            SCENE V. *The green at hole the XIVth.*

SHAK.   Forsooth, good sir, Methinks thou art away.

ELL.   I think you're right, although by just a tad.
            I gotta sink this putt and be a hero!
            Let's see: It's left to right about two inches
            And needs to be hit firmly, through the break.
        [ELLIOTT *hitteth putt as he had planned and . . .* sinketh it!]
            Oh joy!

SHAK.   [*Aside.*] O woe!

ELL.   Oh happy, happy day!
            At last I holed a putt with pressure on!
            And I can feel momentum coming back
            With every breath I take. I'm feelin' *good*!

SHAK.   Out, damned putt! Out, I say! Let thy mem'ry
            Be rudely, swiftly pluckèd from mine brain!
            Now: Let mine own putt tumble in the hole!

[SHAKESPEARE *hitteth putt, which rolleth toward hole and stoppeth . . . an inch short!*]
O woe! Alas! Alack! I've lost the hole!
The score of "six to sev'n" behaunts me now,
And happiness is thine, Ell'iott my sweet,
And mis'ry is all mine, forevermore!
[SHAKESPEARE *taketh vial of poison from his pocket. He drinketh it and collapseth to the green in agony.*]
O true apothecary! Do thy work!
O Ell'iott, do approach and hear me well!
[ELLIOTT *approacheth and listeneth intently.*]
I leave for thee my last and final speech:
I prithee not forget words once I spake
A long, long time ago—"Our doubts are traitors,
And make us lose the good we oft might win
By fearing to attempt."

ELL.   *Measure for Measure,*
        Act I, Scene IV?

SHAK.   Sweet Goodman, thou art *good!*
        But I am slipping fast, so heed mine words.
        Do not forget to listen to thine heart
        And calm thy doubts and ne'er fear to attempt.
        This above all: To thine own self be true . . .
        The potent poison quite o'ercrows my spirit . . .
        I die, sweet Ell'iott, heed whereof I spake . . .
        Now death's pale flag's advancèd in mine breast
        And beckons me to sleep—perchance to dream.
        But . . . I go mad . . . a tale told by an idiot . . .
        Of sound and fury . . . signifying nothing . . .
        Come, bitter conduct, come, unsavory guide . . .
        The drugs are quick . . . the circumcisèd dog . . .
        The rest is silence . . .
[SHAKESPEARE *dieth, disintegrateth, is blowneth away.*]

ELL.   Shit! The Bard is dead!
    Yet I live on! And hope is still alive!
    I met the wind and conquered it this hole!
    And, as the Bard so beautifully put it,
    I persevered and won it, warts and all,
    And showed my creativity and pluck,
    And calmed my doubts, not fearing to attempt.
    And so I have won two holes in a row
    And trail by only two, with four to play!
    It was great fun to play against the Bard
    And speak continuously in blank verse!
    I learned a lot from him, but I can't wait
    To get back to my non-iambic speech!
    And so I take my leave of this fair green
    To play another, tho' I know not whom.
    I'm ready for the fight and need to win,
    And be victorious I shall, by George!
                          [Exit.]

15

GEORGIE ONE-NOTE

GEORGE HERMAN RUTH, JR., WAS POLISHING off his third hot dog (with the works) and guzzling his third cold one when Elliott approached the fifteenth tee-box.

The Bambino! The Sultan of Swat! The Behemoth of Bust! The Caliph of Clout! The Maharajah of Mash! The Rajah of Rap! The Wazir of Wham!

The Babe!

Larger-than-life Babe Ruth delicately placed his mug of suds on the cart dashboard, emitted a stentorian and satisfied belch, wiped his big sauerkrauty mitts on his white-with-black-pinstripes golf shirt, and, winking his trademark wink, swaggered over to Elliott and extended his hand in friendship.

"Pleased to meetcha, kid," he bellowed.

ELL.   It's nice to meet you, too, George Herman Ruth,
        I've been a big, big fan for many years,
        And—

Jeez! I can't believe I'm still speaking in blank verse! Get a hold of yourself, boy! The Shakespeare drama is over, so get back to the real world—if playing golf with Babe Ruth with your life on the line can be called "the real world"!

"And," Elliott stammered, "well, it's a real thrill to be playing with you. I'm truly honored."

"Aw, shucks, kid, it ain't such a big deal. It's just me, good ol' Babe!"

To Elliott, there was something immediately real and disarming about the Babe. Behind the bluster and the swagger seemed to be a warm, watcha-see-is-watcha-get, lovable kid. A guy who had, like Lennon and Picasso before him, somehow retained his inner child and his innocence.

While Babe lit up a stogie and puffed away, Elliott mused.

Awesome! In just a few gestures, a wink here, a belch there, the Bambino has become a fictional character, just like I thought. Joining the other fictional characters of the round, Fields, Lennon, Picasso . . . Just like Fields came straight out of a Dickens novel, Lennon from the pen of Lewis Carroll, and Picasso from Cervantes's brain, The Babe reminds me of one of Rabelais's giants. The appetite of the man! The bigness! Now that I think of it, it's funny how the two words that come to mind to describe this grand scale of being are gargantuan and Ruthian. And *the Babe* is the one who gets the capital letter!

The fifteenth hole at Inwood is a longish, 463-yard par-4, formerly a par-5, a dogleg right with OB swamp down the right side. Like holes 1, 2, 7, 8, 12, and 14, which all have out-of-bounds areas on their right sides, there is a severe penalty for slicing the ball.

Since the Sultan of Swat did not, like the Bard, preempt Elliott's assumption of the honor, Elliott stepped up between the markers with ball and tee in hand and prepared to hit away. The Sultan—a gracious smile on his lips, a cigar in his mouth, and a mug of beer in his pudgy paw—spectated.

Elliott addressed his Titleist NXT, doing his best to ignore the physical disparity between himself and his Ruthian opponent.

Just play your own game. Hit your shot. Keep it left. *Have fun!*

He hit his drive as well as he could hit a golf ball, one of his trademark fades that landed in the middle of the fairway and bounded to a position 255 yards from the tee-box.

"Gee, kid, ya really socked it!"

"Thanks, Babe. Coming from you . . ."

The Bambino threw down his Cuban beauty, placed his nearly empty mug outside the left ball marker, and took his left-handed stance. Elliott noted that he was the first lefty he'd faced since the very first hole (Leonardo), but there was nothing sinister about his movements. In fact, for a large man—6'2", 225—they were rather dexterous.

"Well, here goes nothin', kid."

Ruth's swing was the epitome of testosteronal compactness, and he got every inch of his body into it—his powerful legs and hips, his muscular arms, his whippy wrists. He hit the ball so hard and flush that his body corkscrewed completely around, his legs crossing, and twirling around, each other and his belly nearly facing the right marker.

Swat!

This was the longest drive Elliott had ever seen a human being hit, not counting Moses (who was half-human, half-miracle). It was hit with such force that it went through the fairway on a fly—over the proverbial fence, outta here, big fly, four-bagger, round-tripper—and, defying feasibility, took its first bounce in the thirteenth fairway, ending up 375 yards away. The second shot, coming back toward the fifteenth green, would be a dilly, but the sheer power of Ruth's drive gave Elliott goose bumps.

Speaking of which, a flock honked overhead, in an apparent celebration of the blast.

On the passenger's side of the cart were a keg of Ballantine, a trio of Cuban cigars—huge, 178-millimeter Cohiba Esplendidoses—a book of matches, a plate of hot dogs and rolls, and assorted condiments. As Elliott drove to his ball, the Maharajah slathered some mustard on a brand new dog, then some relish, and finally a heaping, steaming mound of kraut. He refilled his mug to the brim.

Perhaps because he was such an incredible baseball fan, Elliott was awed by the Bambino in a special way that he didn't feel with any of his other extraordinary opponents. Part of it, he figured, was Ruth's unique batting—*and pitching!*—stats, which, as any serious baseball fan knew, just needed to be stated, without explanation, to be instantly recognized: 60, 714, 2,213, .690, .342, 94–46, 3–0. The man had simply transcended raw numbers to become an American folk hero and an international icon!

The Caliph wolfed down the first bite of his nitrite-filled snack and downed it with a mammoth slurp of suds.

"How on earth do you do it, Babe?"

"Parmee?"

"How do you hit the ball so damn far?"

Taking another quick gobble of frank and a swig of brew, the Sultan wiped his mouth with the back of his paw.

"Well, kid, it's like this. Y'see, I always liked to live big. The more the merrier, I say—women, food, booze, homers, whatever. Maybe it's 'cause of my early years, I dunno. You grow up pretty fast when your folks let you down and quit on you. And then, after that, there was the Red Sox management that also quit on me. Guess I just wanted to grab that brass ring and show 'em I could do it. Let 'em all see what they gave up.

And so, when it came time to play, all I ever wanted to do was hit the stuffing out of that baseball, the living daylights.

"In those days, it was my own way, and nobody else's. All the other fellows, they was hitting singles and sliding into bases and nickel-and-diming it. That bastard Cobb, what a ballplayer! But he was just like all the rest of 'em. Like I always said, if I'da chose to hit singles, I'da hit over .600! But I said that ain't for me, nosirree. So I started to hit homers and never looked back. And I sure showed 'em I was different, didn't I? Then, once I heard the cheers of the crowd, well, that made me feel plenty good inside. I guess I needed their approval, 'cause it sure as hell wasn't coming from no one else. . . ."

How sad, and yet how touching! To be abandoned at the age of seven, and then to make something out of a wretched life, and something special at that. What an accomplishment, yet . . . how sad!

As they were about to reach Elliott's ball, and with no forewarning whatsoever (except, perhaps, for the constant borborygmus that had been churning ruthlessly inside the Wazir's tummy for the past few minutes), the Babe—having just consumed his fourth and fifth wieners and chugalugged his fifth mug—emitted not one of your polite burps, but a belch of such Ruthian proportions, an eructation of such profound volume and foul odor that, after the initial shock, what immediately flashed through Elliott's mind was that cartoon of a mother shielding her son's eyes from some ungodly sight—a grisly accident? A naked woman?

With some relief, Elliott hopped out of the cart when they reached his ball and ambled to his bag for the club selection. He was 210 from the pin, and the swirling wind was gusting mightily.

He could always hit a three-metal and try to reach the green in two. That would be the Ruthian thing to do. But with the Babe on the thirteenth fairway and facing a tough second shot, and with the odds against his knocking the ball on the green, what with the tricky wind and the tricky green and all that distance to cover, Elliott went with the odds and chose three-iron.

Just get the ball up the fairway and in the vicinity of the green, and give yourself a chance to hit a good chip and, at worst, two-putt for bogey.

It turned out to be the right choice. Elliott flushed the iron perfect, his ball landing only forty yards short of the green, right in the heart of the fairway.

"Wow! That was a real dandy, kid!"

"Thanks, Babe. Yeah, I hit that one pretty solid."

Elliott realized that this was the second Babe he'd faced during the round. But whereas the lady from Port Arthur was tightly wound, this Babe was relaxed and as loose as one of those geese flying overhead. Both were as competitive as you could possibly get, yet they were planets apart temperamentally.

Elliott was amazed at how down-to-earth and unpretentious the Babe was. Nothing fazed George Herman Ruth, and he seemed to be proud of who he was, unashamed of all his excesses, not even hiding an occasional fit of flatulence. All of him was out there, with nothing left behind, in his paradoxical grandeur—powerful yet gentle, crude yet lovable, repellent yet engaging.

There was only one Babe Ruth, that was for sure, and no one, not ol' William Bendix, not John Goodman—though they both had tried admirably—could ever play his part fully and to perfection. No one, that is, except for the Babe himself.

Back in the cart and heading toward his Ruthian drive,

the Babe bolted down doggie number six, lapped up more than half of bevo number six, and lit up his second stogie.

"Hey, Babe, how 'bout them Bosox?" Elliott asked. He'd been an avid Red Sox fan ever since he'd arrived in Cambridge in the eighties; he'd suffered the heartbreak of the '86 Series against the Mets; and every season since, until the 2004 campaign, he'd shared the continued heartache Sox fans had been experiencing since the Babe was infamously traded to the hated Yanks in 1919. He was curious to hear Ruth's take on the recent and merciful termination of the Curse that bore his name.

"Pricks! That's what they were, kid!" the Bambino said, puffing contentedly on his Cohiba.

"After what they did to me, unloading me like that, after the season I had, they didn't deserve to win another Series, ever again. I'm glad the Yanks won twenty-six of 'em since I was dumped. Then again, kid, I'm not a bitter man deep down. I even have a little tender spot in this here heart for the ol' Bosox. So a small part of me forgives 'em and is sorta glad they ain't suffering through that curse anymore.

"Also takes my name out of the news. I used to love being in the news, kid, but after a while, it gets kind of tired. But most of all, I feel good about the kids of Beantown. The Bosox winning that Series in '04 must've made 'em feel so happy. I loved those kids, and I'm glad for 'em. 'Specially the ones in the orphanages and the hospitals."

Elliott stopped the cart at the Sultan's ball. After some more gorging and quaffing, Ruth climbed out and took a gander, just as a goose let out a mighty honk overhead.

"Well, kid, this is a tough one," he said, assessing the situation. His ball was sitting in the middle of the thirteenth fairway, in a good lie and a mere ninety yards from the pin. That was the good news.

The bad news was that he had to clear a row of tall willows and pinpoint his wedge shot onto a difficult two-tiered green almost entirely surrounded by bunkers.

"Well, here goes nothin', kid."

The Bambino took his pitching wedge back and, with his patented swing-for-the-fences swing, pasted the living daylights out of the unfortunate ball, a magnificent flop shot that propelled it 125 yards up in the air and over the trees. It was hit way too hard, however, and landed over the green in a patch of crud.

Goose bumps again.

Back on the fifteenth fairway, Elliott's ball was positioned perfectly and had drawn a lovely lie. He needed to land a delicate little pitch onto the upper tier of the green and keep it there. The pin, like on number eight, was positioned at the crest of the rise, so he had to get his ball close, but, in any case, not on the bottom tier, whence a three-putt could be a distinct possibility.

Nice and easy, now. Don't punch it too hard and give it too much spin, or else it'll roll back down onto the bottom tier and maybe off the green.

Elliott hit one of the nicest, softest wedges he'd ever hit, ten feet right of the pin, top tier. Mission accomplished.

The drive to the green was filled with light chatter and laughter, with the Babe joking, smiling, puffing, slurping, chomping, belching, and farting all the merry way. A good time was had by all.

But now it was time to get to work. George Herman addressed his ball, hardly visible in the furze behind the green, and, in an effort to extricate it from its nest, smacked the cover off it, sending it whistling past the green, down the hill, and back onto the fairway, twenty yards beyond the apron.

"Hit that sonuvabitch pretty good, too," the Behemoth bragged. "A little too good, I guess."

He chipped his ball back onto the green—a little too hard again—just inside Elliott's but past the hole, and he now lay four to Elliott's three, moments after enjoying a huge yardage advantage thanks to his Ruthian drive.

Elliott stepped up to his putt and confidently drained his ten-footer. He had just won his third hole in a row, and now—presto and *mirabile dictu!*—he was only *one down* with three to play!

Still tingling from the victory, Elliott plucked his Titleist out of the cup and received the gracious Bambino's firm and heartfelt handshake.

As soon as he released the Babe's mammoth mitt from his own modestly proportioned hand, the figurative architect of Yankee Stadium again winked his trademark wink at Elliott and let out one final foul, Ruthian belch that could be heard all the way to Montauk.

As he did, the air inside him was sucked right out of his body, and he swirled around and around, faster and faster, in the air above Elliott, belching all the way and getting tinier and tinier as he aviated in increasingly smaller concentric circles, like an engorged, untied party balloon that has been released into the air, emptying itself crazily, to the delight of some mischievous five-year-old.

When the air had completely vacated his body, the Babe was nothing but a jovial, fond memory.

Elliott was sad to see the gregarious and fun-loving icon go, but this melancholy quickly gave way to bliss.

Only one down!, he exulted to himself as he walked off the green toward the sixteenth tee. He thought of something he'd discussed with Socrates on number-seven tee.

Y'know, I've been thinking so much about *gnothi seauton* and knowing my true self that I sort of forgot about the other golden rule of the Delphic Oracle. *Meden agan,* "nothing in excess"! I really won this hole because of that simple concept.

The Babe, impressive as he was, was a one-trick pony. Power, power, and more power. And me? Not much to talk about for the macho guys in the locker room, but I sure got the job done. Come to think of it, I was the model of versatility out there! Power, in moderation, on the drive, intelligence by choosing a safe three-iron on the second shot, the finesse to keep it on the top tier with the pitch, and accuracy with the putt. The complete package!

Elliott thought about how lucky he had been to be versatile and multifaceted during his life, too. About how he could do and be lots of things, using various talents and energies and fields of expertise, and have lots of passions and play different roles in dealing with different people.

He was fortunate not to be a Georgie One-Note.

So now on to the sixteenth! Only one down, can you believe it? What a struggle! I've actually clawed my way almost back to the top of the hill. What an amazing voyage this has been so far!

Little did Elliott suspect what new turn this amazing voyage would take, what strange new world awaited him. . . .

16

UNCHARTED WATERS

THE MAN WHO DISCOVERED the new world as we know it, Cristoforo Colombo, was preoccupying himself with his complicated pre-shot preparations as Elliott approached the sixteenth tee.

Columbus!

The great explorer was carefully calculating wind speed with his anemometer, wind direction with his portable weathercock, atmospheric pressure with his aneroid barometer, tree height with his arboraltimeter, and hole yardage with his flagstickometer. He was mapping out his plan of attack prior to his Grand Exploration of the hole.

Spying his opponent behind him with his periscope, the trilingual globetrotter greeted Elliott. "*Buon giorno . . . buenos días . . . bom día*. So, it looks like the wind, she's coming at about thirty knots from the north-northeast. Pressure, she's twenty-nine and dropping fast. Trees are, I don't know, maybe sixty-six feet big. And the hole, she's exactly . . . let's see . . . 376 yards long."

Elliott noted how startlingly unusual Columbus's accent was, a total and mellifluous melding of the three languages he spoke with equal fluency: Italian, Spanish, and—featuring its peculiar, quaint, and euphonic nasal diphthong, *ão*—Portuguese.

Christopher Columbus had held a special place in Elliott's heart ever since Mrs. Fishkin had taught him and his class that silly ditty:

> *In fourteen hundred and ninety-two*
> *Columbus sailed the ocean blue.*
> *He took three ships with him, too,*
> *And called aboard his faithful crew.*
> *Mighty, strong, and brave was he*
> *As he sailed across the open sea.*
> *Some people still thought the world was flat!*
> *Can you even imagine that?*

Through the years, through his readings and listenings, Elliott had discovered just how "mighty, strong, and brave" the explorer was, despite various personal and professional shortcomings and miscalculations.

He most admired the extraordinary courage and vision it must have taken to navigate the Atlantic Ocean and venture to the New World.

At that time in the late fifteenth century, Elliott had learned, no one had dared to venture west—as opposed to safely hugging the coastlines to the south and east—in order to reach the Orient and its riches. No one had dared to sail perpendicular to the land, out to the open ocean, the dreaded Ocean Sea, the "Sea of Darkness," with its purported monsters and boiling water. No one had dared to sail away from civilization, to seek a new route to the west, with the wind at his back, heading directly into the uncharted, forbidding waters.

To think of the risks he had to take! Eliott was particularly impressed by the fact that Columbus was a true pioneer in his field—like Leonardo, Lennon, Freud, Poe, Didrikson, Picasso, Beethoven, and Ruth before him—with the distinguishing difference that in Columbus's case, the risk was not just one of failure or opprobrium, but of . . . death!

"On this hole, my friend Elliotto," Columbus said, interrupting Elliott's musings, "I'm gonna attempt what *no* man has ever done! Because of the wind blowing from left to right so hard today, I've calculated that it is quite improbable—about a 14 percent chance—to play the hole left to right, that is to say, to hit a fade onto the fairway."

The sixteenth hole is a severe, blind dogleg right, a 376-yard par-4, with tall trees and swampy cattail-filled OB marsh all the way down the right side. Just now, it seemed unusually ominous because of the tricky, swirling, treacherous crosswind.

"So," the intrepid adventurer continued, "what I'm gonna do is instead of going left to right, I'm gonna take the uncharted route, going right to left, around and over the trees and the swamp, and let my draw—how you say?—*neutralize* the wind. That way, my ball, she should land right in the middle of the fairway!"

Elliott was amazed at the boldness, the daring, the originality of the explorer's concept.

Hit a draw against the wind, over the trees and the swamp, on a dogleg right? Only a madman would attempt that, but I guess it sometimes takes a little madness to accomplish great things. For me, I just couldn't depend on my ability to draw the ball, and I do agree with him about how tricky a normal fade would be in this wind, unless you started your ball out into the seventeenth fairway, over *those* trees, and faded it back onto this one.

Naaah. I'm gonna go with a Tiger special, a nice little

stinger that I won't hit too high but that will just hang on and land up somewhere on the left side of the fairway and avoid any trees, right or left.

Elliott executed his drive perfectly, punching a low, stinging three-iron with a three-quarter follow-through, and his ball landed 190 yards away and just into the innocuous primary cut of rough on the left.

"That's very nice," Colombo allowed, more with self-confidence than with any feeling of condescension, "but right now, Elliotto, *scusi . . . dispénseme . . . perdão . . .* you stand back and watch *this!"*

Columbus packed all his explorer's paraphernalia back into his golf bag and grabbed his impressive King Cobra 454 COMP driver. He stepped up to the tee-box and sank his tee into the ground so that precisely 1.125 inches of the wood protruded out. He licked his index finger and held it up in the air, then uprooted a small clump of grass from the ground and tossed it up into the gale, both gestures made to ascertain whether the wind velocity and direction had changed since he took his most recent measurements. They had not.

The 5'11" Columbus possessed better than average good looks, sparkling eyes, and a ruddy, blotchy complexion. He wore a three-cornered hat, a robelike cloak, funny-looking pants, and (the way Elliott recognized him in the first place) a medal depicting Saint Christopher—the patron saint of travelers!—around his neck.

While Elliott's daring opponent was doing his waggles, his always active mind recollected that—like W. C., John, Jehanne, Marilyn, Abe, Will, and George Herman—Cristoforo had accomplished great things despite coming from very modest roots. This son of a wool weaver had had little formal education yet had, during the course of his life, attained the titles of admiral, governor, and viceroy and was known, these

500 years after his death, to virtually every person in the civilized world who did not claim a cave as his or her primary residence.

Columbus took his stance and, his piercing eyes fixed on a spot exactly twenty-five degrees NNE of the invisible green, gazed into the distance, as if it were the very same dark, uncharted waters he'd faced as his first great challenge over fifty-one decades ago. His sensitive nostrils flared like a bloodhound's, trying to detect any scent of change, any threat to his bold and daring plan of attack.

With a smoothness of technique that reflected either excellent and long-term professional training and development or a phenomenal gene pool, he took his club back, rotated his hips, and exploded into the shot, pronating his strong wrists in order to turn the ball over from right to left and send it on its magnificent journey into the vast unknown.

In terms of distance, the shot was not as impressive as Moses' or the Bambino's, but its trajectory was something to behold. Floating majestically from right to left, where no sane man had ever dared to venture, the ball cleared the huge trees comfortably, wended its way, as if by radar, over the swampy area and toward the dark green of the fairway, and, just as it passed over a large willow tree—the final obstacle between it and safe harbor on this outrageous new route—something unexpected happened, for no rhyme or reason and without warning.

To the bewilderment of the great adventurer, the wind stopped blowing, and the ball stopped dead in its tracks, descending straight down, like the winged Icarus in his ultimate death spiral, and disappearing somewhere in the vicinity of the appropriately weeping willow.

Columbus was aghast. Elliott was delighted at his good fortune but felt some degree of compassion for his opponent,

whose bravery and derring-do, he knew full well, had deserved a much kinder fate.

"Bummer," Elliott offered, and then, in apparent consola-
tion, "but it was a helluva shot. I really didn't think you could
pull it off, but if anyone could, it would be you." Elliott knew
that what he'd said didn't sound quite right, but he couldn't
unring the bell, and, instead of backtracking, he hopped in
the cart with Cristoforo and started driving.

Still in awe of Columbus's creative attempt to conquer
the elements, Elliott sat in deep meditation while he drove.

Talk about dodging a bullet . . . This guy is unbelievable.
What guts! Now I know why they inscribed on his tomb,
"History knows of no man who ever did the like." Can you
believe what he just attempted to do? The adventure! The
risk! The vision! A bit like Picasso's creativity, but with all that
danger thrown in.

And the planning that went into it! How long had he
been here before I arrived? Hours? Reminds me a little of
Leonardo's figuring out that bunker shot at number one, so
methodically, yet so creatively.

Columbus's shot, or rather his attempt, also reminds me of
Honest Abe's quote about "towering genius" disdaining a
beaten path. Or, even more to the point, the ending to Frost's
"The Road Not Taken":

> *Two roads diverged in a wood, and I—*
> *I took the one less traveled by,*
> *And that has made all the difference.*

A gust of wind, occurring too late to do Columbus any
good, got Elliott's attention and blew him back to reality.

"It is funny how the wind, she stops to blow. I know the
winds pretty good, and this never happens," the brave traveler

said ruefully. "But, you know, that's the way the cracker, she crumbles."

"I know. Been there, done that."

"Take my life . . . please," Colombo continued, a wry smile creasing his face. (Apparently, he was a fan of Henny Youngman.) "Badaboom! But, seriously, folks, I learn long ago, during my life, that justice, she does not exist. Was it fair that I spend so many years trying to sell my plan to sail west, and getting rejected? Was it fair that the *Santa Maria,* she smash herself on the rocks? Was it fair that I go to prison and that Isabella, she die when I needed her and that I spend my final years in the obscurity? Was it fair that even now, people don't know where I am buried?" he ranted, cynicism dripping from his lips.

"But you know what hurts the most? Do you not think that your great country, located in the region I discovered before anyone else, she should be named after me? That she should be called the United States of Columbia? But *no!* She is named after Amerigo Vespucci, and all because of the mistake of that *stupido,* Martin Waldseemüller!"

"But—"

"No buts about it!" Columbus said sternly, his dander standing straight up in the air. "I did a little study, you know? And I discover that there are fifty-one places named after me in the *Stati Uniti.* Fifteen cities and eight counties named 'Columbia,' six more cities with 'Columbia' in the name, two cities named 'Columbiana,' one city named 'Columbiaville,' sixteen cities named 'Columbus,' and three more cities with 'Columbus' in the name. Vespucci? He got a grand total of *five!* But at the end of the *giorno?* He got the whole *enchilada!*"

Elliott felt sorry for poor Columbus and made a valiant attempt to commiserate with the brave but wounded discoverer.

"Let me ask you this," he asked the intrepid one, "did they name that great book and movie *Goodbye, Vespucci*?"

"Well . . ."

"And do they celebrate 'Vespucci Day' once a year all across this great land, and have 'Vespucci Day Sales' at all the department stores?"

"I guess . . ."

"And do they call that benevolent and fraternal society of Roman Catholic men the 'Knights of Vespucci'?"

"Ummm . . ."

"And do they call that great big roundabout with the huge statue just south of Central Park in New York City 'Vespucci Circle'?"

"Errr . . ."

"And is one of the eight Ivy League schools named 'Vespuccia'?"

"Mmmm . . ."

"And did they name that space shuttle *The Vespuccia*?"

"Ahhh . . ."

"And do they call our country's capital Washington, 'D.V.,' short for 'District of Vespuccia'?"

"But . . ."

"And finally, my friend, do they call the patron saint of travelers, *your* special saint, 'Saint Amerigo'?"

"Ah, I see your point, Elliotto. You make me feel *so* much better! But I still think life, she is not fair!"

"Well, I think she is sometimes, and sometimes she isn't, but if I learned one thing from both Moses and Honest Abe, it's that you never know, and sometimes you just have to forget about 'fair' and play the cards you're dealt. Anyway, that was an incredible shot, and it's sad that the wind just stopped like that, but you should still be proud of making that amazing attempt. My hat's off to you, sir!" Elliott doffed his visor.

Columbus was touched, but the cart had just stopped at Elliott's ball, and the battle had to rage on.

The wind had picked up again, making Elliott's second shot no bargain. Again, he was faced with the challenge of not allowing the left-to-right wind to whip his ball into the trouble on the right.

Maybe I can't hit a drive like ol' Chris did, but I think I can do something pretty interesting here. I'm about 190 to the pin, and instead of lofting a five-metal up there and have the wind do God-knows-what to it, what if I just take my three-iron again, choke up five inches on the grip, come down on the ball hard, and hit another low stinger, no higher than maybe five feet off the ground, and sorta bounce it up there and roll it up that neck between the bunkers surrounding the green? Just like ol' Lee or Seve might've done at Troon or Carnoustie?

And that's exactly what he did. Elliott's Titleist bounced seven times and rolled right up that neck to ten feet left of the flagstick.

"*Bien hecho!*" Columbus said.

Elliott responded with an appreciative nod.

When they reached Cristoforo's shot, the news was not good. His ball was stymied against the bottom of the willow's trunk, with no option except to hit the shot from a lefty stance. Even then, it was pretty much of a crapshoot.

Intrepid adventurer that he was, Columbus welcomed the challenge. He took his four-iron back, clubhead backward with the tip pointing straight toward the ground, and, swinging lefty, gave it a good old *whomp!* The ball jumped out of there like a rocket and, miraculously, landed just off the apron.

"Just like you said," Elliott quipped, "life, she is not fair!"

The two laughed all the way to the green.

Colombo chipped up to within a foot and tapped in for
his phenomenal par.

"Coulda been a birdie, but that's the way—"

"The cracker, she crumbles!" Elliott interrupted, com-
pleting the discoverer's mangled solecism. "Great par, though.
I am honored to have witnessed what you have attempted
and accomplished."

Enough said. The time for action was at hand.

Facta non verba, Elliott thought, lining up his putt. You
know this putt. Roll it firm, and it's left edge, or maybe left
about the length of . . . a wooden nickel!

With a slight smile and for a split second, he thought of
the old codger in the Halfway House but then quickly directed his mind back to his ten-footer.

To his great relief and joy, Elliott poured in the putt for
his second birdie in four holes and, more important, his
fourth consecutive win. He was really in the groove, and it
dawned on him that he had climbed all the way back from
four down with just six to go to . . . *actually catch God!*

All square! Oh, my sweet Lord! The match hasn't been all
square since . . . the sixth hole, against Poe. *Ten holes ago!*

Elliott summoned up in his memory not only sweet Will's
lovely sonnet at the number fourteen tee-box, but also
Marcel Proust's magnificent expression of the two emotions
he was feeling—relief and joy—as experienced by the author's protagonist, the young Marcel, in *Swann's Way:*

> . . . *at that very moment, when . . . I had finished writing it [his
> first page of writing, about the steeples of the church in Martinville],
> I was in such a state of happiness, felt that it had so completely
> unburdened me of these steeples, and of what they concealed in their
> mysterious essence, that, as if I myself were a hen and had just laid
> an egg, I began to sing at the top of my lungs.*

Elliott felt like singing himself, but just as he finished quoting from *Swann*, he looked up and watched Columbus do his own "swan song."

"*Addio . . . adiós . . . adeus*, my friend," the explorer said sweetly, as he flapped his great cloak and floated into space, like a proud human maritime vessel—perhaps the *San Cristoforo?*—growing increasingly smaller as he sailed away into the distance, until he was barely visible, a tiny speck in the vast cosmic ocean.

It occurred to Elliott that he'd taught a number of courses on the bildungsroman, inner spiritual journeys, and various fictional characters' quests for the Grail, and that on this day, on this golf course, it was he—*Elliott Goodman, protagonist*—who was being taught by others on his own spiritual journey.

He thought back to how he'd been taught and inspired by his various opponents. How Leonardo had inspired him to be inventive and decisive. How John had inspired him to be joyous. How Marilyn had inspired him to be circumspect. How Picasso had inspired him to be self-reliant. How Beethoven had inspired him to be passionate. And, just now, how Cristoforo Colombo had inspired him to . . . *discover!*

The great explorer had indeed taken the road "less traveled by," but, then again, so had Elliott. Inspired by Columbus's spirit of discovery, he'd figured out how to play this hole, not in his usual way of taking his chances with his fade into the wind, but by avoiding the wind altogether. So by playing *beneath* the wind, he'd risen *above* it, playing the hole a new way, taking a new route, and discovering his inner creativity, his inner resourcefulness.

On the heels of this epiphany, he thought of another quote, from the German philosopher Arthur Schopenhauer, one that had bothered him throughout his academic career because although he'd always loved learning from and teaching great literature, he'd also felt that somehow it was a step removed from "real life." Schopenhauer had said, "A truth that has merely been learned sticks to us only like an artificial limb, a false tooth, a wax nose does, or at best like transplanted skin; but a truth earned by thinking for ourselves is like a natural limb: it alone really belongs to us. This is what differentiates a thinker from a mere scholar."

That quote miraculously now ceased to bother him. Elliott felt an inner glow from the clear understanding that, as he had often sensed before on this golfing journey of self-discovery, he was, deep down, a true "thinker," this time as a result of his experience with Columbus.

Walking past the line of shady trees separating the sixteenth green from the seventeenth tee, Elliott felt as if he were in a momentary state of grace.

Phew! Okay now, take a deep breath. All square, you rascal, but don't you get cocky or relax for one second! There are still two holes to go, and they're not gonna be easy. *Not one bit.*

Who knows what God has up His formidable sleeve? He's probably saving for now that big bruiser I'd expected Him to send down on number eight. Yeah, now's the perfect time for Him to crush me like a bug with that Big Boy of His. Yep, it's time for Him to throw in the ol' kitchen sink! But I'm at the top of my game now, and I'm ready for anything.

So who's it gonna be this time? Goliath? Genghis? Sonny?

No, let me guess . . . Hercules? Samson? Paul Bunyon? Bronko Nagurski? Popeye?

17

NO BLOOD

A SHORT, SKINNY, FRAIL, gaunt, bald, hunched, wrinkled, un-prepossessing, bespectacled, big-eared, ribs-sticking-out, bag-of-bones of a man was waiting patiently for Elliott at seventeen tee. He was modestly dressed in nothing but a white loin-cloth and sandals, and his name was Mohandas Karamchand Gandhi.

The Mahatma!

Elliott was so jazzed up about squaring the match with just two holes remaining that he could still feel the adrenaline pumping through his body, almost out of control. His heart was skipping beats, he was hyperventilating, and his hands were trembling slightly with excitement. His first sight of the frail old Gandhi in dhoti and sandals pumped up his surging hopes even more, but he'd been down that road before.

Okay. Deep breaths. And don't you *dare* go there and take anything for granted! Remember old man Leonardo and then fuddy-duddy Freud and then geezer Socrates and then frail little Marilyn? Three fogies and a sweet, non-golfing ac-tress, and you come out of it with three losses and a tie! So don't forget about what you learned from Marilyn about the book and the cover. . . .

Elliott approached the Great Soul respectfully and, smiling cheerfully, put out his hand.

"A real honor to meet you."

The Mahatma returned the smile and, palms together in a praying attitude, bowed and said, "*Satyagraha.*"

Taking this to be an ancient Hindi greeting, Elliott maintained his cheerful smile and stepped up to the tee-box to begin the proceedings on this, the presumably penultimate hole of the match.

The seventeenth hole is a 405-yard par-4 that features tall trees up and down both sides of the fairway and a green surrounded by menacing bunkers on three sides—left, right, and back. It is a relatively hilly hole, sloping first down, then up for nearly the latter two thirds of its length, making it play longer than the yardage might indicate.

Elliott stepped up, full of piss and vinegar, and absolutely striped his drive, a full 265 yards down there and bisecting the fairway.

"*Satyagraha,*" Gandhi intoned once more.

So it means not only "Hi," but also "Nice shot!" A versatile word, sort of like *shalom* in Hebrew or *aloha* in Hawaiian.

The head of Gandhi's Ping G2 driver was nearly half the size of his own as he stepped up to tee off. The man who had virtually single-handedly freed India from British rule, perfected the nonviolent civil disobedience movement, and spawned such worthy successors as Martin Luther King, the Dalai Lama, Nelson Mandela, and John Lennon—the latter having, in fact, mentioned Gandhi during his controversial "Bed-In"—actually surpassed Socrates, Marilyn, and even Freud as the "famous person least likely to be caught dead holding a golf club in his/her hand."

The incongruity of watching the Mahatma attempt to hit a golf ball, in loincloth and sandals no less, did not escape Elliott, who was trying nonetheless to avoid getting smug or cocky regarding the present situation, or falling prostrate on the ground in hysterical laughter.

Compared to all the unusual setup routines and swings Elliott had witnessed during the round—including Lennon's cricket-bowler, cavalry-bugle ritual; Freud's molasses-slow, tic-ridden technique; and Lincoln's backward, ax-chopping act—Gandhi's was right up there with the most bizarre of them.

First, he clasped his hands together and shut his eyes in prayer. Then he mumbled some inaudible mantra. Finally, with a high-pitched little laugh—*and his eyes still shut!*—he took back the driver, held it straight up in the air for four seconds, and gently cupped the ball out of its wooden perch, leaving the tee unharmed and propelling the ball gingerly on its way.

Sadly for him, the drive had a little tail on it and drifted into the trees on the right that divided the seventeenth and eighteenth fairways, landing only 170 yards away.

"*Satyagraha!*" he said softly, turning to Elliott and still smiling.

What an extraordinary word! Apparently, it also means "*Oh, shit!*"

"Mahatma, what's the deal with this *satyagraha*?" Elliott asked as he drove himself and his esteemed passenger toward the latter's ball.

"It is a very important word to me," Gandhi began, in a voice less high-pitched and more British than Elliott had expected. In fact, to the actor's credit, it sounded more like Ben Kingsley's than Gandhi's.

"I say it to express my deep belief in the truth. It means

'holding to the truth' or 'truth in firmness.' It is at the core of my belief system, as it relates to nonviolent resistance, to moral conduct, and . . . to golf!"

"To golf?"

"Oh, yes indeed. Especially to golf. You see, my good friend, the game of golf is the epitome of the essence of *satyagraha*. That is why I love this game so exceedingly much. Because in golf, as in life, there is much to be learned from truth in firmness, from nonviolent resistance.

"In both golf and life, there is strength through gentleness. There is results through patience. There is moving forward through yielding. There is achievement through self-restraint. There is fruitfulness through abstinence, gain through compromise, victory through humility, reward through sacrifice.

"It is about getting what you want and receiving joy and happiness by doing the correct thing—forgiveness, goodwill, selflessness, love. It is about complete service to the game, and it all begins with being very nice to the little white ball down there."

Elliott was flabbergasted by this monologue. He had never heard anyone speak of golf in such a loving and respectful manner.

"You know," Gandhi continued, "most people think that golf is a hard game. But in reality, it is a *soft* game, just like life, as I have indicated. What is *hard* about golf is the way that many people play it . . . with hardness, anger, bitterness, resentment, conflict, and violence!

"And, finally, let me tell you that golf also totally reflects two other tenets of my philosophy of life that I hold dear to my heart. One, you have to play it with no hatred in your heart. And two, you must be prepared to suffer!"

Elliott was digesting all of this when the cart arrived at

Gandhi's ball. The Mahatma hopped out and surveyed the situation, which was not pretty.

"*Satyagraha!*" he said, on finding his ball sandwiched between two native locusts and behind a sugar maple. "As I mentioned, sometimes sacrifice is the way to reward."

Avoiding any macho, threading-the-needle-through-the-trees bravado, Gandhi grabbed four-iron out of the bag, set up, addressed, clasped his hands, shut his eyes, prayed, mumbled, laughed, paused at the top, and gently cupped the ball out into the middle of the fairway. It traveled a paltry fifty yards.

The tortoise, lying two, was still forty-five yards behind the hare, who lay one, as they rolled toward the Great Soul's ball.

"There is," Gandhi said, "an ancient Chinese proverb that goes, 'Patience, and the mulberry leaf becomes a silk gown.'"

It is the spring of 1964, and it is the recess period from Mrs. Nussbaum's second-grade class. Ell Goodman and his best pal, sweet little Marie Prudhomme, are opening their snacks from home, she a red Tootsie Pop, he a purple one. In less than eighty-five seconds, Ell consumes his. Like a just released prisoner who hasn't had a square meal in decades, he ravenously and violently crunches through the hard candy exterior, devours it in six lightning-fast bites, and polishes off the chocolate Tootsie Roll innards in one. Holding only the naked white stick in his little hand, he is a record playing at 78 rpm to sweet little Marie's 33.

She, conversely, is licking the confection at a snail's pace, savoring each luscious tongueful to the limit, her right eyebrow raised ever so slightly, gently taunting Ell with her glare, a look of satisfaction and pleasure that could only come from an innocent seven-year-old, but that nonetheless would have made the Marquis de Sade proud. The young, impatient Ell watches her as long as he can bear to, probably two minutes, and then, unable to take it any more, runs away in frustration and horror.

And so, throughout his life, the mercurial Elliott Goodman would claim impatience as his biggest failing, his Achilles' heel, his Scarlet "I." He never walked if he could jog, never jogged if he could run. Hated waiting on lines. Hated waiting for birthdays to open cards or for holidays to open gifts. Hated people who spoke painfully slowly, telemarketers and their spiels, boring lectures, lengthy explanations . . .

One of the wheels of the golf cart ran over a large pile of goose excrement, almost ejecting Elliott and his distinguished opponent and rudely interrupting Elliott's brief nightmare.

So far, so good. He's playing smart, but short, and if I can put my second shot near the green, I might just be looking at being dormie against the Almighty!

It was still Gandhi's turn to hit, and he took his four-iron again and clasped, shut, prayed, mumbled, laughed, paused, and cupped his ball gently down the fairway another 130 yards, leaving it fifty-five yards short of the green.

Elliott could smell blood as he drove toward his ball. He lay one, and Gandhi was only eighty-five yards ahead . . . *but lying three.*

He had a perfect lie and hit a nice easy seven-iron, which, to his delight, landed ten yards short of the green, but in ideal position for an uncomplicated chip.

Driving to Gandhi's fourth shot, Elliott turned over in his head every fascinating point the Mahatma had made in his monologue.

I love what he has to say about golf! About how it is a soft, not a hard, game that requires patience and sacrifice and yielding and all that. I mean, for me, it's sometimes hard to be soft, but when you play golf, it does make sense. Reminds me of Aesop's fable "The Wind and the Sun," where just shining proves to be more powerful than trying to blow as hard as you can.

Gandhi hopped out and prepared to hit his fourth shot, a straightforward little wedge from fifty-five yards. In the middle of his address, he stopped, scratched his head, and asked, "Elliott, I was wondering . . . are you afraid of death?"

Elliott's bubble of protection that he had been constructing so industriously for so long—the insulation from the potentially dire consequences of the match that his intensity, hard work, concentration, and simply living in the moment had collectively created—suddenly burst.

Huh? I'm busting my hump out here to win a golf match and stay alive, trying not to put too much pressure on myself, and now he asks me if I'm afraid to die?

"Well, I haven't given it much thought lately, but . . . I suppose so."

"You suppose so? Elliott, I think I can say with certainty that every human being who has a heart and a soul has a fear of death. Would you not agree?"

"Ah . . . yeah, I think I would."

"Good, well then, I have always thought that the best thing to do is to admit this fear and not to run away from it, but, rather, to face it. What is it, do you think, that is causing this fear the most?"

"I dunno. Maybe the idea of physical pain . . . how much it's going to hurt. Maybe of psychological pain, a fear of the unknown . . . when will my heart give in? And when it does, and when I die, will my ashes just sit there? Do I have a soul? If so, where will it go? Maybe of emotional pain . . . not knowing if Joy and the kids will be okay without me and get over their loss. Maybe of separation pain. Will anyone remember me, think of me from time to time?"

"These are all good fears, Elliott. It is good that you know what they are. Hearing you speak, I am quite sure that your family loves you very, very much, and that they will miss you very much also."

Initially, Elliott had been annoyed at Gandhi's bringing up this nettlesome topic. It was, after all, the first time since the OR that he had thought in any serious way about his demise—and he was doing it with only one-plus holes to play, when he was on a roll, and at the very climax of the entire round, when everything was on the line. But now Elliott actually felt at ease with the subject, as if facing the proverbial music were a source of comfort to him, not one of fear.

"You know, the good news for you is that when I was as-sassinated, and the third bullet was going through my flesh, just before I prayed to God, I had the feeling that for the first time in my life, I was in a situation where I had no control, where somebody else was, if you will pardon the expression, calling the shots.

"And here comes the good news. You, Elliott, *do* have control of the situation. No one but yourself will be respon-sible for the outcome of this match, and of your life. That is a *good* thing!"

Elliott felt strangely solaced by this little speech, as he dropped off the Mahatma for his fourth shot of the hole.

This was Gandhi at his satyagrahesque best. After his prayerful setup, he scooped the chip up into the air, firmly yet nonviolently, and it bounced once and landed stiff, two inches past the cup.

Speaking of fear, the pressure shifted to Elliott, who had an easy chip, only ten yards to the apron and another fifteen feet to the flag. But the toughest part of the shot was know-ing that he had to get up-and-down to win the hole.

He hit a nice chip, not a great one, and ended up eight

feet to the right of the cup. Under the circumstances, not too bad, but surely not what he wanted.

Elliott parked the cart to the right rear of the green, conceded Gandhi's putt for his bogie five, and, on his haunches, read his own.

Left-to-right breaker . . . two inches outside, if you hit it firm . . . and you better not be *short*, buster!

Sadly for him, he was.

He tapped in for his own five, having missed a golden opportunity to go one up for the very first time. Instead, he had halved the hole with the gentle man from Porbandar, and the match was now all square with one final hole to play.

No blood, Elliott mused. How nonviolently appropriate!

When Elliott looked up after retrieving his ball from the hole, there sat the Mahatma at the edge of the green in the classic lotus position, smiling graciously.

Closing his eyes, Gandhi took one giant yogic ujjai breath, inhaling deeply as he uttered the word *satyagraha* from somewhere way in the back of his throat until all the air was sucked out of his body, which in turn dissolved into Nothingness, leaving only his white dhoti and his timeworn leather sandals in a peaceful little heap.

Although Elliott had blown the chance to pull ahead with just the final hole of the match remaining, he felt no regret, no feeling of lost opportunity, no nagging ache in the pit of his stomach. Instead, he experienced a lightness, an inner peace, a calm poise that he had felt only rarely during the entire match.

Why? Did it just happen, for no apparent reason? Was it because of Gandhi? Was this calm transferred from the Mahatma to him, just as Beethoven's passion had somehow entered his body via a strange osmotic process? Was it the result of Gandhi's little spiels about *satyagraha* and Elliott's subsequent reflection about the "softness" of golf, or perhaps of their strangely comforting exchange about facing the fear of death?

The wind, which had been so strong and which had played such an important role in the golf match since the twelfth hole, died down completely. Not a breath.

As Elliott walked past the greenside bunker, down the incline, and then back up toward the shaded opening between tree lines that was the eighteenth tee-box, he felt newly confident, his competitive juices flowing calmly but strongly.

Okay, kid, this is it! All square with one more to go. This is the whole enchilada. It's do or die, and it's gonna be do, not die, if you have to *kill* yourself! The humor of this last sentence didn't escape Elliott, always sensitive to the evocative and connotative power of words. He smiled faintly, admiring his own cleverness and keen sense of irony.

Feelin' *good*. In fact, I'm feelin' *so* good that I hereby wish for myself—on this last, crucial, vital, key, decisive, do-or-die hole—the greatest challenge I could possibly face.

I hereby wish I could be pitted, right here, right now, against the most competitive, hardest-working, best-prepared, smartest, most focused, meanest, toughest, orneriest sonuvabitch who ever held a golf club in his hands. . . .

18

ICE MON COMETH

LIKE ALADDIN WITH HIS three wishes, Elliott had used up all of *his* on the front nine. The Genie Upstairs had already granted him Freud, the egghead he'd prayed for walking to the fifth tee; Socrates, the dialogist he'd wanted as he approached the seventh; and Didrikson, the babe he'd yearned for on his way to number nine.

Perhaps because He is a merciful God, however, and seeing that Elliott hadn't yet requested anything on the back nine, He graciously accommodated the professor's fourth wish with a supplementary, bonus allowance by producing the greatest golfing competitor the world had ever seen.

In truth, only one player could possibly, *ever* correspond to Elliott's description, could ever represent the ultimate combination of shot-making, toughness, focus, competitiveness, work ethic, preparation, course management, and performance under pressure.

Awaiting Elliott at the eighteenth and final tee, chomping at the bit and loaded for bear, was his wish come true—and his worst nightmare—the only person who could ever fit that

unique and nearly unattainable golfing profile. William
Benjamin Hogan.

The Wee Ice Mon!

As he stared in awe, Elliott was delighted to have the great
Mr. Hogan in this final pairing. Delighted, but not surprised.
Being a total sports fanatic, Elliott knew his golf well and
knew that, if his wish were to be granted, the choice God had
to make would be an easy one.

Ben Hogan! All square, last hole, and I have to play the
Hawk! What a challenge!

Speaking of challenges, Elliott also knew the unbelievable
ones Hogan himself had been faced with, and had met brilliantly, throughout his roller coaster of a life.

Being in the room, at the age of nine, when his father,
Chester, blew his brains out with a .38. Being poor as dirt
throughout his youth and early marriage years. Being a natural lefty and having to teach himself to play golf right-handed.
Being slight of build and trying to make it in professional
golf. Being afflicted with both an uncontrollable hook that he
had to correct by teaching himself to hit a fade and a yippy
putter that plagued him toward the end of his career. Being in
the near-fatal car accident in '49, outside of Van Horn, Texas,
that left him broken and crippled. Being told by the doctors
that he'd never walk again, much less play golf. Being cursed
by the permanent state of pain that would be his constant
companion for the remainder of his life.

So, it's the Wee Ice Mon versus Elliott Goodman, for all
the marbles, eh? It's All Er Nuthin'?, Elliott asked himself
rhetorically, as he played Ado Annie and Will's duet from
Oklahoma on the Victrola in his head.

If holes 3, 4, and 5—the three consecutive par-5's—make
Inwood a unique golf course, the eighteenth is unquestionably its signature hole. It is a charming but straight, rather

innocuous-looking 408-yard par-4, lined on both sides by tall trees.

What makes it so challenging is the insidious canal that runs across the length of the hole, just in front of the green. Far too many second shots to list here have ker-plunked into its aqueous depths, resulting in double-bogeys, or worse.

To add insult to injury for the slice-prone hordes, the canal is flanked on its right by a large, inviting pond that separates the eighteenth green from the seventeenth tee. The two treacherous bodies of water are in turn separated by a lovely flagstone-and-concrete footbridge. In short, if ever there was an ideal "finishing" hole (the irony of the expression did not escape Elliott) to decide a life-or-death golf match, the eighteenth at Inwood would be it.

Having been greeted by one of Hogan's famous steely-eyed glares, Elliott stepped up to the tee with his driver, perhaps, but he hoped not, for the very last time. The pressure was turned way up, not only because he was now "all in" with his chips of life, but also because he knew with 100-percent certainty that Bantam Ben would be way down there in the center of the fairway with his drive, and if his own ball didn't precede Hogan's there, it would be curtains.

Elliott focused as well as he could under the circumstances and, with every ounce of effort he could summon up in his body, wailed away at his drive, pronating his hands to avoid a slice, and executed a carbon copy of his drive on number one. A perfect draw, 240, center cut.

Phew!

Now it was the Little Texan's turn.

Hogan could well have been wearing a sign on his forehead that read ALL BUSINESS. Dressed in workmanlike colors from head to toe—trademark white "Newsboy" golf cap, blue golf shirt under a light gray cardigan, dark gray slacks, black golf shoes—the 5'9", 150-pound dynamo stepped up to his ball, looked at it with an intimidating and laserlike focus that could burn a hole through steel, tossed the Camel that had been dangling from his lips onto the grass behind him, did a quick waggle, stared imperiously out at the hole with his steel gray eyes as though he owned it, paused briefly at address, and, with flawless timing and balance, rocketed the ball down the center of the fairway, watching it as it arced its way left to right in that classic fade of his and pursing his lips approvingly as it skipped past Elliott's ball and landed thirty yards beyond.

His drive explained why he was often called the Mechanical Man.

Yowser!

Elliott looked at Hogan, and Hogan returned the look. That was all you ever got from the tight-lipped gentleman from Dublin, Texas.

Elliott noticed that, for the first time during the entire round, a cart was not provided to transport the players from shot to shot—just a driver, a few irons, and a putter for each competitor. He guessed that was the way Hogan had wanted it.

After all, here was a guy whose tough-as-nails work ethic was second to none (Hogan was fond of saying, about his unparalleled golf game, that "the secret is in the dirt") and who, at the tender age of twelve, to help support his family, had to walk seven miles each way to caddy—for sixty-five cents an hour!—at the Glen Garden Country Club in Fort Worth.

Down the fairway they strode, side by side, *mano a mano*, Elliott and the Hawk, Fire and Ice.

This was definitely not Twain's definition of golf as "a good walk spoiled." This was a good walk, *period*.

Elliott was enjoying the walk, despite all the pressure and the deafening silence. Since the start of the round, he had gotten used to bantering and exchanging ideas with the most unforgettable cast of characters imaginable. Now for the first time, with the exception of the thirteenth hole against Beethoven, not a single word was exchanged between him and his opponent. Not because Hogan was deaf, but because he was IN THE OFFICE, MAN AT WORK, ON DUTY, QUIET PLEASE, DO NOT DISTURB, and he would not be distracted by banter, idle or otherwise.

Facta non verba, Elliott thought, just as he and Bantam Ben reached his Titleist. He recalled Jimmy Demaret's quip about his golfing colleague Hogan: When someone had told him how taciturn Hogan seemed, Demaret replied, "What? He talks to me on every green. He always says, 'You're away.'"

After three hours and eighteen minutes of golf, with all the ups and downs and learning and pressure and discussing and shot-making, it had finally all come down to this. Elliott's watershed, make-or-break, sink-or-swim, fight-or-flight, do-or-die moment.

Perhaps . . . his *last* moment?

The challenge was whether or not to go for it, to negotiate the canal and reach the green in two. Because of the high risk involved, your average player would usually err on the side of caution, laying up and hoping to get up-and-down for par or, at worst, two-putt for bogey. On occasion, you might go for it and risk the penalty, if you were feeling just right or had a nice helping tailwind.

In addition to the perilous canal, going for it involved yet another risk. If you didn't hit the ball high enough and land it softly on the green, you might make it over the canal, all right, but risk hitting the green on the fly and bouncing over it, in which case you'd probably end up on the other side of the cart path, with a probable double-bogey or worse staring you right between the eyes.

With all this racing through Elliott's mind, he stood over his ball—exactly 168 yards from the flagstick and with three-iron in his hands—and, as he addressed it, for that single instant, time stood still. He was frozen in place, not because of fear or nerves, but because of the enormity of it all.

He wouldn't pull the trigger until he was absolutely, positively ready. But would he go for it? Should he go for it? Did he *dare* go for it? Of course, a quote popped into his brain. Again from T. S. Eliot's "Prufrock," whose protagonist at one point meekly asks himself, "Do I dare to eat a peach?" He realized what a strange coincidence it was that at this crucial moment, he was quoting the one major poet whose name, except for the absence of that extra *l* and *t*, was . . . the same as his!

He also realized that *of course* he had to take the risk, to dare, not just because he was competing against the great Hogan, the Mechanical Man, but because he owed it to himself to be bold. He thought of the very first hole he'd played, against Leonardo, when he hadn't been, and how he'd paid the price for his indecision. Now, at the very end of his round, at this vital moment, he *had* to give himself the opportunity to rectify that. He *had* to commit himself, to be brave.

In a final internal pep talk, he tried to think of moments in his life that cried out for going for the green. Times when he didn't have the courage to dare. To say the *F* word just once in a lecture. To give his department chair a piece of his mind. To buy that house in Cambridge Joy had always wanted. To tell the kids precisely how very much he loved them . . .

Elliott took back his three-iron and put his heart and soul into the swing. Speaking of which, his heart, which had been the cause of this entire round of golf in the first place, stopped beating as his Titleist NXT flew in a towering arc toward what seemed to be the pea-sized green. The ball appeared to be traveling so slowly that he thought it would never get there.

At last, it landed, barely—*but just barely*—on a spot not more than two feet over the canal, then bounced, then bounced again, then rolled . . . to within eight feet of the cup.

Elliott's heart, which had stopped beating for a good nine seconds, started lub-dubbing once again. It had been through so much on this day—between the infarction, the OR scene, and the emotionally draining golf match—that, in relief and joy, it began to sing, inside Elliott's exhausted body, the triumphant lyrics of Elton John's "I'm Still Standing."

It was Hogan's turn to hit, and he was not at all amused, but he was not at all rattled, either. Not the Wee Ice Mon.

He grabbed eight-iron, took a puff from his second Camel, and tossed the butt onto the grass behind him. No nonsense, no hesitation, just another Day at the Office.

Whap!

Again his gorgeous fade, like it was propelled from a machine, same arc, same trajectory, same result. The ball landed nine feet from the cup, a foot behind Elliott's ball and on the same line.

The march to the green resembled an intimate, somber funeral procession. Not a sound was heard, except for Hogan occasionally sucking on his third Camel, not a word exchanged. You could hear a pin drop, even if it were to fall between the blades of the fairway grass.

Elliott felt shivers up and down his spine. He was on the putting surface in two . . . inside the great Ben Hogan . . . on the very final, deciding hole . . . and the Hawk couldn't even tell Elliott, "You're away."

As the two competitors approached the footbridge, another quote surfaced in Elliott's fatigued brain. It was from

Boris Becker, the great German tennis champion, and it spoke volumes about putting sports into perspective. The wunderkind had just lost in the second round of the1987 Wimbledon tournament to a virtual unknown, the Australian Peter Doohan, in an astounding upset. Afterward, Boris told reporters, "I lost a tennis match. It was not a war. Nobody died."

Elliott smiled because although he believed the quote to be noble and mature and agreed with it philosophically, in his present situation, it was laughably inappropriate.

On the contrary, this *is* a war! Somebody *could* die! And that somebody is . . . *me!*

As the two warriors walked across the footbridge, Elliott realized how ironic it was that the stone structure beneath their golf shoes and leading them to their fateful showdown on the eighteenth green was in fact similar to the one leading to the twelfth green at Augusta National that was named after his fierce and tenacious opponent.

The Wee Ice Mon went first. Elliott secretly hoped that the Hogan who was about to putt was the one whose yips had become his downfall late in his unmatched career.

No such luck.

In the back of his brilliant and analytical golf mind, the Hawk, who knew his golf history cold, must have been thinking about how the great Bobby Jones, whom some folks still consider to be his golfing equal, had birdied this same eighteenth in the final round of the '23 U.S. Open—by hitting a two-iron from the right rough from 190 yards out to within six feet, no less!—thus forcing a playoff with Bobby Cruikshank. *And how he'd be goddammed if he couldn't match Jones's feat right now!*

Hogan lined up his nine-footer, flicked his lit Camel onto the green, took dead aim with his steely gaze, stroked the ball smoothly with his ancient flat stick, and drained it.

Gulp!

After all this, it had finally come down to one lousy eight-foot putt. Make it, and Elliott gains some time and goes into a sudden-death playoff back at the eighteenth tee.

Miss it, and it's *requiescat in pace.*

Elliott had already decided that he wouldn't, that he *couldn't* lose. That it would be a crime not to complete his amazing comeback, that he'd come too far already—*from four down a mere five holes ago!*—to blow it all now.

Lining up his putt, he couldn't escape one fact that his nimble and ever vigilant mind was unable to conceal from his consciousness. Every single eight-footer in the match so far—the attempts on holes 9, 10, 11, and 17—he had missed!

Clear your head. Never mind about the missed eight-footers, you turkey! *Focus!* Never up, never in. . . .

Elliott stroked the putt beautifully, putting it on the same line as Hogan's, with the same pace, rolling . . . rolling . . . rolling . . .

Elliott's putt for all the marbles rolled inexorably toward the cup, then stopped a millimeter short and teetered on the brink, hugging the very edge of the hole.

There it stayed, for what appeared to Elliott to be an eternity.

As he walked toward the ball, with a shred of a glimmer of a hope that the putt would somehow drop, he flipped mentally, once again, through the pages of *The USGA Rules of Golf,* this time to Rule 16-2: Ball Overhanging Hole: "When any part of the ball overhangs the lip of the *hole,* the player is allowed enough time to reach the *hole* without unreasonable delay and an additional ten seconds to determine whether the ball is at rest."

Holy crap! Is this really happening? One: So this is it? Is that all she wrote? Is that the Fat Lady warming up her voice?

Two: What was all this struggle for? For *nothing*? Three: Four down with six to play, then I come back, and after all that, you're gonna hang there on the lip? Four: Come on, you little white sonuvabitch, *drop already!* Five: Joy! Jake! Molly! *I love you so much!* Six: I pray to the spirit of Isaac Newton. Seven: And to God. Eight: And to everything that is good in the world. Nine: And to me, the one and only . . . *Elliott Goodman!*

Plop!

It was Bobby Thomson's Homer, Fleck Beats Hogan in '55 Open, Havlicek Stole the Ball, Aleksander Belov's Lay-up, Franco Harris's "Immaculate Reception," The 1980 U.S. Olympic Hockey Team, Cal's "Play" vs. Stanford, Flutie's Hail Mary, The '86 Mets, Christian Laettner's Buzzer-Beater, Justin Leonard's 45-Footer, and Bosox Finally Win Series, all rolled into one.

Elliott's knees buckled. He checked his heart to see if it was still beating. He listened to a recording of what just happened coming from a microphone in his head. The voice belonged to Russ Hodges: "Elliott's putt drops! . . . Elliott's putt drops! . . . Elliott's putt drops! . . . Elliott's putt drops! . . . I don't believe it! . . . And they're going *crazy*! . . . Ohhhhh! . . ."

This was no time for fist-pumping or celebration. It was a time for gratitude and regrouping for the playoff. Elliott calmly took his miracle ball out of the cup, and, just as he was about to turn and shake hands with Hogan, he heard, from behind him, the only two words Bantam Ben would ever utter to him.

They weren't, "You're away," but simply, "Nice putt."

When Elliott turned to face Hogan, he saw, there on the edge of the green, a large block of ice with a white golf cap on top of it. The ice melted instantly, leaving only the cap sitting there in a puddle.

Back from the brink . . . four down with six to go . . . then Beethoven . . . Shakespeare . . . Ruth . . . Columbus . . . and now barely hanging on against the Wee Ice Mon . . . and the putt . . . finally . . . dropping . . .

Elliott was physically and mentally drained. The important thing now was to get ready for the extra hole or holes. After all, he still had a life to save.

Realizing that he had no cart to drive back to the eighteenth tee, he looked around for one. Nothing. Just as he started the long trek back to the tee, he heard the faint electrical buzz of a golf cart coming from behind him, from the direction of the Halfway House beyond the cart path.

Turning around, he confirmed that it was indeed a cart, and driving it was none other than that old codger who'd served him the peanut-butter cheese crackers and the small black coffee to go at the conclusion of the front nine. Elliott reasoned that since the old guy seemed to be the only person on the premises besides himself, caddiemaster Peppe, and his various opponents, he must have been appointed the "designated driver."

Elliott hopped in the cart, and the old codger drove him slowly back down the eighteenth fairway in the direction of the tee-box, with Elliott's mind a blank. He had emptied it of the considerable information and knowledge that was crammed into all its little cerebral fissures and nooks and crannies. Except for one single, simple thought, which was in the form of a question.

Who, in God's name, would be waiting at the eighteenth tee to face him in this all-or-nothing, do-or-die, sudden-death playoff?

19

SUDDEN DEATH

SUDDEN DEATH! How ironic is that?, Elliott remarked to himself as the cart reached the eighteenth tee. He stepped out, stretched his legs, and noticed that for the first time all day there was no one waiting for him at the tee-box.

"Hmmm . . . ," he said, half to himself and half to the codger, "Wonder where my next opponent is."

"Well, son, I hate to disappoint you, but you're looking at him."

Elliott was stunned and a little disappointed. He'd been curious to find out who it was God had in store for him on this potentially deciding hole, and now to learn that it was not to be a famous icon, like on the previous eighteen, but an old codger, an ordinary guy, an employee of the golf club . . .

"Not a problem, really," Elliott said, "I was just expecting . . ."

"Somebody important?"

"Yeah, I guess, but, y'know, a match is a match, and I'm happy to be playing you."

Elliott really wasn't, but he didn't let on. Bad manners.

Besides, he had the match to play and wasn't going to let any minor disappointment distract him from the job at hand.

"My honor, still," Elliott said as he grabbed driver from the bag.

"Hit away!" the codger said cheerfully, a sweet, gentle smile filling his face.

Then something extraordinary happened. Elliott stepped up to his ball and, without thinking or hesitating, cranked a perfect carbon copy of his previous drive on eighteen, a lovely draw, 240, center cut. It was as though he were locked in to the same shot, as though his muscle memory were on cruise control.

Tired as he was, it was one of the few times during the round that he'd acted completely by instinct. But, as good as it felt, he knew that good things could be fleeting, so he enjoyed it for what it was worth.

Actually, it was worth quite a lot, since putting it on the fairway was the sine qua non of eighteen.

It was the codger's turn.

Who is this guy, anyway? Why did God send him down now? He must've died, since those are the rules we've been playing by, but why send down someone I don't recognize, an unknown? Just to throw me a curve?

Watching the codger take his practice swings, Elliott knew the guy could play. Looked pretty smooth. *And that swing!* Forget about where the ball landed. The swing—perfect balance, impeccable tempo, precise mechanics, gorgeous to look at—was as sweet as any Elliott had ever seen, including those of Slammin' Sammy and the Big Easy.

As it turned out, the drive ended up 239, center cut, just a yard behind Elliott's.

Sliding into the cart, Elliott couldn't believe what he had

just witnessed. The codger was a Bigtime Player, *and this would not be easy.*

"So what do they call you?" Elliott asked the driver.

"Oh, just Dog. Got the name a long, long time ago, and I guess it stuck."

"You been playing long, Dog?"

"Yep, a pretty long time. But I don't really play much anymore. Just once in a blue moon."

Sandbagger! You probably play thirty-six holes a day up there!

"And what do you do?" Elliott asked, assuming the codger was dead and didn't do too much anymore.

"Oh, this and that. I get by."

Just like in the Halfway House, after studying his face, Elliott had the nagging feeling that he'd seen the old guy somewhere, but he still couldn't put his finger on it. He had a kindly face with sweet features, lots of wrinkles and age spots, a whitish beard and mustache—the standard old guy's costume.

They arrived at Dog's ball, and he got out and chose five-metal from the bag. "Wind's picking up a trifle. Guess I'll have to use the Big Boy today."

Again, the gorgeous, sweet swing. Again, the wonderful result, ten feet left of the flag.

"Man, you can really hit the golf ball."

"That's mighty nice of you to say. Must be something in the ol' genes!"

Elliott chose three-iron out of the bag, as he'd done against the Wee Ice Mon, and strode confidently up to his ball. The pressure was huge, seeing as Dog's ball sat safely up there on the green in birdie range, while Elliott's own sat here, 168 long yards away, with the treacherous canal lurking up ahead.

Elliott paid no attention to the canal, or to anything else, for that matter. He was focused on the shot. He'd come too far to screw up now.

He set up, addressed his Titleist, took his three-iron back, and—with the same courage to go for it that he'd called on against Hogan, and his big heart, and his burning desire to fight to the bitter end—put everything he had left in his exhausted body into the swing and made solid contact with the ball, which started its greenward flight into the freshening wind on the very same trajectory as in the shot against the Hawk.

As he watched intently, the ball seemed to stop in midair. He was having one of his trademark Elliottic epiphanies. . . .

Omygod! *Heart!* It's what this shot is all about, what competing in this golf match is all about, what living is all about! *Heart!* It's about having the courage to dare, to be bold, to go for it, to attempt, to push yourself, to hang in! Sure, the mind is important, helping you to make decisions, to think things through, to plan. . . . But the *heart!* What started all this was the *heart* attack I had in Widener! So is *that* why I had it? To see what I was made of? The irony of it all is that the organ that almost killed me may be the very one that, in the end, is going to save me. . . .

"Nice shot, son!"

The codger's compliment pierced through the epiphany and brought Elliott back to his follow-through position, with his ball—so he discovered as soon as he snapped out of it— once again eight feet to the left of the cup, two feet inside the codger's.

On the drive to the green, Dog wasn't too talkative, but he had a warm glow about him that made Elliott feel comfortable and at ease in this, his time of reckoning. Still, Elliott's mind couldn't help wandering back to the issue that had frozen him during his previous, crucial shot.

Heart! Right under my nose! Been reading and teaching about affairs of the heart, the heart of the Romantic hero, and the heart as the seat of passion and intuition all these years. Just the other day—Tuesday, was it?—I was teaching a seminar and quoted the French philosopher Blaise Pascal: "*Le coeur a ses raisons, que la Raison ne connaît point,*" "The heart has its reasons that Reason doesn't have a clue about."

If only I had known the half of it! Of what was about to happen in Widener two days later as I stood there in the stacks with that book in my hand! Then, all because of my heart, being rushed to the OR, and then God on the ceiling with his challenge, and then this incredible golf match. No wonder the lyrics in that song from *Damn Yankees* aren't "Ya gotta have *brain*"!

At that very instant, the taciturn Dog shattered the silence by whistling the opening notes of that very tune.

Huh?

"Hey, Dog, how come you're whistling *that* song now?"

"Oh, I dunno, just came to me. Often whistle it . . . one of my favorites. I loved the show—that Gwen Verdon, what a knockout! And that song, it always makes me feel good . . . peps me up!"

The cart bumped across the footbridge and over to the other side of the canal. Dog drove past the bunker on the right and behind the green and parked on the cart path.

"You're away," Elliott said, taking a strange pleasure in saying the two words that the great Hogan had never gotten the chance to utter.

"Guess I am," Dog said as he lined up his putt.

"Well, son, sure has been a pleasure to play with you. The golf was mighty good, too!"

He put a sweet stroke on the putt. Never a doubt. Front door.

Okay. Nice birdie, Dog. But you don't know who you're dealing with here. It's *me*, the one and only Elliott Goodman!

After nearly nineteen long holes and countless words and thoughts and feelings, Elliott's tank was on *E*. There was not a drop of gas left for anything to be happening in his brain. He was still fighting, with every fiber in his body and soul, but his thought process had ceased.

Nothing in there but the single, instinctive desire to make this putt—*another eight-footer!*—and prolong the match and avoid death, sudden or otherwise.

Eight feet . . . no break at all . . . straight in. *Don't leave it short!*

Elliott set up, heeled his putter on the green, making damn sure the "moving ball" disaster against Honest Abe on number twelve didn't repeat itself, drew it back slowly, and stroked the putt *pure*.

His Titleist headed straight for the hole, dead on line. The ball decelerated and . . . stopped—like it had in the putt against the Wee Ice Mon—a millimeter short of the cup, teetering on the brink, on the very edge of the hole.

Same deal. Same slow walk to the flagstick. Same ten seconds allowed by the USGA.

Holy crap! Is this really happening . . . again? One: C'mon, ball, do your thing, just like you did last time! Two: Lao-tzu said, "Failure is an opportunity." Is it? Or is it my death knell? Three: Kipling said, "If you can meet with triumph and disaster/And treat those two impostors just the same." Is defeat an impostor? Or my executioner? Four: *Screw* these quotes! Is this gonna be . . . sudden death? Five: Jake! Six: Molly! Seven: Joy! Eight: Elliott Goodman! Nine: *I tried! . . . I tried! . . .*

At the stroke of ten, the ball didn't budge.

Elliott Goodman fell to his knees, his heart beating faster and faster . . . then the crushing chest pain radiating to his jaw and left arm . . . then the terrible fear of never . . .

Then everything went black.

EPILOGUE

"*I TRIED! . . . I TRIED! . . .*," Elliott rasped, barely able to get the words out of his hoarse, desiccated throat.

He had just come to.

Lying naked in a bed in the ICU of Mass General Hospital, he looked down and shed a lone tear as, for the first time, he laid eyes on the network of paraphernalia hooked into or attached to his body. The IV tubing and drip, the chest tubes, the nasal cannula transporting oxygen, the Foley catheter going to his urethra, the endotrachial tube, and particularly the two long, impressive rows of stainless steel staples covering the scalpel incisions that snaked all the way down his chest and also the entire length of his left leg.

Even moving his head an inch to look down was unspeakably painful, as the bypass surgery—through the trauma of his chest having been opened up and his ribs spread apart—had left every single one of his millions of nerve endings raw and exposed.

"I know you tried. And that's why I'm giving you a mulligan. Yes, Elliott, I'm giving you back your life," God said, sitting by Elliott's side. "Yep, it's God speaking. Now don't try to turn your head. I know how painful it must be."

"So . . . you're . . . giving me . . . *a mulligan*?"

"Yep."

"Well . . . thank you! But . . . I thought . . . I was a goner . . . I lost . . . the match . . . remember?" The rhetorical question was punctuated by a visceral groan, the result of Elliott's trying to reposition his aching body a fraction of an inch.

"Elliott, you must relax. I know exactly how much pain you're in, but, remember, pain hurts, yet it is a constant reminder to you that you have survived your ordeal and are alive."

Elliott smiled weakly but gratefully.

"You must have a bunch of questions for me?"

Elliott nodded.

"Well, save your energy. I'm going to answer all of them, in one fell swoop. I've gotten pretty good at that, if I may say so. And now, listen carefully, as I know how exhausted you must be. When I'm done, I want you to close your eyes and rest. Deal?"

"Deal," Elliott answered weakly in a crackly, breathy voice.

"Okay, then. So why did I give you a mulligan, even though you lost the match? Let's start out with that. Actually, Elliott, you said it best—'I tried.' So you missed that final putt? So I'm not going to give you another chance at living because of one millimeter? I may be mighty, but I am flexible! Anyway, the difference between winning and losing isn't all it's cracked up to be.

"Next question. Do I save everyone? Sadly, no. There are people I haven't saved because they didn't try. Or they gave up. Not *you*. Everyone has potential. Great potential. But they don't always realize it. Or they don't want to fight for their lives. *You* do.

"Does everyone get the chance to be tested? Again, sadly, no. You were one of the lucky ones, Elliott. Just look at a few of your new friends—John, Socrates, Joan, Marilyn, Abe, Mahatma. They weren't so lucky. They had their lives taken from them either by others or by themselves. *You* didn't.

"Why a golf match? Different strokes for different folks, I always say. And speaking of strokes, for you, Elliott, golf was the perfect arena. It is, in fact, one of my very favorite ways of challenging people. It brings out so much, and it reveals—and this is what I love about the game—the mystery and the paradox of life itself. It giveth, and it taketh away. It juxtaposes humility and glory, urgency and patience, reason and instinct, conflict and understanding, penalty and reward, misfortune and joy.

"Why did I send down those particular substitutes? They are the people who helped form who you are, Elliott. People you look up to and admire. Would you have learned as much, say, from playing chess against Sol Finkelstein of Hicksville, Long Island? Maybe. Sol, indeed, has much to give, but you already knew the people I sent down, and you were more likely to listen to them.

"Last but not least, Elliott, I'd like to revisit why, in the end, I actually gave you back your life. Yes, certainly, because you *tried*. But beyond that, was there a more profound reason? If you don't know the answer to that by now, I'm afraid you'll have to figure it out for yourself. Well, Elliott, that should do it. You need to rest now. And I have someone else to attend to, so I should be going. Bless you."

Before leaving, the Almighty deposited a small object on Elliott's chest, right over his heart, then disappeared into thin air.

Despite the insistent pain pulsing through his body, Elliott felt real joy in his heart.

A mulligan! A new lease on life! Getting back Joy and the kids and friends and teaching and everything else . . . I *did* it!

He paused to grit his teeth, then felt the small object God had placed on his heart. He fondled it with his fingers: It was round and smooth. He clutched it and moved his hand slowly upward toward his face so that he could get a good look at it and discovered how much pain this single, uncomplicated gesture could produce.

When the object at long last reached a position six inches from his face, he squinted hard and, without his glasses, tried to focus in on it. Slowly, it became a little clearer, and, after a few more seconds, he could see the blurry outline of a de-sign, and then some of the fine details, and finally, he was able to identify the object as . . .

A wooden nickel!

First the pain. Then the joy. Now the *shock*.

Elliott could scarcely believe it. He instinctively knew what it meant, and he closed his eyes to sort it all out.

A wooden nickel! So it was . . . *God* I was playing against all along during sudden death! He was the old codger who served me coffee and spoke of wooden nickels . . . Dog . . . "God" spelled backward! I *thought* I recognized Him in the Halfway House. It was the same face as the one I'd seen on the ceiling of the OR! So *that's* why He knew I was thinking about *Damn Yankees* and coincidentally starting whistling that "Heart" song!

But why did He come down to play? I thought He didn't play golf. Didn't Leonardo tell me it wouldn't be fair if He played against me? That He sent down the substitutes to "make even the field of play"? Didn't Socrates say that He didn't play and was just a spectator? Did He come down just to check in and see for Himself how I was doing? Or to push me to the limit?

Elliott stopped thinking. He needed to rest, to take it all in. The pain in his body, the joy in his heart, the wooden nickel in his hand . . .

"Don't take any wooden nickels," the old codger—Dog . . . God—had told me. I never understood what that meant, not really. Just thought it was one of those funky, old-fashioned expressions, but maybe giving me the nickel was God's way of saying, "Don't take anything fake from anyone else. There are so many things that are worthless out there, fake, phony, without meaning." *Out there.* What's really important is what's . . . *in here!*

Elliott craned his neck to look at his heart. The pain of this simple gesture was nearly unbearable, so he put his head back on the pillow and again closed his eyes.

A wooden nickel! Take only what's real, real for you. I guess that's what my teaching is all about. I give to my students, and they take, not everything I offer them—there are a few wooden nickels among the pearls!—but what they need for themselves. . . .

A wooden nickel! *Of course!* The truth was there all the time, right under my nose, but it took this unbelievable golf match, playing against these amazing people, for me to see it. These people gave me so much, the game of golf gave me so much . . . but it's what *I*, the one and only Elliott Goodman, took from it all that matters.

I took only what was true and meaningful for me, and if I failed, I questioned and I struggled and I learned. I took Decisiveness from Leonardo, Non-thought from W. C., Justice from Moses, Joy from John, Focus from Freud, Compassion from Poe, Self-knowledge from Socrates, Effort from Jehanne, Humility from little Babe, Hubris from Marilyn, Self-reliance

from Pablo, Integrity from Abe, Passion from Ludwig, Humanity from Will, Versatility from big Babe, Discovery from Cristoforo, Poise from the Mahatma, Risk from the Wee Ice Mon,
Heart from God. . . .

Elliott looked down at all his tubes and then at his staples
and shed one more painful tear, which rolled softly and
slowly down his left cheek, caressing his skin before it descended into his beard.

I'm damn lucky to be here. No, not lucky at all, actually. I
earned back my life! As Branch Rickey once said, "Luck is the
residue of design." So I guess there *is* justice in the world,
after all! And I guess it *is* "how you play the game"! What a
wonderful paradox: I lost the match, but because I played it
with an open heart and with everything I had in me, I actually won my life back!

Elliott was unspeakably tired, between his bypass surgery
and his little conference with God and his infinitesimal but
draining physical activity. Once again, he closed his eyes.

And in one final epiphany before his body and mind gave
themselves up to the arms of Morpheus, Elliott vented.

Yes! Now I know, after struggling through this awesome
golf match, what I should've answered back in the OR when
God asked me why He should let me have my life back. My
life is worthy of being saved because it's . . . *my* life! With its
ability to absorb, and to learn from, failure. With its capacity
to improve. With its passion and its perseverance and its heart.
Because it's unique and it's mine and it's . . . *no one else's!*

Well, God may have given to Job, after he finished testing
him, great wealth and 14,000 sheep, but He gave me an even
greater gift, one He could only have given to *me*—the chance
to be . . . the best . . . Elliott Goodman . . . I can . . . possibly . . .
be. . . .

Then the one and only Elliott Goodman gave himself up totally and completely and drifted off to a profound, peaceful slumber.

After all, he had to save his strength for living the rest of his life.

Acknowledgments

The heart—that hollow, muscular, conical organ, but so much more!—plays a major role in this novel, and a major role in my life. So, my heartfelt thanks to:

• The cardiologists who have helped keep my heart beating, literally, through their caring and their expertise: Stu Seides, Avram Merav, Michael Feld, George Smith, Argin Sharma, Ron Goldberg, Alan Brown, and Joe Ilvento.

• The friends who have helped keep my heart beating, figuratively, through their loyalty and their love: Lance and Mary Donaldson-Evans, Frank and Barbara Fleizach, Leo and Margaret Schwartz, Bill and Beth Jaquith, Mark Cripps, Seymon and Lynne Ostilly, Rony and Rachel Herz, Phyllis Clurman, Val Light and Bob Joseph, David and Joanne Frantz, John and Betty Gabel, Chris and Kay Bea Zacher, Hugh and Meryl Herbert-Burns, Mike Appelbaum, Hank and Elayne Gardstein, Ken and Paula Horn, Al and Bonnie Gorfin, Pete and Linda Haller, Fred and Dottie Rudolph, and Anthony Caprio.

• The extraordinary teachers who have helped fan the flames of my passion for knowledge: Gertrude Bowler, Gil Feldman, Bob Pasotti, Larry Hayden, Kenneth Lucas, Miles Kastendieck, Robert Desmé, George Pistorius, Jack Savacool, Neil Megaw, Whit Stoddard, and Jean Bruneau.

• The outstanding coaches who have helped fan the flames of my passion for athletic competition: Bill Thompson, Morty Goldman, Ernie Fleishman, Lon Hanauer, Jon Plaut, Larry Silver, Julie Copeland, Harlow Parker, Bob Bell, Ralph Dupee, and Clarence Chaffee.

- The characters in this novel, who have filled my heart with joy: Elliott Goodman, the Almighty, and the eighteen "substitutes"; and (with apologies) those who were at various times also among the dramatis personae—Cleopatra, Dante, Machiavelli, Montaigne, Newton, Marie Curie, James Joyce, Jack Johnson, and Albert Einstein.

- My Labrador retrievers, Koslo and Mocha—those two "gods of frolic," to quote Henry Ward Beecher—who have given my heart the inestimable gift of their unconditional love.

- My truly amazing agent, Joëlle Delbourgo, and my truly wonderful editor, Michaela Hamilton, who both—wholeheartedly—believed in this project from the very outset. And art director Janice Rossi and artist Franco Accornero, who perfectly captured the heart and soul of the story in this book's inspiring jacket.

- My kids—Noah, Jenny, and Sarah—who, bless their hearts, make me *sooooo* proud to be their daddy.

- And, finally, my wife, Susan, my sweetheart, who not only read every single chapter patiently as it rolled hot off the printer, but who was the original champion of the unfinished manuscript, rescuing it from certain oblivion as it collected dust on a bookshelf.

Again, from the bottom of my heart, a great big "thank you" to all of the above, who, to paraphrase the inimitable Yogi Berra, have made this book necessary.

7/06